T0368710

Without The King's Consent

TELL ME PRETTY BABY

1954 Mystery Record Revealed

The Surprising Truth:
Was The Recording Artist Really
Elvis?

a true story by

ANDREW JACKSON

FREDERICK ALLEN

Order this book online at www.trafford.com
or email orders@trafford.com

Most Trafford titles are also available at major online book retailers.

Note for Librarians: A cataloguing record for this book is available from Library and Archives Canada at www.collectionscanada.ca/amicus/index-e.html

Printed in Victoria, BC, Canada.

ISBN: 978-1-4269-1130-9 (sc)
ISBN: 978-1-4269-1131-6 (hc)
ISBN: 978-1-4269-1132-3 (eb)

Our mission is to efficiently provide the world's finest, most comprehensive book publishing service, enabling every author to experience success. To find out how to publish your book, your way, and have it available worldwide, visit us online at www.trafford.com

Trafford rev. 6/15/2010

 www.trafford.com

North America & international
toll-free: 1 888 232 4444 (USA & Canada)
phone: 250 383 6864 ♦ fax: 812 355 4082

"YOU CALLED ME A LOW DOWN HOUND "

A phrase from the lyrics of

"TELL ME PRETTY BABY"

✱ ✱ ✱ AUTHOR'S NOTE ✱ ✱ ✱

This book is based in part upon my recollections, various newspaper accounts, and trial court documents and transcriptions. I have taken extra precaution in relating the positive and negative aspects of this controversial recording in order to avoid any misconceptions which, in my opinion, would adversely affect Elvis' unique and memorable talent and personage. **In reference to the back cover design**, I might add that unlike most exaggerated back-cover hype, I have simply presented the pro & cons of this story.

ACKNOWLEDGEMENTS

It is impossible to personally thank all the many people who in the past twenty-nine years were instrumental in making "Without The King's Consent " a reality. I would, however, like to give special thanks to the following persons:

Charlotte Thacker, my ex-fiancée, who helped me retain the legal representation in my battle with Vernon Presley, Executor of the Estate of Elvis A. Presley, and RCA Corporation. Wherever you are today, Charlotte, a special and warm thanks to you.

Thomas J. Bevans, my former business attorney, who stood with me over the years with excellent legal advice.

The Dallas Morning News, The Dallas Times Herald, The Nashville Banner, The Tennessean, Billboard, Variety, and especially, John Elfers of The Dallas Public Library.

Brenda Weiss, who encouraged me throughout the many years as I struggled to put this story together.

Broadcast Music, Incorporated (BMI), Nashville Branch, with whom I have been an affiliate publisher (d/b/a Golgotha Publishing Company since 1968).

And finally, to Frederick Allen, my co-author and editor, and, William R. Abegglen, their contributions to this book have been extensive, and for them, my thanks.

ANDREW JACKSON
2010

CONTENTS

PROLOGUE

Chilly winter air clung to the thriving desert city of Phoenix, Arizona. It was late January or early February of 1954 as a sullen young man of nineteen and his male companion, possibly his cousin, blasted through the bright lights, searching for a night of excitement on their restless voyage westward. The West Coast was where it was happening, Elvis Aaron Presley had heard. He wanted to see if it could happen for him.

His soul vibrated to a rhythm all its own, and he loved to sing for those who appreciated his unique voice and talent. The big band Jazz era was dying, Country and Western wasn't paced to his heartbeat, the black sound of Rhythm & Blues wasn't accepted across the cultural divide he wanted to bridge. Elvis longed for a sound to make his fire burn its brightest -- a sound that the world would soon know as Rock-n-Roll.

It was just such a sound that tickled his ear that night as Elvis and his friend drifted past a small club teeming with youngsters. It seemed worth investigating, if only for the chance to mingle with the pretty girls passing through the door. Though not yet of legal age, Elvis looked old enough that he never had trouble gaining access to the places he wanted to go. Few teenagers old enough to drive -- or to be drafted -- were denied access to such establishments. In a world where adulthood was earned, such clubs represented a vital rite of passage. Tonight was no exception.

The two adventurers jostled their way through the crowd and staked out a convenient spot, close enough to the stage to hear the band, yet close enough to the dance floor to keep an appreciative eye on the pretty girls. A young man, after all, had to keep his priorities straight.

The musicians called themselves the Red Dots, and the sound that blasted from the bandstand had a unique flavor. It wasn't quite what Elvis hoped to find, but it was close enough for him to sing along and tap his feet to the deep, thumping beat of the bass guitar. The bass player, Pete Falco, spotted the young man in the crowd, and between sets he invited Elvis to join the band for a few songs. Shyly admitting that he was indeed a musician, Elvis agreed. The crowd responded with wild enthusiasm, enchanted by his magnetic stage presence. His voice was pure and intense, with a fair measure of Tennessee/Mississippi country twang, a dash of big city Rhythm & Blues, and a twist of black soul. Electricity crackled through the smoky nightclub.

A local disc jockey, Don Reese, watched from the floor. Something very special was unfolding before his eyes, he realized, and he quickly inserted himself into the quick friendship being formed between Pete and Elvis. This new style of music had a beat the kids seemed to love. Don had been in the business long enough to know something hot when he saw it. As he stood amidst the throbbing young crowd -- a young crowd that the music industry longed to satisfy -- the gears in his mind engaged, dollar signs dancing a rapid beat that matched the frenetic pulse coming from the stage. This segment of the music industry had lain dormant since the boogie-woogie craze of World War II. But this, Don thought, this was going to be hot. Very hot!

All too soon the night came to a close. Small clots of excited youngsters drifted out the door as the band members packed away their instruments. Reluctant to part, Pete Falco filled Elvis in on the background of the group. The Red Dots would be working at a local recording studio the next day, he said, and he wanted Elvis to tag along.

In addition to his duties as bassist, Pete had written most of the original material the band had been playing. He had some new music he believed was very good, he told Elvis, and he wanted to cut some demo tapes. Pete thought it would be perfect for this mysterious newcomer with the sultry voice and unique style to perform the vocals. The other members of the Red Dots agreed. Pete gave Elvis directions to the studio, and encouraged him to show up early to allow time for rehearsal before the recording session began. After handshakes all around, Elvis and his companion stepped out into the cold Phoenix air and roared off into the night. It had been an occasion to remember. Pete hoped the kid would show up in the morning. The local disc jockey, Don Reese, had lingered long enough to watch the impromptu recording plans unfold. Dreams of riches danced through his head. He wouldn't miss the session for the world.

Morning dawned cool and crisp. Pete Falco found few things as inspirational as a desert sunrise. This, he felt, was a day that would change the world. Pete and his fellow Red Dots rolled into the parking lot of Audio Recorders and began unloading their equipment. The studio was by no means the most advanced of its day, but it would do nicely. True stereophonic equipment lay in the near future, but this studio relied on two mono systems, mixing them together for a very realistic sound that lent itself to Pete's style of music. In those days everything in the recording industry was, for the most part, experimental in nature.

The members of The Red Dots cast frequent glances toward the parking lot, anxious for Elvis to show up. The band's lead singer, far from harboring resentment or jealousy, appreciated the young man's unique voice and style. Everyone had enjoyed performing with him the night before and looked forward to his arrival.

Don Reese showed up early as well. The disc jockey found himself continually amazed at the energy level of these young musicians. The Red Dots, in his opinion, was certainly not a great band, but Falco had written some good songs and had a great personality. But that dark-haired youngster from the nightclub, well, that was something else again. The whole place had jumped to his uncanny voice and flamboyant stage presence. Don wondered if Elvis had contracted with an agent yet. He knew the kind of quick money that could be made in the recording industry, especially with a new sound that was really hot.

The sharp, crackling exhaust of a hot rod jalopy interrupted Don's daydreams. The car crunched to a halt and two boys jumped out. A chill tingled through Don as Elvis strutted across the parking lot and entered Audio Recorders. This, no doubt, would be a day to remember.

Don followed the young man into the studio. Electricity filled the air as Pete Falco and the Red Dots exchanged warm greetings with Elvis, rekindling the fast acquaintance from the night before. The musicians discussed the technical aspects of the recordings they were about to make. Pete had three songs in mind, and everyone agreed that the best was "Tell Me Pretty Baby. " It had an upbeat tempo and a distinctive rhythm that charmed everyone -- especially Elvis. This was the kind of tune he was looking for; the kind of song that made his adrenaline surge.

The band members discussed the material while tuning their instruments. Pete would play the bass, of course, and also fill in with some limited backup vocals. Pete noticed Elvis trying to sing "Tell Me Pretty Baby " through clenched teeth, in the bluesy style the Red Dots' lead singer had used the night before. That wasn't what Pete wanted, however, and he had to keep reminding the young man to open his mouth and enunciate the words more clearly. He wanted to get away from Elvis' black sound, a sound that would not appeal to the market he wished to reach. The voice mesmerized Pete, and he thought he could sell the record with Elvis on vocals.

Pete pulled his barstool up right behind Elvis, close enough to tap him on the back to signal the breaks in the song. It took the youngster several takes to get it right, but everyone seemed pleased with the results. This was Elvis' first professional recording session, and he seemed willing to accept restraints on his style if that was what it took to produce a marketable record.

As agreed, Pete Falco paid Elvis fifteen dollars for recording the three songs. Not a lot of money, to be sure, but it would buy enough gas for the boys to make it across the desert and mountains to check out the music scene in Los Angeles. And, Pete reminded Elvis, there could be a lot more money if the records sold.

Pete thought the young man's name didn't sound right for a professional singer. He kicked a few suggestions around, and then asked if he would mind using "Jamie Falco" if the records were produced and sold. Elvis said that would be fine.

Everyone present agreed that the close personal bond formed between the hungry young man and the mature song writer went deeper than the mere recording of a few songs. Even Don Reese seemed touched by the scene. Emotion threatened to overcome the group as the two boys climbed into their hot rod and drove into the blazing sunset, Elvis still singing "Tell Me Pretty Baby."

The demo tapes didn't turn out quite like Pete had hoped, but they were a far sight better than some of the others he had produced. At any rate, he thought, the intentions had been to sell a few records, not to produce a number one hit. He had, of course, harbored high hopes that something good would come of the tapes. Pete's flat back up vocals embarrassed him a bit, but he hoped the exceptional voice of Elvis would cover his own shortcomings.

Pete shopped the demo tape of "Tell Me Pretty Baby" around to various record producers. Most told him to re-record the song, tighten it up some, then bring it back for reconsideration. One company in Los Angeles told him that the tape wasn't quite up to par, but if he would bring the singer back into the studio they might be able to do something with him. Few who heard Elvis' voice had any doubt as to his phenomenal potential. By this time, however, so much time had passed that Pete didn't know how to contact Elvis. He shelved the recording, hit the bandstand playing bass, and later took up truck driving.

And then "Heartbreak Hotel" crackled across the airwaves and changed the face of music. Elvis had hit it big. Pete took the demo to the acquisitions man at the label Richie Valens worked with. Without Elvis at his side, though, Pete had no luck. He contented himself with following the young man's brilliant career from a distance.

Later that year, in July of 1954, Elvis signed a recording contract with Sun Records in Memphis. A year later RCA bought all known rights to Presley's recordings. They did not, however, tap Pete Falco on the shoulder to request "Tell Me Pretty Baby." Maybe they didn't know about the Phoenix recording session.

But Pete knew, and his children knew, and that was all that mattered. The years rolled by at a dizzying pace. And then, in August of 1977, came the tragic news that stunned the world: Elvis Aaron Presley was dead.

Andy Meets Shanti

CHAPTER ONE

It was a tiny one bedroom home, tucked away in the correspondingly tiny town of Ardmore, Oklahoma, that witnessed the birth of Andrew Jackson on December 5, 1938. In his youth, Andy's grandmother regaled him with the fascinating story of blood ties to his namesake, the seventh president of the United States. This comforting reassurance of a proud heritage would serve throughout life as a constant reminder, an ever-present inspiration for Andy to excel in whatever endeavor he undertook. In adulthood, his Dallas-based used car business helped put food on the table. A tall, slim man with a pleasant smile and friendly eyes, Andy did well for himself in buying, selling and trading automobiles. His passion and part-time business, though, would always be the recording industry. And so matters stood in April of 1977, that fine spring when fate finally got around to dropping a treasure in Andy's path: an unreleased recording by the late great Elvis Presley.

Andy sat in the office of his Auto Village dealership, nestled alongside East Main Street in Grand Prairie, Texas. Outside, the afternoon air shimmered with the roar of jet engines from nearby LTV, a military aircraft manufacturer that nourished the economy of the Dallas suburb. Another slow day, thought Andy. The car lot stood deserted; neither the usual "just looking" customers nor drifting wholesale dealers seemed interested. The morning had been no different, so Andy granted his secretary the afternoon off to attend to some personal business.

Andy stretched back in his office chair, listening to the drone of jet engines and mulling over the strange twists his life had taken in the past. He wondered what surprise might lurk around the corner. He loved the entertainment field, especially the music recording industry. Records lined the wall of his small office, mute testimony of his modest success as a record producer and publisher. His pride and joy, these records, constant inspiration for the inner voice that urged him on to loftier goals. His eyes darted back and forth, from one shining platter to the next, as day dreams filled his head. He never imagined that the King of Rock-n-Roll was about to cross his path and turn his world upside down.

The used car business had supported Andy throughout his adult life, but the entertainment industry held his heart. In late 1968 he embarked on a journey to learn the ropes of the music business. He soon discovered one thing beyond doubt: there is no guarantee of success. Nonetheless, he devoted every spare moment to studying the intricacies of the field.

Andy was not a particularly gifted guitarist, nor was his voice a threat to the recording artists of the day. His real talents lay offstage, behind the scenes in the business end of production and publication. Down this path lurked vicious competition, though, and Andy would learn repeatedly that the chances of hitting it big were slim indeed. Try as he might to remain optimistic, doubts kept creeping along the fringes of his glorious daydreams. Would he ever get that big break, that one-shot wonder that would put him over the top with something rare and unique?

The sight of an attractive young lady gliding across the dealership lot brought Andy back to reality. His mind firmly on business, he greeted her with a warm smile and a formal introduction. Shanti Falco, she said her name was. He directed the young lady to a seat and reclaimed his own behind the desk.

Confirming Shanti's interest in purchasing a car, Andy discussed the various models he had on the lot, others he had access to, and their prices and payment plans. As he worked his way through his standard spiel, though, he noticed Shanti's eyes straying to the records on the wall. Finally she worked up enough courage to ask the obvious question: was Andy somehow involved in the music business? Andy smiled and stretched back in his chair, more than happy to relate glittering tales from his decade of dabbling in the industry.

And then Shanti interrupted with a story of her own, a story about her father. Pete Falco, his name was, and he had played in a band called the Red Dots. He had, in fact, worked on some recordings with Elvis Presley way back in 1954. Andy perked up, intrigued by the fascinating tale of an unreleased song titled "Tell Me Pretty Baby," stashed in a dusty box and hidden away in a dark closet at her father's home. Perhaps Andy would be interested in meeting her dad and listening to the old recording? His heart somersaulted into his throat. Yes indeed, he managed to blurt, he would be interested, very interested.

Shanti went on to explain that her father found himself out of work at the moment. Perhaps they could reach some kind of agreement on the recording, something to help her dad through the lean times. Andy assured her that such an arrangement was entirely possible if the recording did indeed turn out to be Elvis Presley. After further questioning about Pete Falco's involvement as a songwriter and musician, Andy scribbled down a phone number and promised to give him a call.

Andy escorted Shanti out to the lot and showed her around. She found a model to her liking, and they cut a fair deal. Andy waved as the young lady drove away in her almost new car, his heart pounding at the prospect of getting his hands on an unreleased Elvis recording. Yes indeed, he thought, such twists in the path of life. And so it was that fate danced a jig across Andrew Jackson's used car lot on that fine spring afternoon.

Disconnected

CHAPTER TWO

Like so many other dreams -- strung out in a broken line that marked the cruel disappointments of Andrew Jackson's life -- the culmination of this one proved elusive. Andy had trouble contacting Pete Falco; the two men's schedules never seemed to coincide. And then disaster struck: Andy lost Pete's phone number. A cloud of frustration turned his bright smile to a dreary frown. So close and yet so far away, he mused, like a pot of gold at the end of the rainbow. Dark shadows tormented his sleepless nights, unfulfilled hopes danced just beyond his fingertips.

Andy ripped frantically through a stack of thick phone books. No luck. Pete Falco seemed lost forever, hidden somewhere amidst the millions of souls that roamed the streets of the vast Dallas-Fort Worth metropolitan area. Andy had no idea which of the tangled and overlapping cities, suburbs and rural communities might hold Pete's residence.

He tore through his files for the bill of sale on Shanti's new car. There it was, her address and phone number clearly printed across the form. With a mounting sense of joy he reached for the phone and dialed. Disconnected. He slowly replaced the receiver and sank down in his chair, a cold feeling slowly eating its way into his stomach. He turned his eyes toward the neat rows of records gracing the walls of his tiny office, sullen reminders of the glory he had briefly tasted. It all seemed so long ago.

A couple of weeks slipped by. The disappointment slowly released its tight grip on Andy's heart, but not a day passed that he didn't kick himself for his carelessness. He was lost in just such a round of gloomy reminiscence when he spied a car turning into the lot one morning. Something about the sight tickled his memory, but it took his mind a moment or two to slip into gear. Andy sat bolt upright. That was the car he had sold to Shanti Falco!

Andy scrambled for the door as Shanti and a distinguished looking gentleman emerged from the car and headed for the office. He could hardly contain his enthusiasm as he rushed to greet the pair. He blurted out a breathless explanation about the lost phone number and the fruitless attempts to contact Pete. Andy made it clear that his interest in the Elvis recording remained stronger than ever.

Be that as it may, Pete said, that wasn't the reason he had come to Auto Village. His daughter was having transmission problems with the car, problems that might become very expensive before long. Did Andy have a repair shop, Pete asked, and could he help out since the car had been purchased from him? Andy set their minds at ease. Of course the car could be fixed there, he said, and he made arrangements for it to be done within a few days.

With that bit of business out of the way, Pete's eyes turned to the records that graced the walls of Andy's office. They discussed the recording industry, slipping into the jargon that marked them as veterans of the business. Before long the conversation returned to the old Elvis tape. Pete carefully related the events that led up to the Phoenix recording session and the aftermath of that memorable event. Andy hung on every word, fascinated by the story of "Tell Me Pretty Baby." This was something rare indeed, he thought, and he couldn't wait to hear the original recording.

Andy questioned Pete carefully, going over each facet of the incredible tale. Why, in the long stretch of years that had passed under the bridge, hadn't Pete done anything with the master tape? Pete pointed to the lukewarm responses given by the record company representatives he had approached, and their unanimous agreement that the recording wasn't professional enough to warrant the expense of production and promotion. Pete's main excuse, though, was that he could never scrape together enough cash to produce the record himself.

Andy's eyes lit up. His means were rather modest, of course, and by no means did he have the funds required for a major production. He did, however, possess the inside knowledge and contacts necessary to accomplish the task with limited resources. This could be that big break he'd been wishing for.

But a healthy dose of caution tempered Andy's strong curiosity. This wasn't something he would jump into overnight. He would proceed with both eyes wide open. As Pete babbled on, Andy carefully considered the possible pitfalls. Elvis was unknown to the world when "Tell Me Pretty Baby" was recorded. He cut the demo with Pete's equally obscure band, the Red Dots. The recording equipment seemed antiquated by modern standards. And although Pete knew whose voice graced the recording, the public would surely be skeptical of such an important song coming to the surface after so many years. Last, but certainly not least, Pete expressed extreme reluctance to tangle with RCA Records in what promised to be a nasty and expensive round of litigation.

Andy twisted these variables around for a while, inverting the angles and chewing on each until he had formed a pretty clear mental picture of the risks involved. He considered the thoughts entertained by his distinguished forebear, General Andrew Jackson, as he floated down the Mississippi River in late 1814 to meet the elite group of British soldiers that held New Orleans. And so he reached a decision. "Tell Me Pretty Baby" deserved to see the light of day, and Andrew Jackson deserved to be the one to make it happen.

Andy made arrangements to visit the Falco home that weekend. He pictured himself reaching into the dark closet, groping around for the dusty box, and carefully threading the old tape onto Pete's machine. It might sound a little strange on the modern multi-head stereophonic machine, but that wouldn't matter much.

Andy walked Pete and Shanti to the door, thoroughly convinced that the fantastic story was authentic. "Tell Me Pretty Baby." He turned the title over in his head, let the taste of it roll off his tongue in a dozen subtle variations. He watched Shanti struggle with the balky transmission for a moment. The car eased out of the lot and disappeared into the hazy distance. Andy glanced at the calendar hanging near the office door. He couldn't wait for the weekend to arrive.

The Big Deal

CHAPTER THREE

Andy could hardly contain his exuberance as he wheeled across town, passing in and out of a half-dozen sprawling municipalities that made up the Dallas suburbs. One moment he whistled appreciatively at the million dollar estates of the affluent; the next he shook his head at the dilapidated shanties of the desperately poor. As he neared his destination, though, the scenery improved. This was a solid middle class neighborhood, Andy realized, perfect for a hardworking man of average means like Pete Falco.

Andy slowed the car, creeping along the street as he strained to make out house numbers. There it is! His stomach churned as he coasted into the driveway. Pete met him at the door with a warm handshake; the two had obviously established a lasting rapport. They would be able to work together.

A million thoughts flashed through Andy's mind as he entered the living room. If this deal panned out his dream to strike it rich in the recording industry just might become a reality. He said a silent prayer that things would go his way for a change.

A round of refreshments and a few minutes of small talk helped to break the ice. Then all thoughts turned to business. Andy settled down on a slightly tattered sofa while Pete rummaged through a back closet for the demo tape. Andy let his eyes roam around the small room. Most of the furnishings were somewhat threadbare, and tears in the faded wallpaper revealed glimpses of bare sheetrock. The whole room gave the impression of barely-concealed poverty.

Then Andy noticed the entertainment center, jammed with expensive audio gear. Top of the line brands, each component sparkling like a jewel. Several equally impressive guitars rested on stands along one wall. Andy walked across the room for a closer look. Fender. Gibson. Martin. B.C. Rich. All the best. Andy smiled, imagining Pete scrimping and saving to afford such fine instruments. A true musician never settles for second best. Andy hefted one of the guitars, savoring its perfect balance and smooth action. He strummed a few happy chords. The sound lured Shanti into the room, her bright smile cutting through the gloom like a spotlight through a bank of fog. This would be a day to remember.

Pete soon returned, a tightly wrapped box nestled lovingly under one arm. As he unwrapped the package with agonizing slowness, he related the story of how the precious possession had almost been lost. A few years back, during his messy divorce, his former wife had packed it away with her own things as she made a spiteful sweep of the house. Fortunately, one of the children had spotted the old tape and returned it to its proper place amongst Pete's treasures. Andy realized that the recording held a sentimental value for Pete far beyond any monetary reward it might bring. Such a loving attachment could only mean one thing: the tape was indeed authentic. Andy filed that thought away for future reference.

Finally, after what seemed an eternity, the tape emerged from the package. It looked real enough to Andy. He had handled enough demo tapes to know that this was the real McCoy. Andy sat down, trying to relax while Pete carefully loaded the reel onto his expensive tape machine. A potent blend of excitement and anticipation and joy and dread coursed through Andy's veins. He popped back up and restlessly paced back and forth, looking over Pete's shoulder and wishing he would hurry up.

And then the first strains of "Tell Me Pretty Baby" drifted from the speaker and wrapped themselves around Andy's soul. He froze. The hair on the back of his neck bristled to attention. All doubts vanished, swept away before the sultry voice that rose and fell like angry waves on a storm-tossed ocean. That was Elvis Presley.

The upbeat tempo and haunting lyrics mesmerized Andy. The musical style was different from later recordings, of course, and the instruments seemed thin and oddly ghostlike. But there could be no doubt about the voice. Elvis.

Pete played the song through several times, rewinding the delicate tape by hand to save wear and tear. Andy tried to break free from the magical spell cast by the song. He wanted to analyze the recording with cold detachment. It didn't work. Each replay only strengthened his resolve: Elvis Presley.

Andy nodded his head and returned to the sofa. He had heard enough. It was time to get down to brass tacks. He certainly was not in a position to make a substantial offer, but neither was Pete looking to become wealthy from the sale of his precious heirloom. Each accepted the other's limitations, and each realized that the song might not even be marketable in today's music scene. It might turn out to be nothing more than a flash in the pan, a quaint curiosity sought by only the most diehard Elvis collector.

Pete had some questions of his own. What would Andy do with "Tell Me Pretty Baby" if he acquired exclusive rights to the recording? Without a moment's hesitation Andy said he would do everything in his power to put the song on the market. Andy believed that Elvis fans would drool over the recording, especially if it did turn out to be the first by "The King." The style differed from standard Elvis fare, but that only served to emphasize its early date. And the song certainly had a catchy rhythm and strong emotional impact. If this was Elvis -- and Andy made it clear that he believed it was -- then his fans certainly had the right to know about the rare recording.

Pete agreed. So did Shanti. But then Pete pointed out a harsh reality: Andy could count on being targeted by RCA in a nasty lawsuit. The recording industry titan considered everything remotely connected to Elvis Presley to be its exclusive property. Jackson stood firm. If this tape held the voice of Elvis, he had the moral courage to put it on the market whether RCA liked it or not.

Pete smiled. Maybe they could work out a deal. He pressed a button on the tape machine. Everyone sang along as the pulsing rhythms of "Tell Me Pretty Baby" bounced off the walls for the umpteenth time.

Amidst the jubilation of the moment Andy maintained enough self-discipline to exercise a bit of restraint. He still wanted to have the tape examined by experts to verify his gut feeling. He could not afford to sink his life savings into an elaborate fraud. Pete agreed. He would allow Andy to take the tape in for scientific analysis if Andy would foot the bill.

Pete introduced another tantalizing angle. He knew the whereabouts of someone who had witnessed the historic 1954 recording session. The man, a former Phoenix disc jockey named Don Reese, managed an ice cream parlor on the north side of Dallas. Don had kept tabs on Pete throughout the years, primarily to keep track of the rare recording. A couple of times he had tried to buy the tape, but he never seemed to be in a position to make a reasonable offer. Andy took down directions to the ice cream parlor. He certainly planned to check in with Don Reese.

This brought up another subject. Did Pete know the whereabouts of the others present in the Phoenix recording studio? Pete shook his head. More than twenty years had rolled by. He had no idea of how to contact the other members of the Red Dots. Perhaps when news of the recording hit the media one of the men would step forward. Maybe ads in music industry trade publications would bring someone out of the woodwork. It seemed like a long shot.

Andy steered the discussion toward the most important item of all. What was this going to cost? Pete, being a reasonable man, readily admitted that the long-term expenses of marketing the recording would far outweigh its present value. First, he suggested that Andy cover the cost of repairing Shanti's balky transmission. A small expense, to be sure, but one that Pete could not afford at the moment. Pete would accept the repairs as his down payment. Andy, recognizing Pete's appreciation of fine musical instruments, offered to throw in an expensive guitar he had tucked away in storage years ago. Pete snapped at the offer. Later, when Andy had established the ironclad authenticity of "Tell Me Pretty Baby," a cash payment would close the deal. Andrew Jackson would have physical possession of the master tape along with exclusive rights to market the recording worldwide. The deal suited both parties. For now, at least, a handshake sufficed to seal the bargain. Andy stood one step closer to realizing his dreams.

CHAPTER FOUR

Andrew Jackson backed out of the Falco driveway and pulled away, the old master tape nestled on the seat beside him. Andy's mind danced with visions of the future. He kept reminding himself that the project hinged on a lot of unknown variables. If "Tell Me Pretty Baby" truly represented Elvis' first recording, if Andy could transfer it from the master tape to vinyl, and if he could put together a viable marketing plan -- well, then he might have something. A long shot, but one with potential rewards too great to ignore.

The first step on the long road to fame and fortune would begin with audio tests comparing the voice on "Tell Me Pretty Baby" to a known Elvis recording. A simple enough proposition, Andy thought, and one he planned to launch first thing in the morning. The night sky glowed with special radiance, lit by millions of lights glittering from the towering skyscrapers of downtown Dallas. Andy zoomed past, heading for the Grand Prairie car lot to deposit the priceless treasure in his office safe. Later, as he dropped off to sleep, visions of grandeur continued to dance through his head.

Dawn crept up slowly. Crisp air invigorated Andy as he walked across the lot and unlocked his office door. Today would be a busy day, and he was far too excited to enjoy his usual second cup of coffee. He cracked open the safe and gently extracted the tape. He unwrapped it, gingerly placed it on the desk, and stepped back to admire the sight. He wondered what methods a recording powerhouse like RCA might employ to get their hands on such a treasure.

The door crashed open behind him. Andy let out a startled gasp and spun around, his heart racing. For a couple of seconds he stood transfixed, gaping at the intruder. Then he burst out in laughter; it was only his secretary, as startled by his unusual behavior as he had been by her sudden appearance.

Her eyes darted to the curious gizmo on the desk. Andy launched into an hour-long recitation of the demo tape's remarkable background. His secretary sat spellbound through the entire story. She seemed delighted to see Andy in such high spirits.

Before long the lot crawled with customers, far more than usual for a Monday morning. Andy got busy making deals. His smile seemed infectious, his buoyant mood charming even the most hard-nosed horse trader into submission. One lucrative sale followed another. The day flashed by in the blink of an eye, a dizzying kaleidoscope of tire-kicking, hood-popping, price-haggling, sign-on-the-dotted-line car deals.

Andy totaled up the day's receipts, suddenly realizing that he had neglected to make a single phone call concerning the audio tests. He sighed. "Tell Me Pretty Baby" had lain dormant for twenty-three years; another day or two wouldn't make much difference one way or the other. He hoped.

A flurry of business devoured that week and part of the next. Sales continued at a brisk pace, and Andy certainly appreciated the extra revenue. Perhaps the unexpected windfall would allow him to take a few days off and concentrate on the recording. Andy touched base with Pete Falco several times, assuring him that the voice tests would be conducted shortly. Shanti's transmission had been repaired and the car was ready for pickup, along with the guitar that Andy had promised. Pete said he would drop by in a few days.

Andy finally got around to contacting Sumet Sound, a North Dallas recording studio, to set up an appointment to have the tape reviewed. Andy had dealt with several of Sumet's engineers on past projects. If anyone could pass judgment on "Tell Me Pretty Baby," these experts could. To avoid coloring their perceptions, Andy would not reveal the supposed identity of the artist in advance. He would simply ask them to play the tape and, based on their intimate knowledge of the recording industry, take a guess at whose voice it might be.

Pete and Shanti showed up at the car lot a couple of days later. Pete's eyes lit up when he saw the guitar. He caressed the shiny wood body for a moment before tossing off a few chords. His long fingers glided up and down the neck, picking out the rhythmic melody of "Tell Me Pretty Baby" with graceful perfection. Shanti seemed equally satisfied as she tested her newly-repaired transmission. Bright smiles lit up both faces as they departed.

The day finally arrived for Andy's appointment at Sumet Sound. The studio engineers crowded into a small room packed with expensive audio gear. Andy had to bite his tongue to keep from revealing his secret. These music experts held sterling reputations for technical brilliance and long industry experience. Andy felt confident that their opinions could be taken to the bank. Indeed, if everything worked out right, the bank was one of the places he hoped to visit often.

One of the engineers threaded the delicate tape onto the playback machine. Andy explained that he wanted the men to sit through the entire two minutes and twelve seconds of "Tell Me Pretty Baby," discuss it for a while, and then offer professional opinions as to the artist's identity. Everyone nodded as Andy hit the play button and settled down on a stool.

The men tapped their feet to the rhythmic opening, leaning forward in curiosity. They exchanged questioning glances as the first velvet strains of the artist's voice washed across the room.

Their eyes narrowed, their heads tilted forward to catch every subtle nuance of the recording. Andy glanced from one man to the next, judging their reactions.

And then it happened. One of the engineers jumped to his feet and shouted, "Elvis! Elvis Presley, in the early days!" The others seemed baffled for a moment, but then heads started to nod. An excited babble broke out, everyone trying to speak at once. From the ensuing exchange emerged a unanimous decision. This was indeed Elvis Presley!

Andy tried hard to contain his emotions. He questioned the men carefully. Could this be some sort of hoax? Perhaps the work of an Elvis impersonator? Someone rewound the tape, and the excited conversation dropped off as the song played through again.

This was no fraud, everyone agreed. This was Elvis in the early days, back before he had fully developed the distinctive voice that imitators would later mimic. Only spectrographic analysis would yield a certain verdict, they said, but in their collective opinion this was indeed the voice of a young Elvis.

Andy nodded. That was enough. The wheels could now be set in motion. In the morning he would relay the news to Pete Falco, sign a check for the agreed purchase price, and ink the sales contract. Andy's heart pounded with renewed vigor. He was in business.

Andy meets Don

CHAPTER FIVE

Andrew Jackson had one more task in mind before he left the north side of Dallas. He wanted to drop in on Don Reese. The ice cream parlor Don managed wasn't far out of the way; it wouldn't take long to swing by and hear the former disc jockey's version of the "Tell Me Pretty Baby" recording session.

Bumper-to-bumper traffic clogged the roads, a common phenomenon at that time of the afternoon. That was one of the reasons Andy had settled down in the more relaxed suburb of Grand Prairie. Dallas had its own advantages though, Andy mused, like the big city way of doing big business. Scores of nice apartment complexes lay within a short distance of the downtown business district. If this project turned out as big as Andy hoped it might, perhaps he would consider moving closer to the action.

The sight of the ice cream parlor yanked Andy out of his daydream. He swore softly as he frantically maneuvered across four lanes of traffic and slammed on the brakes to make the turn into the driveway. He sat in the car for a moment, studying the quaint ice cream emporium while he regained his composure.

A welcome blast of cold air met Andy at the door. He stepped to the counter and ordered a frosty treat, a sort of celebration to honor the good news from the engineers at Sumet Sound. A pretty young girl took his order. Andy asked if Don Reese was in. She flashed an innocent grin and affirmed that indeed he was. She spun on her heels and disappeared into the back room to inform the manager that he had a visitor. The girl soon returned, presenting Andy's rich banana split with a flourish. Don would be there shortly, she said.

Andy kept an eye on the door to the back room as he dug into his ice cream treat. Before long an average looking man with intelligent eyes emerged and started across the room, his head tilted curiously. A gaudy name tag affixed to the lapel of his cheap polyester suit confirmed his identity: Don Reese.

Introducing himself in a manner that betrayed his disc jockey past, he perched on the edge of a chair across from Andy. He seemed overly cautious, as if this unexpected visitor might be about to hit him up for a loan, or perhaps serve a warrant. Andy recognized Don's reluctance and quickly set his mind at ease. He simply wanted to discuss the music recording industry, he said, and an incident that took place in Phoenix back in 1954.

Don sat bolt upright. His face twisted into a momentary expression that Andy didn't quite recognize, an expression that vanished as swiftly as it had appeared. Don assumed a more genial air and reached out to grasp Andy's hand. A kindred soul, he called Andy, and launched into an excited babble about his love of music and the recording industry. He confirmed that he had indeed been in Phoenix in 1954, working as a radio disc jockey. How could he help?

Andy gave a brief recap of his dealings with Pete Falco. When it became clear that he had purchased the "Tell Me Pretty Baby" recording, Don's face fell. He seemed thunderstruck. The obviously unwelcome news rendered him speechless for more than a minute.

Andy took advantage of the pause to devour the remainder of his banana split, his eyes never straying from Don's crestfallen expression. Then it hit him: this man knows exactly what the old recording is worth.

Don finally overcame the shock. All he wanted to know, it seemed, was when and how. The when had been just recently, Andy explained, and the how was a private arrangement. He could not divulge the particulars. A down payment had been made, all obligations had been fulfilled. The tape belonged to Andy. A substantial final payment remained, he said, but that would be attended to very soon.

Andy started to tell Don that the master tape sat right outside in the front seat of his car. He caught himself just in time. No need to place temptation in the path of this man, this stranger who had obviously never given up hope of producing the song himself.

Now Andy got down to brass tacks. Did Don actually witness the Phoenix recording session? Did he really believe that the young man who sang with the Red Dots that day was indeed Elvis Presley? Don answered both questions emphatically: absolutely! As a matter of fact, said Don, he had even been present at the club the night before when Elvis took the stage.

Don grew quiet and his eyes glazed over; he seemed lost in a haze of nostalgia. Andy studied him intently, convinced that the man was telling the truth. Some emotions just can't be faked.

Don snapped out of his pensive mood. He had some questions of his own. Did Pete Falco send Andy to see him? But he answered that question himself with a laugh; who else would know? He tried a different tack. What had Andy done with the recording? Not much, Andy replied, beyond having some experts offer their opinions on just who the singer was. He provided a brief sketch of his visit to Sumet Sound, and the unanimous agreement amongst the sound engineers that the voice did indeed belong to a young Elvis. Andy omitted the fact that he had just come from the studio. And now, Don wanted to know, what was Andy going to do with the song?

Rather than answering right away, Andy launched into a recollection of his long involvement with the recording industry. He had the experience, the inside contacts, and the knowledge to put "Tell Me Pretty Baby" on the market. He planned to do just that, he said, as soon as he got ironclad verification of the singer's identity.

Don pointed out that Elvis was under contract with RCA Records. The company owned everything associated with the superstar. Could Andy release the song under those conditions? Andy laid out his strategy: if he could prove that Elvis had recorded the song before he signed any contracts with Sun Records or RCA, he could legally release the song under Elvis' name.

Moreover, Andy continued, if this song was indeed Elvis' first recording, it could very well represent the actual birth of Rock-n -Roll. A scary thought, to be sure, but one that could be worth millions if it panned out. The song might serve as a benchmark not just to Elvis fans, but to the entire industry. Before such brilliant predictions could come true, of course, the song had to be produced and marketed. That would take time and money. Andy explained that he made his living selling cars in Grand Prairie.

Don jumped in quickly, his eyes glowing: perhaps he could join forces with Andy? That was an angle Andy hadn't considered. It might be worth thinking about. Don said that while he certainly wasn't rich, he did have a small amount of capital he would be more than happy to invest in the project. He had been present at the birth of "Tell Me Pretty Baby," he explained, and it had long been his dream to have a hand in the rare recording. He said that he also had some contacts in the music industry, and that he was willing to take on the grueling legwork that would be involved in the production. His enthusiasm seemed boundless, and he seemed to possess formidable expertise in management and marketing.

Andy promised that he would consider the proposal. The men exchanged business cards and a warm handshake. Andy chewed on the situation as he started the long drive home. Things seemed to be coming together quite nicely, he thought. But an elusive shadow flittered around in the back of his mind; something seemed slightly out of place. The strange feeling persisted as he zoomed up the entry ramp and merged with the freeway traffic. He wished he could put a finger on the vague premonition.

CHAPTER SIX

Andy reached work a little later than usual the next morning. Weeks of accumulated stress had begun to take a toll on him. He hadn't been sleeping well, and a low grade headache plagued him constantly. And the trouble with his girlfriend certainly didn't help.

Wanting to share his good news, he had dropped by Gina's small Arlington apartment the night before. It turned out to be a mistake. Gina seemed to take pleasure in turning his good moods into bad ones. Andy suspected she did it on purpose, but he knew that any mention of the subject would only provoke a nasty fight. He asked himself why he had ever entered into a relationship with her in the first place, and why he continued to tolerate her sharp tongue and sour attitude. The night had ended on a negative note.

He continued to think about the incident as he pulled into the car lot. He wished he wouldn't allow her to get under his skin. The fiery young beauty seemed to have him wrapped around her finger, he mused.

The sharp smell of brewing coffee greeted him at the door; his secretary had already opened shop. After a brief exchange of pleasantries Andy poured himself a steaming cup of java and headed straight for his office. He plopped down on his overstuffed armchair with a sigh and launched into the daily routine of preparing his desk for business.

That task out of the way, Andy picked up the phone and dialed Pete Falco's number. Pete answered on the second ring. Everything was falling into place, Andy said, and if he would drop by the car lot he'd fill him in on yesterday's happenings. Oh yeah, he added, Pete's check would be ready and waiting. Pete promised he'd be over shortly.

Andy smiled as he hung up. The phone call had cleared away the blue mood hanging in the air. He felt ready to take on the world. One scene kept unfolding inside Andy's head over and over. He closed his eyes and savored the moment once again, the excited voice of the Sumet Sound engineer as he leapt to his feet and identified the singer of "Tell Me Pretty Baby" as Elvis Presley, the quick agreement by the other experts. Andy couldn't wait to relay the story to Pete. He also planned to discuss Don Reese's offer to become a partner in the project. Maybe Pete could offer some insight.

A steady flow of customers interrupted Andy's thoughts. He was just closing a deal on a nice Lincoln when he spotted Pete's car rolling into the lot. Pete stood at a respectful distance and waited for Andy to finish. A good sign. The more Andy learned about Pete, he thought, the more he liked him. Men of such caliber were few and far between.

The men greeted each other with a friendly handshake. Andy showed Pete into his office before relating the events at Sumet Sound. Pete didn't seem at all surprised that the engineers had identified Elvis so easily. After all, he had stood next to Elvis as he recorded the lyrics. Nobody had to convince him. Nonetheless, Andy's exuberance proved contagious. Before long loud and hearty laughter filled the office.

Andy had prepared a contract to transfer exclusive rights to "Tell Me Pretty Baby." Pete read the document carefully, pausing here and there to ask questions. At last he seemed satisfied. He took a pen from Andy's desk and carefully signed his name. Andy filled out a check and handed it to Pete with a flourish.

The check represented the bulk of Andy's personal savings, but he considered the investment worthwhile. Moreover, business at the lot had been booming lately. That would help cover the money shortage, Andy thought. He hoped the increased business continued for a while; he might end up in a financial bind if it slowed down. The overall economic outlook wasn't exactly bright, as the man sitting across the desk could attest.

Pete was happy to receive the desperately-needed money. Truck driving normally provided a decent living, but skyrocketing fuel prices had pinched even the larger freight lines. Pete's jobs had suddenly become few and far between. The check would help cover some of his overdue bills, and he would be able to keep himself and Shanti fed. He hoped the money would last long enough to find steady work. He still played bass for a couple of local bands, but that didn't bring much money in anymore, especially with competition from all the new talent. Nonetheless Pete felt a twinge of regret and loss as he signed away the legal rights to his beloved recording.

Andy recounted his meeting with Don Reese. Pete said he would have been surprised if Don hadn't tried to nose in on the deal. The surprising part was that Andy was actually considering the offer. Something about Don had always seemed funny, Pete said, and he had never fully trusted him. Don had never done anything to justify such an attitude, he admitted, but he could not deny the feeling.

Andy agreed, relating the misgivings that had been creeping around in the back of his mind ever since the meeting at the ice cream parlor. Some people just don't make good first impressions. He had encountered men like that before. In fact, he had felt that way about the biker that worked in his repair shop. He was the type of man who at first glance made you want to lock the doors and pull down the shades. The biker had turned out to be solid and trustworthy, however, and Andy couldn't ask for a better friend. Some people were just that way.

Maybe that was the case with Don. The former disc jockey had a voice and style that just didn't match his appearance. Nonetheless, if Don stood willing to put his money and his time on the line, perhaps Andy should accept the offer at face value. He would continue to think about the proposal, he told Pete; he still had time to reach a decision one way or the other.

Andy glanced at the clock and realized with a start that lunchtime had arrived. He offered to take Pete out to eat. Pete gratefully accepted. On the way out Andy asked his secretary if he could pick anything up for her. Such thoughtfulness was the main reason she had endured a low salary and stuck with the Auto Village for so long. She declined the offer with a gleam in her eye; she had plenty of rabbit food. Andy smiled. The fact that she survived on raw vegetables amazed him. He just could not understand how anyone could stay healthy on such a meager diet. He often teased her about it.

The men climbed into Andy's car for the quick trip to a pizza joint. The restaurant's all-you-can-eat lunch special and generous salad bar attracted a crowd of blue collar laborers. Pete and Andy worked their way across the packed room to a booth near the back.

As the men settled down, Pete asked an unusual question: how could Andy serve two masters at the same time? Andy seemed puzzled; his parents had instilled him with deep religious convictions, but he hadn't attended church regularly since going through a particularly nasty divorce. Pete laughed at the baffled expression on Andy's face. He explained that the two masters he had in mind were the used car business and the recording industry.

The same question had been crawling through Andy's mind ever since Shanti Falco had first related the magical story of "Tell Me Pretty Baby." Andy's lifelong dream was to jump into the music industry full time. That dream lay closer than ever. Pete smiled at the response. The two men made a solemn vow to do all they could to make Andy's dreams come true.

The King is dead

CHAPTER SEVEN

The next few weeks passed in a blur, Andy devoting every spare minute to piecing together his own record company. A careful study of his records revealed that he had about thirty thousand dollars worth of used car inventory that could be readily liquidated. That seed money would be enough to take the first tentative steps toward forming the company, but it wouldn't be near enough to actually put "Tell Me Pretty Baby" on the market. His next move, then, would be to find one or two business partners. Don Reese aside, he should have no trouble finding investors.

One of his old daydreams popped to mind, that of converting the car lot into a full-scale production company with an outdoor concert arena on the back acreage. That particular fantasy didn't seem so far away now. First, though, he had to get the record company into operation. And then, if "Tell Me Pretty Baby" enjoyed the kind of success he hoped it might, he would expand into the production end of the business. All in due time.

A month passed before he relayed the news to Pete Falco: he would sell his automobile inventory and jump into the recording industry feet first. The move marked a big step for Andy. With every penny of his meager funds committed to the venture, he would have no safety net. No problem, Pete said; "Tell Me Pretty Baby" would be a sure hit.

The two men met a few days later to lay down some firm plans for the venture. Pete was giddy with excitement, thrilled to get back into the business he loved. They would form a good team, their skills complementing each other nicely. Andy would handle the business end, while Pete's technical expertise would be vital when the time came to produce the record.

Andy brought up the matter of naming the production company. They kicked a few suggestions around, laughing at some and writing others off as too vague. They finally settled on a name they could both live with: Trans-Media World Record Producers. A grandiose title, to be sure, but certainly no bigger than the dreams they shared.

Andy proceeded with the liquidation of his inventory. Auto brokers snapped up most of the cars, while a handful went to other dealers and old customers at discount prices. That chore out of the way, Andy turned his attention to the delicate task of starting a business from scratch.

Nothing seemed to work out right. Everything from letterhead to office conversion to recording equipment -- cost twice as much as anticipated. The money dwindled away at an alarming rate, and there seemed to be little to show for it.

Andy embarked on a desperate crusade to drum up investment capital. A few individuals showed interest, but each insisted on controlling the company. Andy refused to accept money under those terms. Pete agreed. It was their dream, their company, and they would not let anyone else have the final say. Sink or swim, they would do it on their own.

Before long the fledging company lay in ruins. Maybe the dream had been too big, the obstacles too great, the money too meager. Whatever the reason, by August Andy was bankrupt. Everything had vanished -- the car dealership, the record company, the dream. It was a hard pill to swallow, but there could be no denying the bleak reality.

Broke and downbeat, Andy took his few remaining possessions and locked the door to his empty office. He still had "Tell Me Pretty Baby," of course, along with a few other recordings he had accumulated over the years, but these seemed small consolation. His spirit was shattered, his courage devastated. He wondered if he had what it took to succeed in the record business. He still loved the music industry, of course, but it seemed to care little for his having invested his life savings and his soul. Pete Falco still stood by his side, but Andy had never experienced such bitter loneliness.

And so matters stood on August 16, 1977, when a tragic announcement flashed around the globe: Elvis Presley was dead. The news hit Andy like a stroke of lightening from a clear blue sky. He was devastated.

Andy had always hoped to contact Elvis someday and talk about "Tell Me pretty Baby." The superstar had become increasingly reclusive for the past several years, of course, but it would have been worth a try. Maybe Elvis would have wanted to acquire the old recording, or perhaps he knew of someone who did.

With the King gone, Andy doubted that he would ever be able to recoup his initial investment. But then he watched in awe as mobs of distraught fans descended on Graceland. As the vivid images from Memphis flashed across Andy's television set, it suddenly dawned on him that "Tell Me Pretty Baby" might be more valuable than ever. He had admired Elvis, and the loss brought a terrible wave of grief crashing over his soul. Nonetheless, there was no denying that the untimely death had created a renewed financial opportunity. If the world gives you lemons, Andy thought, make lemonade. He planned to do just that.

Andy meets Dr. John

CHAPTER EIGHT

Andy refused to allow the setback to keep him down. Before long he picked himself up and set out with renewed determination to round up additional investors. "Tell Me Pretty Baby" remained his strongest selling point, of course, but he realized the necessity of obtaining absolute verification of the singer's identity. Armed with such evidence, the money should come pouring in from all quarters.

The death of Elvis Presley had caused a sudden rise in the potential value of the recording. That might prove to be a two-edged sword, though, for the legal ramifications had taken on a new dimension as well. Andy did not let that deter him; he knew he was sitting on a gold mine, if only he could get the song into production. "Tell Me Pretty Baby" should have been released long ago. Fate had dictated otherwise.

With such thoughts in mind, Andy turned his face toward his dream with renewed determination. He needed ironclad evidence that Elvis recorded the song. Now he knew where to turn: Dr. John Godfrey, a professor at the University of Texas at Dallas as well as a nationally recognized audio expert. Andy called to set up a meeting.

A couple of weeks passed before the appointed date, each day crawling by with agonizing slowness. He could barely contain his anticipation as he parked his car and set out across the university campus, the precious demo tape tucked safely under one arm, a rare Elvis vinyl record grasped in his hand. His heart pounded as he walked into Dr. Godfrey's office. A warm greeting from the eminent sound expert set Andy's mind at ease.

Dr. Godfrey had instructed Andy to bring a known Elvis recording from his early days -- the earlier the better. Such records had grown increasingly rare in the wake of Elvis' death, but Andy finally managed to locate a pristine recording from the Sun Records days, "Ain't That Lovin' You Baby."

Andy watched with growing excitement as Dr. Godfrey made preparations for an informal comparative and spectrographic test, threading the old demo tape onto his playback machine and dropping the vinyl record onto an expensive turntable.

The professor played each song through several times, nodding his head with increasing excitement. He finally narrowed the playbacks to key sections, switching rapidly back and forth from "Tell Me Pretty Baby" to "Ain't That Lovin' You Baby." Every so often he redirected the output to a set of studio headphones before switching back to the monitor speakers. Andy tried to question him a couple of times, but Dr. Godfrey signaled for silence with a finger to his pursed lips. Andy was about to explode.

Dr. Godfrey finally seemed satisfied. He switched the equipment off and plopped down in a plush leather chair behind his desk. He leaned back and stared at the ceiling for a moment, lost in deliberation. After what seemed an eternity, he announced that it was probable that Elvis Presley sang both songs.

Andy asked if he would put that in writing. Dr. Godfrey fed a sheet of letterhead into his typewriter and pounded away at the keyboard for a couple of minutes. When he finished he handed the sheet to Andy.

This was what he had been looking for: a signed affidavit from a respected expert, expressing the opinion that "Tell Me Pretty

Baby" had indeed been recorded by Elvis Presley. Andy beamed
with joy.

Then he noted the caveat attached to the end of the document:
"obviously there was no scientific test, because it was represented
to me as being the voice of Elvis Presley. To conduct a scientific
experiment, you would have to be blind to the factors involved,
and even then you couldn't make a positive finding. In my opinion,
there is not a known methodology for doing that." He questioned
the professor carefully, but was reassured that the qualification
did not change his underlying opinion about the identity of the
singer. Any other audio expert, Dr. Godfrey said, would recognize
the qualification for what it was: legal window dressing.

That was enough for Andy. He now had the solid footing he
needed to raise additional investment capital. His enthusiasm
soared; the dream was back in sight. He whistled a happy tune as
he walked back across campus to his car.

Andy raced back to his girlfriend's apartment -- his new
residence -- and dashed to the telephone. He couldn't wait to
relay the good news to Pete Falco. The conversation soon turned
to deciding which step to take next. They would make an all-
out effort to contact musicians who knew Elvis in his early days,
along with anyone else who might know something about "Tell
Me Pretty Baby." Whatever the outcome of that, Andy and Pete
agreed that nothing much could be done until they had some
money. Andy mentioned the investors he had turned down before.
No dice, they concluded; they would not turn over control of the
production to anyone. The name Don Reese popped up. Maybe
he would be game. The conversation ended on a happy note,
each man expressing a renewed commitment to putting "Tell Me
Pretty Baby" on the market.

Andy dialed Don Reese's number and waited for an answer.
Something about the man still struck him as slightly out of place,
but they needed money more than ever. Don finally answered,
obviously excited to hear from Andy again. He had tried to get in
touch when Elvis died, he said, but both numbers Andy had given

him were disconnected. Andy explained that his car dealership, converted into headquarters for the failed record company, now lay empty. Andy now lived with his girlfriend.

Don seemed relieved when Andy reassured him that "Tell Me Pretty Baby" had not yet been produced. Don expressed his willingness to get back in on the action; he too recognized the increased financial possibilities caused by the death of Elvis. The song was now hot property. Andy pointed out that in order to cash in, the song needed to be on the market.

Andy said that he intended to market the record under the name Elvis Presley. The only way he could do that would be to prove its authenticity before release. He made it clear that he had no intention of releasing the song until he had ironclad proof that Elvis did indeed sing "Tell Me Pretty Baby." He started to mention the informal analysis conducted by Dr. Godfrey, and the resultant signed affidavit. Something made him hold back, though. He still didn't trust Don.

At any rate, said Andy, the market would not dry up anytime soon. Elvis fans would always be Elvis fans. The King of Rock-n-Roll had passed away, but his music would last forever. Don had to agree.

The two men discussed the possibility of forming another record company, with Don owning a percentage. Of course, the whole venture would be built around "Tell Me Pretty Baby," which was legally owned by Andy. They set an appointment for a meeting later in the week.

Don did not come to the meeting empty handed. He introduced Marion Sitton, an intelligent businessman with contacts in the music industry. More importantly, Marion had a pool of ready cash and seemed willing to back the venture. Andy realized that this man could be an important asset to the project.

Thus reassured, Andy now produced the signed affidavit from Dr. Godfrey and related the events of the meeting at the university campus. Marion studied the document with a critical eye. He seemed impressed. He had Andy and Don repeat the story of their previous involvement with the demo tape, questioning them carefully along the way. At last he seemed satisfied. He made a firm commitment: if they would take him, he would join the venture.

Don also reiterated his willingness to donate his time and expertise in return for a percentage share in the company. Andy turned everything over in his mind. Counting himself and Pete Falco, that would make four partners. Each man brought long years of business experience, valuable industry contacts, and a varying amount of investment capital. That should be enough.

Andy accepted the offers, sealing the deal with a round of handshakes. The formal paperwork would be drawn up later. The room overflowed with excitement as the meeting broke up. For Andy, at least, things looked brighter than ever.

Delays continued to plague the venture, and the old problem of higher-than-expected costs loomed large. Nonetheless, through hard work and perseverance, the men finally formed a new company in June 1978. They called it International Classic Productions. Certainly not as grandiose sounding as the last company, but filled with the same high hopes.

Andy was on top of the world. His elation was tempered with extreme caution, however, for hard experience had taught him that hidden dangers usually lurked just around the next corner. He realized that he had set out through a deadly mine field. Each step would have to be taken gingerly. Many unforeseen obstacles would have to be overcome before success was assured. He stood ready to face the challenge.

Ominous signs

CHAPTER NINE

Ominous signs had already emerged from the headquarters of RCA Records. In January 1978 the company embarked on a rampage to acquire -- by means foul or fair -- the rights to all known recordings by Elvis Presley. In many cases this proved to be a simple matter of spending what amounted to pocket change to the corporate giant. In other cases, however, those in possession of rumored Elvis recordings proved reluctant to part with their treasures. Many lived to regret such hesitation. RCA, it seemed, maintained a stable of slick-talking corporate lawyers. These cunning legal warriors held duplicity as a virtue and made their living by being more devious than their competitors.

The most visible case was that of Shelby Singleton, who in 1969 had legally purchased the entire Sun Records catalog. In the wake of Elvis' death, Singleton had released an album featuring songs by the King of Rock-n-Roll -- songs discovered amongst the thousands of master tapes acquired from Sun.

RCA's response was swift and merciless. In late 1977 the company petitioned a Nashville judge for an injunction to halt sales of the album and to reimburse RCA for any moneys generated by its sale. Chancellor C. Allen High granted the request, awarding RCA $45,000 and issuing an order that prevented Singleton from releasing two other albums featuring recordings by Elvis Presley, Johnny Cash, Carl Perkins, Jerry Lee Lewis, Charlie Rich, and Roy Orbison.

Although the judge did allow him to keep some $600,000 in profits, Singleton remained firmly convinced that the recordings would have brought much more in the long run. He was understandably bitter, especially when he learned that RCA planned to send an Elvis expert to comb through his tape vault and retrieve any Presley material. "We'll be glad to rent them our studio to do it," Singleton told a Variety reporter.

Andrew Jackson flew into Nashville to further authenticate "Tell Me Pretty Baby." The town still buzzed with sensational rumors concerning Singleton's legal battles. Despite the suddenly gloomy outlook, Andy's hopes remained high. They would soon be dashed.

Andy's first appointment was with Scotty Moore, Elvis' first guitarist and manager. Moore, who now ran his own independent production company, had seemed somewhat hesitant when Andy called from Dallas to arrange the appointment. This feeling was reinforced by the cool reception Andy received when he arrived at Moore's office. After a bit of guarded small talk, Andy removed the "Tell Me Pretty Baby" master tape from his briefcase and handed it to Moore.

Andy settled down in a chair while Moore loaded the recording onto his tape player. Andy's thoughts returned to the happy scene at Sumet Sound in Dallas. He remembered that beautiful moment when the sound engineer's eyes lit up in recognition. And now, as the first strains of "Tell Me Pretty Baby" washed across the room, Andy watched Moore for a similar reaction.

He could not have been more disappointed. Five or ten seconds into the song, a look of disgust spread across Moore's face. He snapped off the tape player and fixed Andy with an evil glare. "It's a crock!" Andy's smile vanished, his face twisting into an expression of sheer confusion.

"I said I think it's a crock," Moore repeated. "The group on the record is trying to imitate what we did in 1954, but that record wasn't out before 1955 or '56." There must be some mistake, Andy thought. He asked Moore to listen to the entire song. Moore sneered in derision. "I believe our meeting is over, Mister Jackson." Thunderstruck, Andy gathered his materials and departed.

He cruised the streets of Nashville for what seemed an eternity, lost in a daze and trying to figure it all out. How in the world could Scotty Moore dismiss the song after listening to five or ten seconds of music? How could he pinpoint the date of the recording in such a rapid fashion?

And then it hit him. RCA had reached Scotty Moore first. Andy gripped the steering wheel and sat bolt upright. Dozens of possibilities ran through his mind. Perhaps it had been an outright offer of cash. Maybe RCA had agreed to put its marketing and distribution muscle behind Moore's production company. Whatever type of deal had been cut, Andy knew beyond a shadow of a doubt that Moore had been instructed to deny the existence of any purported Elvis recordings that did not appear in the RCA catalog. Andy wondered if it might be too late. Perhaps everyone that could verify the authenticity of "Tell Me Pretty Baby" had already been compromised.

His next stop only confirmed his suspicions. He dropped in on Shelby Singleton, the man who had the nerve to tangle with RCA in court. Andy had alerted Singleton that he would be in town with a recently discovered Elvis recording. He hoped that his familiarity with early Elvis material would allow him to offer an opinion on "Tell Me Pretty Baby." As things turned out, Singleton's response was not the one Andy had been looking for.

Unlike Moore, Singleton had the courtesy to allow the entire recording to play through before he spoke. Nonetheless, Andy noticed that his mind seemed made up long before the last notes of "Tell Me Pretty Baby" faded to silence. "This record has voices on it," Singleton said. "As far as I have been able to find out, Elvis never recorded with voices until he came to Nashville."

Andy seemed confused for a moment. Of course the song had voices on it. How else could it be Elvis Presley? Who ever heard of an Elvis instrumental? But then he realized Singleton was talking about the backing vocals. Andy remembered that when Elvis had started recording with Sun Records in 1954, he was singing with Bill Black on slap bass and Scotty Moore on guitar, with no backup vocals. This style continued until 1956, when Presley was joined by the Jordanaires.

This raised an obvious question: if Elvis performed "Tell Me Pretty Baby" in 1954 with a full band and backing vocals, why did he revert to a more primitive style for two years before resuming his use of vocal accompaniment? Andy started to explain that the song had been written by Pete Falco, not Elvis. Falco had controlled the Phoenix recording session; "Tell Me Pretty Baby" had been performed according to his instructions. Elvis had not been in charge.

Singleton cut him off. "It doesn't even sound like early Elvis to me. Anyway, I've done some checking on your story. From what I can figure out, Presley was not in Arizona at the time this was supposedly recorded." With that pronouncement Singleton stood up, grasped Andy by the arm, and led him toward the door. "Thank you for allowing me to hear this recording, Mr. Jackson," he said. "I hope your stay in Nashville is pleasant."

But the trip was over. In less than an hour Andy boarded a jetliner for the return flight to Dallas, his thoughts focused on the strange meeting with Singleton. It all seemed like an instant replay of the encounter with Scotty Moore. The resemblance was so strong that it seemed to Andy that both meetings had been rehearsed beforehand. He suddenly realized that they probably had been. He remembered that Singleton had been allowed to keep $600,000 in profits from his Elvis releases, and that RCA never seemed to have put up much of a fight over that part of the disagreement.

This startling revelation smashed into Andy's consciousness like an iron sledgehammer into an upraised brow. He wondered if it might not have been a disagreement after all. Perhaps the highly-visible injunction suit against Singleton had been nothing more than a carefully-staged preemptive legal strike orchestrated by RCA's devious attorneys. Andy's mental picture of the scheme, previously fuzzy and vague, slowly sharpened into focus. Suddenly it was all too clear. This perfectly choreographed -- and very public -- lawsuit would doubtless serve as an example to others who might contemplate releasing hidden Elvis Presley material. Now it all made sense. The web of deceit seemed to be growing larger by the moment.

Back in Dallas, Andy called his partners to relate his strange Nashville experiences. Everyone agreed with Andy's assessment of the situation: RCA did not intend for anyone to release Elvis Presley recordings. These behind-the-scenes maneuvers only served to strengthen their resolve. The partners renewed their commitment to putting "Tell Me Pretty Baby" on the market.

International Classic Productions rented office space in the prestigious Blanton Towers, located on West Mockingbird Lane just across from Love Field Airport. Andy found an apartment nearby, although he usually stayed with Gina, his high-strung girlfriend.

This was a bustling part of Dallas, swirling with high-stakes wheeling and dealing. The partners usually held their meetings in the first- floor restaurant, where they could watch the mesmerizing flow of traffic as it raced past just outside. The fast pace energized the men. With "Tell Me Pretty Baby" on the verge of release, the partners sensed the sweet taste of success just around the corner.

Andy insisted that it was more important than ever to obtain additional verification of the song's authenticity. Faced with a wily opponent like RCA, they would need all the ammunition they could get before the record was released to the public. Pete Falco and Don Reese protested. After all, they had witnessed the recording session, and each had signed an affidavit attesting to the fact that Elvis sang "Tell Me Pretty Baby." They did not see the need for additional proof.

Fortunately, Marion Sitton did. He used his extensive contacts to locate two musicians who had worked with Elvis in the early days of his career. Marvin "Smokey" Montgomery and Leo Teel each provided signed affidavits attesting to their belief that Elvis Presley did in fact sing "Tell Me Pretty Baby." Other affidavits and documents came from people who had played with Elvis on "Louisiana Hayride" and other television and radio shows in the early 1950s. A piano player who performed with Elvis in the early days attested that Elvis often mentioned a band called the Red Dots. A lady in Dallas who had been friends with Elvis confirmed that the superstar frequently alluded to Pete Falco's band.

Andy took the master tape to Wayne Edwards, the country music promotions director for RCA's Dallas branch. Edwards seemed cordial enough, and he gave the recording a careful listening. "It certainly sounds like Elvis," he said. "But then, with the right technical equipment, I could sound like Elvis. There's just no way of telling."

Nonetheless, Andy and his partners agreed that the scales had finally tipped in their favor. With the first anniversary of Elvis' death fast approaching, they needed to get "Tell Me Pretty Baby" on the market as soon as possible. With that in mind, International Classic Productions inked a contract with Rainbow Record Pressing in Dallas. Rainbow would produce 25,000 vinyl records in a 45 rpm double A-side format, each side featuring an identical version of "Tell Me Pretty Baby."

Hal Freeman's Nashville-based Cin-Kay Distributors assumed control of worldwide distribution and promotion. Part of Freeman's promotional strategy involved a massive mailing that would put "Tell Me Pretty Baby" in the hands of disc jockeys at 8,200 influential radio stations. With luck, heavy airplay would follow.

Andy and his partners rejoiced. Everything finally seemed to be coming together. International Classic Productions was in business.

Summer 1978

CHAPTER TEN

Memphis found itself unprepared for the madness that swept through its streets in the summer of 1978. Perhaps nothing quite as exciting had occurred in these parts since 1862, that fateful second year of the Civil War when a flotilla of Union ironclads rounded a bend in the Mississippi River, loosed a thunderous volley from massive naval guns, and churned downstream to claim the latest in a series of fallen Confederate cities.

The first wave of modern invaders did not announce its presence in so grand a fashion. They arrived in a trickle, almost invisible at first, but slowly gaining in numbers as the shimmering heat of July gave way to the dog days of August. The trickle soon grew to a steady flow and then a rushing torrent. Before long the charming Southern city, perched atop a bluff alongside the Father of Waters, found itself all but overwhelmed. Hotels and restaurants and bars groaned under the weight of the sudden crush. Teeming crowds overflowed into the streets until the entire city resembled one giant organism, one churning mass of frantic humanity.

The ultimate goal lay along a tree lined boulevard south of downtown, hidden behind an imposing brick wall. The crowd pressed forward intently, everyone dead set on reaching the wrought iron gate where a driveway pierced the wall, the one opening that promised a brief glimpse of the mysteries tucked away inside. Graceland. The one year anniversary of the death of Elvis Presley had arrived.

Andy and his partners gathered several hundred miles to the west, crowded around a small television set in the cramped Dallas office of International Classic Productions. The Memphis spectacle flashed across the screen in a series of heartbreaking images. A somber mood prevailed, a mood only peripherally related to the sad scenes being played out at Graceland.

Every fan that dropped a bundle of flowers at the grave seemed equally intent on taking home some small reminder. The television cameras swept across throngs of fans standing in front of crowded souvenir shops, happily enduring endless lines to purchase mementos of the historic occasion. Any product associated in any way with The King -- from t-shirts and posters to books and records -- sold like hotcakes. Everything imaginable seemed represented. Everything, that is, except "Tell Me Pretty Baby."

The partners had long ago realized the vital importance of having the song on the market in time for the anniversary, of course, but one maddening delay after another ensured that it would not be ready. Andy still deemed it imperative to validate the authenticity of the recording beyond doubt. Inevitably, it took longer for the affidavits to arrive than initially anticipated. And the physical production of the record itself -- from pressing the vinyl discs to printing the jackets -- encountered unavoidable snags.

Pete and Don and Marion watched in mute horror as thousands of fans coughed up millions of dollars on cheap Elvis merchandise. How many copies of "Tell Me Pretty Baby" might have been snapped up that day had the record been available? The answer was too painful to contemplate.

Andy tried to reassure his partners. Be patient, he counseled; long-term sales would surely make up for revenues lost during the anniversary. Those rabid fans would still be there next week and next month and next year. They would still flock to the record stores to grab the first song ever recorded by their beloved idol. It mattered little whether that recording was available today or six months down the road. Patience.

All of this was true enough, of course, but Andy thought his little pep talk seemed somewhat hollow. Disappointment still permeated the room. Only one thing could sweep away the gloom: cold hard cash.

Everyone felt some degree of desperation. The first victim of this panic was Don Reese. The missed opportunity seemed to hit him harder than the others. Don, serving as publicity director, had already advanced the tantalizing idea of a news leak. A little advance publicity couldn't hurt, could it? Andy and the others cautioned Don not to engage in such questionable practices. The release of the song would create a big enough splash without advance hype.

Don backed off for now, but in the end his enthusiasm got the best of him. Perhaps he didn't understand the ruthlessness of the press. Perhaps he believed a little outside pressure would hasten the production process. Whatever his reasons, Don let United Press International in on the secret. He later insisted that he was just fishing around to see if the wire service would be interested in doing a story at a later date. He even hinted that the reporter had given a solemn promise to keep the information under wraps until Don gave the word.

Whatever had gone on behind the scenes, the UPI reporter prepared a dispatch that listed all the particulars: the long-forgotten 1954 recording session, the lineage of the rare master tape, the current production plans. That night -- August 20 -- the sensational story hit the wires and flashed around the globe.

Andy reached the office early the next morning. He knew something was afoot even before he unlocked the door and stepped inside. Both phones rang insistently, certainly an oddity considering that only a couple of people had the number. Andy snatched up one of the receivers and found himself in the strange position of having to calm down the caller in order to figure out just what in the world he was talking about. The full extent of Don's error soon became apparent. The cat was out of the bag. "Tell Me Pretty Baby" was international news. Unfortunately, the record was not yet available.

The day passed in a blur. Andy did his best to control the damage. International Classic Productions was under siege. Reporters called from around the world, frantic to verify the facts and write their stories in the face of looming deadlines. Elvis fans breathlessly insisted that they just had to hear the song -- right now! Andy patiently went over the details with them, being careful to explain that the record was not yet in production. Perhaps that tidbit would keep the news from spreading further than it already had, but Andy doubted it.

Businessmen dangled lucrative offers. Some wanted to buy into the partnership; others proposed purchasing the recording outright, cash on the barrel. Andy found some of these deals quite tempting -- especially an eye-popping $500,000 offer from RCA itself -- but after quick consultation with his partners he declined such offers as politely as possible. The rights to "Tell Me Pretty Baby" simply were not for sale. Don Reese was adamant on this point, a strange turn of events considering that Don's overzealous promotional tactics had caused the current frenzy. Andy could not fathom what might be going on inside Don's head. At the moment, though, he had little time to study the matter.

The phones continued to ring off the wall for three long days. These were easily the most exhausting and exhilarating days Andrew Jackson had ever known. And just then, at the peak of the excitement, came the news everyone had been waiting for: Rainbow Records had the first batch of vinyl ready for pickup.

The partners piled into Andy's car and raced across town to the pressing plant. Adrenaline coursed through their veins as Andy snatched up a bundle of records and tore into the package. None of them would ever forget that first magical glimpse of the gorgeous "Elvis Classic" label affixed to the black vinyl disc. A stunning illustration of Elvis in the prime of his youth dominated the jacket, framed by an eye-catching caption set in bold type: "His <u>First</u> Professional Recording." A quality production all around. Andy beamed.

The office buzzed with activity in those early days of September as the partners launched their long-planned promotional campaign. Dallas radio stations received the first handful of records. Countless phone calls went out to other influential stations across the nation, promising records shortly -- Cin-Kay Distributing would handle that part of the work; Andy carefully packed up a bundle of records and shipped them to Hal Freeman's Nashville office. Within a few weeks nearly every radio station in America would have a copy of "Tell Me Pretty Baby." With luck, the initial wave of media attention would be followed by heavy airplay. That, in turn, should lead to massive public interest. By that time, if everything went according to schedule, the record would be available via direct mail as well as through retail music outlets and Elvis souvenir shops.

Andy surrendered to a peculiar blend of emotions: elation, relief, caution. He had taken another step on the long road to glory. He kept reminding himself that if past experience was any guide, well, some type of disappointment probably lurked just around the corner. Andy's dreams seemed to have a bad habit of turning into nightmares in the blink of an eye. He tried to push such thoughts from his mind. For now, at least, Andrew Jackson was on top of the world.

CHAPTER ELEVEN

Emotions reached a fever pitch as the scheduled distribution plan got underway. As predicted, the interest created by the barrage of media coverage sparked a firestorm of controversy. The simplest of the questions surrounding "Tell Me Pretty Baby" turned out to be the most vexing: Did Elvis sing it? Everyone, from Vernon Presley to RCA Records, held an opinion -- and didn't mind sharing it with the world. The news media descended on the story with savage gusto, all hands intent on airing the various angles of the brewing controversy.

Andy and his partners realized that this worldwide media coverage could be a two-edged sword. It created spectacular interest in the recording, to be sure, but it could also backfire. Many controversial stories wilt under the glare of such intense scrutiny.

International Classic Productions needed a media representative to present their side of the story, someone who had charm and wit to capture the audience's attention, and intelligence to convey the facts in a straightforward and memorable manner. Surprisingly, the perfect spokesman turned out to have been in their midst all along: Pete Falco. As frantic calls poured in from television and newspaper reporters, Pete became the group's informal press representative. He seemed to thrive on the attention, and his intimate knowledge of the music industry allowed him to convey the intriguing story of "Tell Me Pretty Baby" in an overwhelmingly effective manner. As the demands on his time grew, Pete assembled an attractive press kit for distribution to interested parties.

Pete was contacted by Marcia Smith-Durk, a staff writer with the Dallas Times Herald, on September 6. "I wrote this rhythm and blues number," he told her, "but I didn't feel that my singer was right for it. Presley was sitting in on the session and I dug his voice. So I paid him $15 and he sang the song." The interview led to an extensive feature article -- the first of many in the coming weeks. The show had opened with a bang.

Hal Freeman joined the fray on September 18 with the official release of the record. A group of Nashville music writers attended an elaborate press conference at Freeman's Cin-Kay headquarters. Parked out front was an immaculately restored 1950 Ford with the "Tell Me Pretty Baby" logo splashed in bright colors along each side. Freeman greeted the reporters and proceeded to explain the lineage of the song. Then he flipped a switch on his console stereo system, dropped a copy of the record on the turntable, and settled back as the men absorbed the magical rhythm of the controversial song. Predictably, some of the skeptical newsmen expressed doubts as to the song's authenticity. Freeman suggested they call Pete Falco for more information.

Pete was more than happy to oblige. "I wrote the song, the bass is me, and the guy going flat in the backup singing is me," he told Nashville Tennessean reporter Walter Carter. "It was a demo to peddle my stuff. My singer was white but he sang too black. I had Presley cut it because of his voice. I thought I could sell it." Pete discussed the steps taken by International Classic Productions to authenticate the song. He mentioned Dr. Godfrey's sound spectrograph analysis as well as the numerous signed affidavits from musicians who had played with Elvis in the early days. Carter seemed satisfied. The next day his illustrated story appeared in the Tennessean under the bold headline "First Elvis Cut Claimed."

Freeman had already launched the all-important promotional distribution of the record to influential radio stations. Among the first to receive the disc was New York City's WHN Radio. Within two days "Tell Me Pretty Baby" became the station's most requested song, airing at least once an hour. One disc jockey invited listeners to voice their opinions on whether or not the song had indeed been performed by Elvis. The station's switchboard lit up like a Christmas tree. "Our listeners want the opportunity to judge for themselves," said WHN program director Ed Salomon. "Our audience is divided half and half, whether it is Elvis or not." One caller was Ed Harris, member of a unique duo billed as the nation's only male and female black country singers. Sometime in 1956 or 1957 Harris had attended an Elvis concert in Tampa, Florida. At that show, he insisted, Elvis had performed "Tell Me Pretty Baby." The obscure event had lain forgotten until Harris heard the song on WHN. "I never forget a song" he told the Nashville Tennessean. "I tried to learn every song Elvis ever did. I told my wife, 'I heard that song before' when they played it on the radio."

Despite such reassurances, nobody was surprised when negative articles started to appear. One of the more balanced and objective reports appeared in the September 30 issue of Billboard, the most respected music industry publication. According to reporter Sally Hinkle, the Nashville release of the record had kicked up "a storm of action and reaction around here," being "hailed as definitely Elvis and definitely not Elvis by various music industry figures." Hal Freeman told Hinkle that he was even then awaiting additional affidavits from individuals who would "swear to the fact that Elvis did rave about a band called the Red Dots." Freeman also mentioned that he had entertained doubts of his own until he learned that International Classic Productions had voluntarily missed the anniversary of Elvis' death in order to gather additional proof. "They could have sold individual records in Memphis last August and become rich," he said. "So if it is a scam, why weren't they there? On that particular day they could have gotten $8-$10 per record."

Hinkle also interviewed Shelby Singleton, the producer who had recently locked horns with RCA over the release of early Sun Records demos by Elvis. "We heard this tape last September, or thereabouts," he said, "and from what he can figure out, Presley was not in Arizona at the time this was supposedly recorded." Finally, Hinkle spoke with Scotty Moore, Elvis' first guitarist and manager. Moore repeated the same snappy sound bite he had previously offered to Andy: "I think it's a crock!"

Such quotes might prove damaging, of course, but they amounted to little more than minor annoyances compared to the bomb dropped in a follow-up report by Walter Carter. The article appeared in the September 23 Nashville Tennessean under an ominous headline: "Promoters Lying, Says Elvis' Dad." Vernon Presley, reached by phone at Graceland, insisted that the 1954 recording session in Phoenix had never happened. "They're lying," he said. "He [Elvis] did no entertainment of any kind except in school and church. Except for moving here from Tupelo he hadn't been out of Memphis until he made his first record here with Sun." Indeed, according to Vernon Presley, Elvis had been working for Crown Electric Company at the time of the supposed recording session.

Corroboration came from Lamar Fike, a high school friend of Elvis. "The first time he was out on the West Coast, I believe, was 1956, when he did Love Me Tender. We went through Phoenix a number of times in 1957 and '58 and you'd think somewhere in the conversation he would have said something like 'You know, I once did a recording here.' But he never did." Fike went on to say that "in 1954 the furtherest thing from Elvis' mind was recording." (This comment would become particularly ironic some twenty years in the future, when

RCA itself released a collection of 77 long-forgotten Elvis recordings. The producer of the set, Ernst Jorgensen, referring to one of the circa-1954 recordings, said: "The studio wanted to make him out to be a nice boy who loved his mother, not a driven musician. This cut shows he wanted to be discovered so badly.")

Andy and his partners monitored these events from their Dallas office. Comments from people like Scotty Moore and Lamar Fike might be dismissed as nothing more than jealous blathering. Vernon Presley's remarks, on the other hand, caused more concern. Here was the eminently respectable patriarch of the beloved superstar insisting that the whole thing was a fraud. And while Andy believed that RCA had orchestrated the maneuver, he certainly couldn't make such a comment to the press. Such an attack on the character of Vernon Presley might be interpreted as a blow to the sacred memory of Elvis himself. They would just have to ride out the storm, letting the chips fall where they may. It was far too late to back out.

For the most part, though, the positive publicity seemed to outweigh the negative. Thousands of records had gone into circulation. Several radio stations had already placed the song in heavy rotation. Moreover, the vast body of rabid Elvis fans was beginning to show signs of interest -- perhaps the most heartening development of all.

Amidst the excitement, however, a seemingly minor misunderstanding had developed. Freeman placed his radio station mailings on hold because he had not received enough money from International Classic Productions to cover the postage expenses. Most of the records reserved for this purpose were gathering dust in Freeman's Nashville office. As soon as Andy learned of the hitch, though, he dispatched the necessary funds along with the latest batch of vinyl from the Rainbow Records pressing plant.

"Tell Me Pretty Baby" gained momentum as the last days of September slipped away. It had been a memorable month, to be sure, but everyone involved agreed that the real action lay just ahead. As if to confirm their expectations, Freeman reported the shipment of several thousand copies of the record in the first week of October. Andy and his friends were overjoyed. Every indication pointed to an inescapable conclusion: "Tell Me Pretty Baby" might be the next million seller.

Gina

CHAPTER TWELVE

It was an open secret among the partners that Andy kept the master recording of "Tell Me Pretty Baby" tucked away in a safe deposit box. In fact, ever since Andy had taken possession of the tape from Pete Falco over a year ago, it had never left his sight. Every time someone else put their hands on the precious tape -- from Dr. Tosie to the Sumet Sound engineers to Scotty Moore -- Andy had been right there. The recording represented Andy's lifelong dream, and he felt much safer with it out of harm's way.

Andy's thoughts often turned to his girlfriend, Gina. Their relationship had suffered from all the hustle and bustle and seemingly endless work hours associated with promoting the new record. Gina was certainly not the easiest woman in the world to get along with, of course, and with Andy so involved with business matters things had taken a decided turn for the worse. Gina ran her own business in Arlington, and it was a rare day indeed when their schedules happened to coincide. Andy loved the fiery tempered brunette, of course, but there was only so much torment and aggravation he was willing to put up with. And so he decided that the only way to salvage the relationship and to make his work days flow more smoothly

-- would be to start spending more nights back at his own apartment. Perhaps a little distance and time would allow things to cool off. They could pick up the pieces later. At least Andy hoped so.

This arrangement seemed to please his business partners as well. The office had taken on a frantic air. On many mornings the phones started ringing off the wall before the day was fairly underway. Calls came in from all over the nation -- indeed, from all over the world. Everyone had a thousand questions about "Tell Me Pretty Baby." In addition to fielding these inquiries, there seemed to be an endless procession of critical details to attend to. Fortunately, Andy's new arrangement with Gina allowed him to devote more time to the sudden deluge of rabid interest.

Despite the whirlwind of activity, though, things were going well. In fact, Andy thrived on the chaos. Only one thing bothered him: Don Reese. Andy just couldn't figure him out. Don had suddenly become dead set on obtaining additional verification of the authenticity of "Tell Me Pretty Baby." Andy thought this seemed awfully strange, especially since Don had stated numerous times that he had personally witnessed the historic recording session. He had even signed an affidavit to that effect. Why, then, when all the other partners were satisfied with the existing documentation, did Don insist upon gathering additional affidavits?

The whole episode began when Don rushed into the office one afternoon and said that some of his industry contacts had finally come through. Through those contacts, he claimed to have located the other members of the Red Dots. All that was great, of course, but Don wanted to let the band members listen to and inspect -- the original master tape. Only then, he insisted, would they have enough ironclad evidence to keep RCA Records off their back. Furthermore, he would not reveal the location of the mysterious band members, but insisted that he had to act fast or the opportunity would slip away. The men refused to deal with anyone but Don, he said, and since they couldn't come to Dallas, well, Don would have to go to them. And if RCA Records got wind of the plan, Don insisted, they might try to interfere. The recording giant had deep pockets, of course, and it probably wouldn't take much to purchase the men's silence.

It all made sense in a quirky sort of way, Andy thought, but he remained somewhat hesitant to turn over the tape to Don. Why couldn't Don take a cassette copy of "Tell Me Pretty Baby?" The duplicates had been dubbed on high quality tape, and the sound quality between the original and the copy was indistinguishable to human ears. In fact, even the newly -pressed vinyl records were good enough for identification purposes. Weren't they?

Don had an answer for that: the physical tape itself dated the recording. That particular brand of tape had been manufactured for only a short period of time in the early 1950s, he said, and the band members would be able to conclusively identify it as the original recording. Here, Andy admitted, was a valid argument.

And so, against his better judgment, Andy finally consented to the plan. He would retrieve the master tape from his safe deposit box tomorrow afternoon, and bring it to the office the following morning. Don beamed with joy. After assuring Andy that everything would turn out fine, he left to start making plans for his mysterious trip.

Andy thought the whole thing sounded somewhat fishy. He soon became tied up with a thousand other details, but in the back of his mind he continued to study the matter from every angle. Try as he might, though, he just couldn't see what Don stood to gain by deceiving him. Nonetheless, a vague feeling of foreboding remained.

He finally decided that he needed an outside opinion. Andy thought briefly of discussing the matter with Pete Falco or Marion Sitton. He realized, though, that their opinions would hardly be impartial. Suddenly, the solution flashed through Andy's mind. He picked up the phone and dialed Gina's work number. He had an important business matter he needed to discuss, he said. Would she mind acting as a sounding board tonight? Gina said she would love to see him; in fact, she had been on the verge of calling to set up a date herself.

Andy smiled, suddenly realizing that he had missed her warm touch. Maybe the night would turn into something much nicer than a business meeting. He said he'd pick up some food on the way over.

And things might have turned out fine if the conversation had ended there. Unfortunately, talk soon turned to their on again, off again relationship. Some stray remark touched off an argument, and with Gina's hot temper things turned sour in a hurry. After exchanging a few angry words, Andy finally told her to forget the whole thing. He'd see her around, he yelled, and then slammed the phone down. He regretted the childish move almost immediately, of course, but it was too late to take it back.

Andy snatched a pen and dug into a thick stack of long-neglected paper work, determined to put Gina out of his mind. He would just have to work out this Don Reese puzzle on his own.

Cleaning service

CHAPTER THIRTEEN

Andy awoke late the next morning with a headache and a sense of regret over the previous evening's argument with Gina. At least things with the record were running smoothly. There had been rumors of legal action to halt sales, but as of yet, nothing had been filed in court.

Andy hoped that RCA and Vernon Presley would leave the matter alone now that "Tell Me Pretty Baby" was on the market and doing well, but he didn't think they'd be so cooperative. As he showered and shaved, he thought of talking to an attorney about the situation, and again wished he and Gina were on better terms so he could ask her advice.

His personal life was a mess, but he didn't want to think about that right then. He feared his occasional melancholy over his and Gina's relationship was becoming too obvious. Don Reese had suggested to Andy that he spend some time with a woman to unwind a little. Andy only wished it were so easy.

The thought of Reese made Andy think of his partner's insistence on taking the tape to wherever the Red Dot band members were. He hated the thought of placing the master tape in Don's hands, but realized he had to trust his partner. Maybe it was just the accumulation of everything else -- Gina, waiting to see what RCA would do, handling the record's promotion. Whatever it was, Andy didn't feel right.

But, there really wasn't much he could do about it now that he had told Don he could borrow the master, barring something solid that would indicate he shouldn't. He decided to get all the details from Don; exactly where he was taking the tape and how long it would be gone. He considered taking out insurance on the rare recording.

An insistent knock on the door snapped him out of his thoughts. Few people had come to his apartment in the several months he had lived there. Only one person would visit this early -- Gina, offering peace for their argument. His heart raced at the thought. Her apologies could be very sweet. He wrapped himself in a towel, splashed on some after shave lotion, and then padded to the door with a big smile on his face.

To his surprise and embarrassment, it wasn't Gina at the door. It was a lovely young woman with long blond hair and too much makeup. She said her name was Paula and that she was offering to clean apartments in the area. Without being invited in, she simply walked through the door as Andy, speechless, watched.

She surveyed the messy apartment, and laughingly asked if he was a bachelor. She then floored him by using his name.

"Mr. Jackson, I've heard a lot about you," she said. "You're the man who put that new Elvis song on the radio. It'll make you a lot of money, I imagine. And a lot of friends. You can afford a girl like me," she added slyly.

Andy still hadn't digested the fact that she knew his name. He was flustered and keenly aware that her beauty was arousing him. To buy time and regain his composure, he admitted he wasn't a good housekeeper.

"I'll tell you what; look around and see what all needs to be done. Give me a decent estimate and we'll agree on a price, OK?"

As Paula walked into the kitchen, Andy returned to the bedroom. He rummaged through his closet, his mind switching from Reese's proposal to Gina to the abrupt arrival of the wandering housecleaner, now strangely silent. He heard a small noise, turned and was startled by Paula, who'd opened the door and leaned against the wall, eyes older than the rest of her.

"I really don't like to clean," she said, casually running her hands up her sides. "I know a better way to make money, one I'd rather do with a guy like you."

She sauntered over to Andy and tugged the towel off his hips. He objected, but his heart wasn't in it. He needed this. He deserved something for himself, something fleeting and mindless, that wouldn't hurt nobody. What Paula was doing made even his guilt fade, along with all thoughts of Gina and Reese.

"How much will this cost me?" he stuttered.

"Let's not talk price, honey," Paula whispered, yanking at her clothes. Her body was unblemished, and her familiarity with a man's body told Andy that the young prostitute was not only willing but experienced.

After almost an hour, he was spent. Paula went into the bathroom and emerged dressed. As he paid her, she winked, said she'd see him around, then swished out the door.

Andy showered again, savoring the encounter. He dressed and locked the dirty apartment. It was a beautiful day. The autumn Dallas air was crisp and fresh. He inhaled deeply: It was going to be a good day after all, thanks to the young hooker and her "apartment-cleaning" service.

When he reached the office the others were well into the day's business. Marion Sitton had already left to check on record production at Rainbow's plant. They were anxious to get the next shipment off to Hal Freeman, the Nashville distributor.

Pete Falco was on the phone, making arrangements for yet another interview. He claimed to hate the attention, but Andy thought Pete thrived on the way he was fussed over by some of the interviewers, people impressed by his association with the King. Pete looked up at Andy and waved, never missing a word of his well-practiced conversation.

Don Reese, however, seemed extremely interested in what had made Andy so late. "Ain't but one thing makes a man that pink and glossy -- a maid that gives a little extra," Don guessed, and everyone laughed at Andy's flustered response. Surprised, Andy started to question Don about his statement but Don changed the subject to the master tape, asking if Andy had picked it up from the bank yet.

Andy assured him that he would bring the tape with him the next morning and figured it was his turn to do the questioning. He asked Don to come into his office and asked some pointed questions -- exactly where Don planned on going with the tape, who would look at it, how long he'd be gone.

Either Don had been practicing or his story was perfectly legitimate, because he fielded each question without hardly blinking. One thing, however, was puzzling: Don was adamant about not needing insurance on the master. It would cost a fortune, he said, and it would take too much time, which they couldn't afford, not if they wanted to get sworn statements from the band members while they still could.

"Authentication is absolutely necessary, Andy," Reese said earnestly. "No one can authenticate like the guys who were there. Man, do you think any insurance agent would sell you a policy in less than a week? He'd have to call his manager in Houston and they'd talk to some guy in Omaha and they'd want to have a damned lunch meeting over it all, next Wednesday or something. We don't have the time, Andy."

Don's argument was logical, and Andy reluctantly agreed so. He said he'd have the tape the next morning, but only if Don promised to take care of it like it was his own. Don agreed, a flush of victory making his face glow as he scurried from Andy's office.

The remainder of the afternoon was uneventful. The others had taken care of whatever had come up in Andy's absence. All that remained was his signature on some letters to the West Coast, seeking interested record stores.

"Tell Me Pretty Baby" was going to be in great demand, his letters stated, and now was the time to get their orders in. No matter what, he thought, it always came back to selling. He felt no remorse over the loss of his car dealership. Not now that he was actually producing and marketing music, anyway.

It had been a struggle, and still was an uphill battle. The company was in the hole and it would take several months of better than average sales to realize a return on their investments. The whole office was on a shoestring and a prayer, and would be until the real money started to pour in.

Once the record was getting regular airplay and was picked up by the record stores, they would all see a return on the efforts they were making. It was worth it, Andy thought -- he was doing what he wanted, and he was running his own company the way he wanted it to be run. He finished what little was on his desk and left. He had to go by the bank to pick up the tape and wanted to beat the traffic.

The drive from Dallas to Irving was pleasant, but as he drove, doubts again crept in. Perhaps he just wasn't used to the fast pace, he thought. He was still baffled by how Don had managed to hit the nail on the head, guessing that a maid with "extras" had paid a visit. It would have been more reasonable if Don had guessed that he and Gina had spent the night together. That comment, and the look on Don's face as Andy told him he would have the tape tugged at Andy's thoughts as he arrived at the bank.

After retrieving the tape, Andy sat in the warm sunlight, savoring the texture and sight of the recording. It was incredibly satisfying to hold his prized tape again. Who would ever think that a plastic spool, a celluloid-ferric oxide tape, could contain so many hopes and dreams? The first professional recording made by the greatest figure in rock and roll, and it was his. A slight chill ran up Andy's neck as he placed the tape in his briefcase. The tape was the Holy Grail to a man whose life revolved around music.

Dusk bathed Dallas as Andy pulled into the parking lot of his apartment, and in the shadows he almost missed the slight figure getting out of another car. It was Gina, who'd apparently been waiting for him to come home. He had once offered her a key to his apartment, but she had refused. He turned off the engine and got out. She waited on the walkway in front of his car, her arms spread wide. They embraced; Andy truly loved the way this woman felt in his arms. If only she weren't so independent and hot-headed, but he had to admit those attributes were also what made her so special, and Andy so willing to seek her advice.

Arm in arm they entered his apartment, his briefcase clutched in his free hand. He hoped the young blonde's scent was gone, but he had no reason to worry. The smell of unwashed clothes, stale food and overflowing ashtrays filled the rooms. Surprisingly, Gina didn't seem too disgusted, only giving him a bemused look.

Tiptoeing her way through the living area to the kitchen, she peered into the refrigerator. She sighed and checked the cupboards. "Well, that's it," she exclaimed. "I'm not staying in this pigsty, and neither are you. Get your stuff and we'll go back to my place."

She told him that she'd go ahead and make something for supper while he got his things together. It didn't take long for Andy to gather some clothes and his shaving kit. Along with his briefcase there wasn't anything else he could think of that he needed. He was blissfully content just being back on good terms with Gina.

The drive to Arlington didn't seem to take long. He sang along with the radio most of the way. He absentmindedly touched the briefcase, as if the treasured tape would disappear if he didn't assure himself that it was truly there. In a life full of ups and downs, Andy had reached a peak doing what he loved; his dream within reach; driving to be with a woman he adored.

Andy and Gina made small talk before dining, as he mulled the best way to approach the subject of Don and the tape. Gina had never trusted the man, so Andy knew he had to be careful or the whole evening would be destroyed.

He brought up the subject after they finished dining. He told her how Don had asked to take the master to help him get affidavits from the Red Dots.

"You're not going to let him have it, are you? He's a sneaky snake, baby. You don't want to let him have your original for any reason," she argued.

Andy hated to tell her that he had already agreed to let Don take it, and that it was in his briefcase that very moment. But he did, and she sat silently as he explained what had happened since they had last spoken. He was telling her he'd gotten the tape, pointing to the briefcase, when the phone rang.

Gina answered it, and with a surprised scowl motioned Andy over. Covering the mouthpiece, she said, "It's HIM. You tell him no, you understand? Don't let him have your tape, Andy." He nodded and took the receiver.

Don sounded apprehensive. He said he'd called Andy all afternoon at his apartment, and that he was sorry but he was afraid things would go wrong this close to "things really happening, man." He said he needed to know if Andy had the tape and if everything was all right. Yes, Andy assured him, he had it and would bring the tape in the morning. Andy had to raise his hand and signal Gina to be quiet when she heard him say that. Though she kept her silence, her dark eyes narrowed as she sat on the edge of the couch, her fists and teeth clenched in anger.

Andy listened as Don explained, again, that it was their only chance to get the Red Dots to listen to and look at the tape. If they were to all say it was the real thing, then "couldn't hardly nobody, Andy, not the Colonel and not Vernon and not no-damn-body say that ain't Elvis singin'." Andy agreed that it would be a big plus, but said it would be the last time the tape would be out of his sight. He told Don that he believed they had all the authentication they needed, and this was just a way to cover their bets.

"Okay, I hear you," Don said. "But I've got a tight schedule to keep tomorrow, so please meet me in the restaurant below the offices at exactly 11 in the morning, cool?" Andy agreed, and repeated -- no further investigation on the tape. This was the end of it, Andy told him as he hung up.

The phone was still rocking in its cradle when Gina jumped up and yelled, "You can't take that tape to him, Andy! He's up to something; I can feel it."

Andy said he was open to suggestions, but couldn't really see a way out. She gave him one.

"There are plenty of photo shops here," she said. "Take it to one of them and have pictures taken of the tape reel and of the cartridge, and let the Ass take that to show his so-called band members. He can take one of the cassettes for them to listen to; there's no difference in the sound."

Her idea was a good one, and it evidently meant a lot to her that Andy believe her suspicions. She was pleading with him in a way she never had. "I think he's doing his damndest to get his hands on that tape," she said. "If you lose that tape, you lose everything; it's your ace in the hole. It's what keeps those bastards under control."

Making a quick decision, Andy agreed to take the tape to a studio and have quality photographic reproductions made, and to give them to Reese. He said he would also provide a few cassettes, and that Reese would either be content or forget the whole idea.

"I'm also going to bring you into this a lot more," he told Gina, "if you really want. I need someone I can trust to look out for me, okay?"

He hugged her until her rigidity evaporated. His sincerity turned the tide of her anger, and they left the dishes for later. For Andy, being with her washed away the lingering guilt over his morning fling and made the day almost perfect, one of the most perfect he'd ever know.

The Double Cross

CHAPTER FOURTEEN

The smell of perking coffee woke Andy. Unlike most mornings when he'd take forever to get going, he jumped right out of bed and into the shower. Gina had made a huge breakfast, a sign of domesticity unlike her but one Andy thought meant he was definitely back in her good graces.

During breakfast, Gina reminded Andy that he'd promised to take extra care of the master tape and be sure that no one, especially not Don Reese, got his hands on it. He agreed, and asked Gina to recommend a good photography studio, one that could make quick, quality photos without charging him too much.

As Gina went to get a phone book, Andy poured his second cup of coffee and wondered if all this was in fact necessary. If Don was being straight with him, Andy knew he was going to feel foolish, not to mention disloyal, for not trusting Reese. But, he'd settled on a plan, thanks to Gina, and was going through with it. No use wasting more time.

Gina gave him the address and hugged him at the door, a long, quiet embrace that left him a little breathless. She pushed him out without saying anything else, and a sense of unease shook Andy as he heard the door lock behind him. He shook off the premonition of finality, if that's what it was, and left.

He found the professional photography lab on Park Row, not too far from Gina's. The manager assured Andy that the job would take less than an hour. Andy gave the tape to a technician, who carried it into a studio. Andy asked if he could witness the actual shoot, and after a short discussion between tech and manager, was allowed into the studio.

The photographer quickly arranged the tape on a stool, set the lighting the way he wanted it and took close to 20 shots, from every conceivable angle before saying he had all he needed. Again, Andy was promised the prints would be ready within an hour. To his relief, a price was quoted that would not strain his tight budget.

He had just enough time to make the drive to Irving and back. He needed to leave the tape in the safety deposit box and withdraw enough cash to pay for the prints and have a little left over for gas money. He made a mental note, for the hundredth time, to buy a smaller car. The guzzler he had was great for a car dealer, but a struggling music executive who was continually zipping around on errands needed something more economical.

He made it back to Arlington and to the photo shop by ten o'clock, in just a little over an hour. His prints were ready. They were glossies and they were all he could have wanted. Every detail of the old tape, reel and cartridge was perfectly evident. If this wasn't good enough for Reese and the Red Dots, then there was nothing to be done about it.

Andy thanked the manager for doing such an excellent job on such short notice. He hurried to the car -- he had right at 45 minutes to make his appointment with Don in Dallas. He'd just gas up and hit the freeway. There was a short line at the pumps of the corner station, so he pulled in. It took ten minutes before he pulled up to the pumps and filled the guzzler's tank, and he was on his way soon after.

The traffic was light, and he arrived at the Blanton Towers offices a little after eleven. He'd made good time, and although he was a little late, he didn't think Don would be too upset, or would have to alter his appointment schedule.

He parked in the east parking lot, as he always did, and went through the revolving doors on that side of the building. There was a main hall just beyond, which led to the restaurant, with business offices on each side. It seemed strange that there wasn't anyone in the hall, which was usually bustling this time of day. He soon found out why.

No sooner had he stepped into the main hall than he saw Reese rush out of the restaurant. He must have been waiting, thought Andy. Reese stopped 20 to 30 feet away and yelled, "ANDREW! Where have you been?"

Andy didn't have the time to consider the weirdness of Don's behavior before two men in dark suits stepped out from the doorway of one of the business offices and grabbed him. They pushed him, face first, against the wall, one on either side. He was frisked and handcuffed.

They identified themselves as detectives for the Dallas Police Department, read him his rights and said he was under arrest for sexual assault.

Hardly able to breathe at the sudden turn of events, Andy looked to Don for help. Reese was standing calmly nearby, as if he had expected this to happen.

"What have you done, Andy?" Reese asked. "You sure got yourself into a mess. Where's the tape? Andrew, we need the tape, now that you're going to jail."

Andy could do little but gape as Reese continued to ask for the tape. The detective seemed unnaturally willing to let him stand there, handcuffed, while Don questioned him. The pieces began to fall together.

It could only be the hooker, the "maid" who had come by his apartment, who had filed charges on him; for what, he couldn't begin to understand.

He felt that Reese knew more than he was saying, but things were happening too quickly. He told Don to take the photos of the master, which were in his inside coat pocket. The detectives gave the envelope a questioning glance, then handed it to Reese, who backed away as the detectives escorted him out of the hallway and to an unmarked police car parked near the entrance.

The ride to the downtown Dallas jail took place in an endless haze, the crackle of the scanner and the detectives low talk seemingly unreal. This was happening to someone else, Andy thought. I haven't done anything.

He was placed in a holding cell and told it would take hours before someone would book him and that he'd be allowed to make a phone call at that time. His belt and shoes were taken from him, and that, more than anything, convinced him this was for real.

He was in his stocking feet, in jail, stunned by what had happened. He'd gone from the top of the world to the pits, and he had an ugly feeling things were spinning out of control, and that he had no way to stop them.

Stuck In Jail

CHAPTER FIFTEEN

It was almost ten that night before Andy was booked, issued jail coveralls and placed in an overcrowded 10-man tank, with 18 men awaiting bail or trial. He had to sleep on the floor, and found an almost-clean spot on the concrete to throw his dirty, vinyl-covered mattress. He had been formally charged with sexual assault, but bail would not be set until his arraignment.

He was almost frantic with worry. How would the company survive? How would Gina accept this latest setback, especially once she knew the root cause of it -- his encounter with the prostitute?

Andy wasn't sure of the phone-calling procedure, and no one volunteered to help him. There was only one phone, and a huge black man was shouting into it, as if the person on the other end was deaf, or just stubborn. Andy finally realized there was a piece of envelope stuck to the wall next to the phone, with the names of the tank occupants who wanted to use it. From the length of the list, Andy knew he'd never make the call that night.

His natural salesmanship asserted itself. He offered the next inmate some cigarettes for his place in line. The man agreed, but told Andy to hurry, because the phones would be cut off at 10:30, which was only a half-hour away.

Andy gave the operator Gina's number and prayed she wasn't so mad at him that she wouldn't accept his collect call. She did, but her angry questions were more than he'd expected. Evidently, Don Reese had called her, insinuated that Andy had been arrested for rape and then arrogantly tried to have her tell him where the tape of "Tell Me Pretty Baby" was.

Andy asked her to settle down and that he would tell her what had happened. He started with Paula and was afraid Gina would hang up the phone immediately, but she listened as he told of Paula's bursting in, and how he was sure Reese had sent her to his apartment. He then explained how he had been arrested upon arrival at the restaurant, and how Reese had identified him for the detectives. He also told her the tape was back in his safety deposit box.

Gina was crying when he was done. Andy felt terrible as she asked him why he'd done anything at all with Paula, and that if he hadn't he wouldn't be in jail. He guiltily cut her off, explaining that his time on the phone was almost over. He managed to tell her that she needed to come by the jail in the morning, get his car keys and pick up his car at the office.

Between sniffles, she promised she would take the day off and do as he asked, then told him to call her at noon, and she could tell him what she'd accomplished and they could talk about what else needed to be done. He said he would and was trying to apologize again when the line went dead.

He put his name at the bottom of the list, hoping his turn would come at the right time to call Gina, because now he surely needed her on his side. As he fell asleep that night, trying to ignore the stink of the tank, he prayed that Gina would stick with him. He just didn't have anyone else he could depend on.

Gina kept her promise. The jailer woke Andy early the next morning to have him sign a release form for the car keys. The tank was deathly quiet as Andy signed the papers, except for an old Mexican man lying on his grimy mattress, reading a ragged New Testament. He saw Andy looking at him and told Andy that he needed to call a lawyer, not his girlfriend, and make bond before it was too late. The old man told Andy that if the system saw he had no money and could not buy his justice, it would bury him. His words left Andy shaken.

It was late that evening before Andy finally was able to call Gina. He paced away the afternoon, selling a few cigarettes for soap and shampoo. The bug spray the jailer had squirted on him the night before was congealed and sticky, and he could smell himself. He showered as best as he could in the rickety, tin, shower stall, and dried with a torn piece of sheet. He knew he had to get out, because adjusting would be difficult, if not impossible.

Finally, it was his turn on the phone. He was worried that Gina would not be home, since the noontime soap operas had already become the late afternoon talk shows. He was relieved when Gina picked up the phone.

She told him his car looked as if someone had taken a crowbar to the trunk and seats, searching for something. The tape, he guessed. Reese had seen him lock his briefcase in the trunk of his car many times. More and more, he wondered how he could have been so blind to Reese and his ruthless pursuit of the master tape.

Gina assured him that everything was as it should be, except for the damage. She'd taken his possessions back to her apartment.

They discussed getting a lawyer and a bondsman for Andy, and Gina said she would make some calls for him the next day. He asked her to bring him some socks and underwear, and hesitantly asked if she could spare some cash. He could tell she didn't like the direction of this, but he didn't know what else to do or whom else to ask. He pleaded with her to please stand by him. Just before she hung up, she yelled that he didn't need her when he was with "that slut." He went to bed exhausted and frustrated.

The next morning the cell speaker crackled out his name, ordering him to get ready for his arraignment. He was met at the barred door by an officer, handcuffed, herded before a bored magistrate who hurriedly read the formal charges and set bail at fifty thousand dollars, then led back to the tank. He had no idea how he could raise that kind of money. Everything he had was tied up in the record production company. He wasn't sure what it would cost him to get a bondsman to make his bail, but he urgently needed to find out.

He used his phone time later that day to call Pete Falco. Pete sounded relieved to hear from Andy, but quickly burst Andy's bubble of expected financial help -- neither he nor the others had the money to get Andy out of jail. Pete then dropped a bombshell on Andy.

They were readying for trial themselves. The industry was rocking with rumors that RCA was preparing a lawsuit -- and it had to be against them. Pete made it clear that this was the worst possible thing Andy could have done; get jailed, even if wrongfully.

Pete told Andy that Hal Freeman wasn't shipping records any more, and no money was coming in at that point. The company just didn't have the funds to both bail Andy out and prepare for the litigation it surely faced over the record.

Andy would just have to deal with his legal problems himself, Pete said, and also have to somehow get a civil lawyer to represent him against RCA, because the company was sure to sue over "Tell Me Pretty Baby."

It was not what Andy had hoped to hear. Things were looking bleaker by the minute. He thought of telling Pete that he suspected RCA was somehow behind this whole mess; that the company had somehow bought off Reese, who had then set Andy up so the partners would be divided. Andy had been brooding on that idea for days, but didn't really believe it himself, and didn't think he could make Pete see that if Andy was right, it was in the best interests of the company to get him out so they could fight together.

The phone opened up again later that night and Andy called Gina. After telling her the bail amount, he asked her to please try to find a bondsman who could help. She reluctantly agreed, knowing she would be the one to pay the bondsman's fee. Andy again asked her not to abandon him yet. Her answer wasn't as firm as he would have liked, but it was most likely all he could expect, given the circumstances.

Andy had been in jail almost a week when Gina told him she had found a bondsman. It had been expensive, more than she had expected, but she had raised the money. Elated, Andy promised to repay it, and more. He was confident that he'd be freed soon anyway. A jury couldn't possibly find him guilty of sexual assault. The girl had solicited him. She had enticed him, and then charged him for sex. There was no assault, and surely no physical evidence. He just needed to be out and take control of his life again.

The next day was the slowest he had ever experienced, as he waited to be released. Every time the speaker squawked, he jumped to his feet, clutching his pitiful sack of possessions. Lunch passed, then supper. Andy finally admitted to himself that something had gone terribly wrong, and he was afraid to call Gina and ask what it was.

Finally, it was his turn on the phone. He was stunned as she told him that bail had been increased to one hundred thousand dollars, at the personal request of the district attorney. Evidently, Andy's one prior felony conviction had convinced the prosecutor's office that he was a flight risk. The bondsman was not in the position to post twice the bail he had originally expected, and even if he was, Gina didn't have the added cash. Andy would just have to sit in jail until his trial.

Less than a week later Gina told him she couldn't handle it any longer, that the worry and anger and frustration were too much. She cried and said she was sorry, but their relationship was over. Andy would not see her again until his trial.

After two weeks of constant blows, Andy thought he couldn't be hurt anymore. But that night, finally, Andy wept. What good was it all if he'd thrown Gina away?

CHAPTER SIXTEEN

Andy's days slowed to a predictable crawl. Unable to raise bail and unwilling to beg anyone to accept his calls, Andy waited for events to catch up to him. The district court had appointed an attorney to represent him when he claimed he was unable to hire one, but the attorney had yet to contact Andy.

However, the former car salesman was a natural optimist, and he still believed the criminal case would be thrown out for lack of evidence. What gnawed at Andy was the growing certainty that RCA planned to wrest possession of "Tell Me Pretty Baby" from him and that the company would first try to block distribution and sales of the record. Since he had little contact with his partners, he watched every newscast he could and read any scrap of newspaper he could lay his hands on, figuring the news would be reported.

Even so, when the story broke, he was caught unawares. He was sitting on a table in the dayroom, munching stale cornbread, when an afternoon news anchor casually reported that RCA officials and Vernon Presley had asked for and been granted a temporary restraining order halting all sales of "what is alleged to be an old Elvis recording, which is being promoted by a man currently in Dallas County jail, awaiting trial for sexual assault."

Over the hoots of his fellow inmates -- as always, they were on the alert for any mention of themselves -- Andy learned that the suit had been filed on October 11 in Chancery Court in Nashville by attorneys representing Presley, executor of his son's estate, and RCA, which had exclusive rights to market all Elvis performances.

The Nashville court's order was specifically aimed at Cin-Kay Records -- owned by Hal Freeman -- and Dallas' International Classic Productions. The newscast went on to other reports, leaving Andy feeling spent. The battle had begun and he couldn't even fight back.

But the media blitz at least made it easier to keep track of unfolding events. The origin of the disputed record was repeated and took on almost mythic overtones: a youthful King, footloose in Phoenix in 1954 and cutting a demo with the local Red Dots, the tape's meandering ownership and current popularity begging the question -- if it wasn't Elvis, why the hoopla?

Andy was fascinated by the sneering accusations expressed by those close to Elvis and how they relied on their memories of the King to give validity to their arguments. Ex-producers, record company owners and over-the-hill former bodyguards used to the limelight all weighed in, claiming "Tell Me Pretty Baby" was faked. Andy knew the clarity of their memories was helped by the deep pockets of RCA. Vernon Presley insisted that his boy couldn't have been in Phoenix in 1954 because "I didn't know about it," so there.

Even Freeman, who had eagerly asked to be allowed to promote the record, now claimed to be suspicious of its true origins.

Andy followed the story, bitterly amused by the knowledge that it was money -- RCA's money and other's willingness to be bought by it -- that was fueling all the retreats and charges. He knew he could prove the record was authentic, but he needed help.

He knew he would soon be facing serious litigation in civil court, and over everything hovered the black cloud of the false sexual assault charge. In desperation, Andy decided to call a former girlfriend, Charlotte. Not sure if she would even accept his call, Andy was surprised and relieved when she did.

Charlotte said she had followed his situation in the news, and that she sympathized with his predicament. She said she did not believe the criminal charges against him were true, and those words, more than anything, convinced Andy to ask her for help.

It was like a breath of fresh air, knowing that there was someone out there who still cared what happened to him. Charlotte agreed to help in whatever way she could. She couldn't offer financial help, but she was more than willing to call attorneys for Andy and to act as go-between. Andy made it clear he could offer an attorney only a percentage of "Tell Me Pretty Baby" as payment, and she said she felt confident she could help. Now, Andy felt energized and in control of his future. He felt he had a fighting chance.

It was well that he felt confident, because he soon discovered that, along with the Nashville order, Dallas District Judge Dee Brown Walker had signed a similar temporary restraining order, also prohibiting International Classic Productions from marketing "Tell Me Pretty Baby." In essence, the order echoed the Nashville attack and was merely another step in RCA's well-orchestrated legal maneuvering. There was added bad news.

The date set for the show-cause hearing in the Dallas court was November 2, a day Andy already had engraved in his memory. It was the scheduled start of his criminal trial.

As if that were not enough, Andy gleaned some more disturbing information from one particular newspaper account, which reported on an October 19 deposition given by Freeman in Nashville. The record distributor claimed to have received only 3,400 records, less than half the amount Andy knew had been sent to him. Freeman also claimed that International Classic Productions had paid him only $3,000 of a promised $10,000.

Andy knew this wasn't true, but then remembered which partner was the liaison between Dallas and Nashville: Don Reese.

The newspaper reported that Freeman's deposition stated that he had stopped distribution of the record even before ordered to do so by the court. Freeman claimed that not only had he not been fully paid, there were questions he had that had not been answered.

That Andy could believe. He finally knew what he was up against, and why. He had been too trusting, too naive. Freeman was right, as Gina had been. There were too many questions unanswered, and in the middle of all of them sat one man -- Don Reese.

The Criminal Charge

CHAPTER SEVENTEEN

Over the next few days, Tom Mills, the court appointed attorney, visited Andy in jail in an effort to establish a defense strategy. Mills was a veteran defense attorney and Andy was impressed with him. From what Andy knew of court appointed lawyers, he felt lucky to be represented by Mills, who seemed to be putting forth real effort. While Andy may have acted stupidly with Paula, he hadn't committed a crime. Mills said he believed Andy's story, and Andy's hope was renewed again.

Andy told Mills that he believed Don Reese had possibly masterminded the whole thing in an effort to gain control of the tape of "Tell Me Pretty Baby." After listening to Andy's story, Tom thought it plausible, and even more, thought the defense could be structured around it. Mills also believed it should be no problem getting Reese to testify.

Andy asked Mills if he could recommend a good civil attorney who might be willing to help him in the civil lawsuit. Mills assured Andy that he would search for a good lawyer, but Andy still felt a mounting sense of pressure. The show cause hearing was only days away, and he had yet to even see an attorney.

Mills was as good as his word, for only two days later, Wayne L. Kreis visited Andy to discuss representation in the civil litigation.

Kreis had good references and seemed knowledgeable about civil law and the business. He told Andy that he could represent him at the show cause hearing, but that there really wasn't anything they could do at that point. The show cause hearing was for the plaintiff's attorneys to present evidence to support the restraining order.

Kreis assured Andy that after listening to whatever case the plaintiffs had built, they could better prepare for the actual trial, and in all likelihood would win and get "Tell Me Pretty Baby" back on the market. Andy certainly hoped the man was right.

In a huge surprise, Reese came to visit Andy the day before the hearing started. He said Mills had contacted him about appearing as a witness, and said that he would try to get there.

After a few vague comments about the partners, Reese revealed the real reason behind his visit -- the tape. He said the partners desperately needed it for the hearing. Andy said he understood their position, but told Don that he would not turn over the master to anyone.

Andy's refusal sent Reese into a rage. He stormed away from the visiting area screaming that he had no intentions of being at Andy's trial, and his threats to see Andy "hang for what you did to that young girl" echoed in the empty visiting room.

Andy was disturbed by what Reese had threatened when he'd stalked out. The girl was certainly young, but she was an adult. Andy had done nothing to her that she'd objected to. What really worried him now was the idea that the jury would believe he'd taken advantage of her youth. For the first time since his arrest, Andy felt the distinct stirrings of real panic -- could he be convicted?

The next morning -- while the show cause hearing began in the 192nd District Court Andy was escorted into the 195th District Court on the floor below. Mills met him with bad news: Reese wasn't going to testify. Andy's former business partner had been excused by claiming a need to be at the show cause hearing and protect himself.

Gina, however, would be there and would testify in Andy's behalf, and her testimony would lay the foundation for the conspiracy defense.

Also, Mills had done some in-depth checking on Paula and her mother. While his investigation had not discovered anything concrete that would impeach their testimony, Mills felt he could attack their credibility -- neither the girl nor her mother were pictures of innocence or honesty.

Mills also had learned that no medical examination whatsoever had been performed on Paula to support her story. The prosecution had nothing more than the girl's word that she'd been raped. The police had no photographs of bruises that would prove assault; no chemical analyses with damning body fluids; nothing at all. Once again, Andy felt things could turn out okay.

He couldn't help but wish he could be upstairs, defending himself against RCA and Vernon Presley. At least he felt like he had a good lawyer there in his behalf.

The courtroom was almost empty when Andy was escorted in. Nobody was talking, and the few eyes all seemed to be watching him. He was just taking his seat when Charlotte walked in. He was relieved to have some moral support nearby.

Mills and Andy quickly discussed a few points. They agreed that Andy wouldn't take the stand. With his prior felony, they felt the district attorney would attack his credibility. This was going to be difficult enough without past mistakes being dragged before the jury.

The jury selection took most of the day, after which the court recessed. The actual trial would start the next morning.

Andy was able to make two telephone calls that evening. He first called Charlotte, who agreed that jury selection had gone well. She said she was impressed with the effort Mills was showing. She also gave him a brief report on what was going on in the show cause hearing. She'd talked to Kreis, and he had asked that Andy call him as soon as possible. Quickly telling Charlotte goodbye, Andy called his civil attorney.

The lawyer accepted his call and was cheerful, claiming that nothing was happening that he hadn't expected. It was going to be a drawn out process; didn't Andy know that big time attorneys got paid by the hour, he laughed?

No, what he really wanted was to ask Andy to release him the master tape to use as evidence. Anything else that Andy might have that they could use would be helpful. While he didn't need anything immediately, the plaintiffs would be finished in a few days, and it would be their turn then. He wanted to be prepared. It was something Andy would have to decide soon.

He told Andy to make a list of everything he could think of that could be of any importance, and to call him back soon. Wishing Andy good luck in his criminal trial, Kreis hung up, and Andy knew he had to make some quick decisions.

The next day dawned cold and damp. Andy was happy to see Charlotte sitting in the courtroom, and was anxious to get underway. After the judge and jury entered, the district attorney went right to the heart of the matter, calling Paula to the stand.

Andy hardly recognized her when she walked into the courtroom, and he was shocked by how young she looked. Since the state's whole case rested on the jury believing Andy had taken advantage of a young girl, she now looked the part. It was obvious the jury was also disturbed by her youthful appearance.

The made-over teenager took the witness stand, without makeup on her cherubic face, dressed in an ankle-length skirt and bobby socks. Andy was also certain that her full breasts were strapped flat.

The D.A. carefully walked her through her testimony. She claimed that Andy had enticed her into his apartment with an offer to pay her for cleaning services, then sexually assaulted her. Paula made Andy sound like a sick pervert, and she calmly related details; how he threw her on the bed, pulled her pants down and forced himself into her.

It sounded preposterous to Andy, but it frightened him that the jury appeared to believe her story. "I was there!" he wanted to scream. "She's lying! Can't you see that?"

Andy's attorney cross-examined the girl, but she didn't waver from her well-practiced story. She almost faltered when Mills asked if she knew Don Reese. Andy hoped the jury caught her indecision and hesitation, as it was critical that a connection be established between the two of them.

She was finally finished, and Andy would never forget the wicked smile she gave him when she walked away from the courtroom. The prosecution next called the girl's mother. Paula's mother looked and talked as if she had come straight from work at the local honky tonk. Her appearance raised a few eyebrows in the jury box.

She testified that her daughter had come home crying that she had been raped. How was it affecting her, the D.A. wanted to know?

Oh, it was terrible, the mother wailed, drying nonexistent tears. Her dramatics embarrassing, the prosecutor quickly turned her over to Mills.

He quickly attacked. Was her daughter injured? No, the mother responded, sweet Paula had been lucky.

Why hadn't they taken her to the hospital, Mills wanted to know? How could you be sure she wasn't torn up, or in shock?

The girl's mother searched for an answer, glancing toward the prosecutor's table for help. None was forthcoming.

Her daughter didn't seem hurt, she repeated, and didn't appear to need a doctor, so why go to a hospital, she finally responded. Mills then asked if they weren't worried that the girl might be pregnant. The woman's admission that the girl was taking birth control pills had an obvious effect on the jury, who now seemed to see past Paula's innocent facade.

The state then called the detectives who had arrested Andy, and also brought in the police officer who had taken the original complaint. Nothing enlightening was said by any of them. However, Mills hammered on Reese -- did they know him?

Both detectives admitted they did, since Don had assisted them in Andy's arrest. Who had made the original contact that resulted in Reese's assistance and Andrew Jackson's arrest, Mills asked?

They claimed to have forgotten. They just knew that Mr. Reese had agreed to identify the defendant. Again the jury members exchanged quizzical looks, and both Andy and Mills hoped that they were seeing the connections between Reese and everyone else involved in this mess.

After the police left the stand, the prosecution rested, having failed to present any evidence of sexual assault. There was nothing more than Paula's word that a crime had been committed. It was the defense's turn, and Mills hoped to provide an answer as to why someone would lie and send an innocent man to prison. He called Gina to the stand.

She began by testifying to everything Don Reese had done to get his hands on "Tell Me Pretty Baby." She related the phone calls to her house, as Reese frantically hounded Andy; the damage done to Andy's car after his arrest; Don's subsequent call as he gave Gina the news of Andy's arrest and told her she may as well give Don the tape.

The tape could be worth a fortune, she claimed, and the man would do anything to get it, including framing a business partner.

The district attorney objected at her accusations, and the judge instructed the jury to disregard her comments. But the point had been made, and the connection had been drawn. One of the jury members, a woman in the front row, looked directly at Andy and smiled. Even though Gina was out of his life, she had done him an enormous favor.

After her testimony, Mills said the defense would rest. The judge called a recess for lunch. Andy felt confident that the state had not made its case. with no physical or medical evidence of rape, how could they even consider his guilt? The lunch hour seemed to drag on forever, as Andy waited in a cramped cell behind the courtroom.

The state's closing arguments sounded hollow. The D.A. pleaded with the jury to believe Paula, but without evidence, it was an empty charge. The jury didn't look impressed by the prosecution's case, and Andy's hopes soared.

Mills was firm in his remarks. The burden of proof was on the state, he said, and the state had not met that burden. There was no physical evidence of any kind that the girl had even had sex, much less by force, and even less with the defendant. She was on the Pill and obviously sexually active. Mills then turned to Reese and his invisible but undeniable presence.

Yes, the defendant had sex with the complainant and had never claimed otherwise. But, it was Paula who had enticed HIM. It was Paula who had charged HIM for her service. Furthermore, it was not to clean that she'd gone to his apartment, nor for a piddly $20. She had been bought and paid for, and was still being bought, and her services were being paid for by Reese, in a cold-blooded, premeditated frame designed to leave Andy in jail and Reese free to benefit from the sale of a record worth millions, whose worth was even now being proved in this very same building.

These people didn't care if Andrew Jackson went to jail, or for how long, Mills thundered, as long as he was out of the way so they could steal the master tape of Elvis Presley's first recording, a tape that could make them rich.

His closing argument was convincing, and the jurors appeared to agree. Andy watched them closely, and his heart jumped as a few of them glanced at him and nodded in assent. Tom closed with a final plea -- exonerate Andrew Jackson of these vicious charges, and return him to his life.

The district attorney had one final say. Conspiracy? How absurd, he said. He wasn't buying it, he said, and the jury would be foolish if they did. The accusations against this Don Reese were unsubstantiated and flimsy. The girl was young and gullible.

She had gone to Jackson's apartment to make a few hard-earned dollars and he had raped her. That, he told them, was the truth, and they should find the defendant guilty, guilty, guilty.

The jury trooped out to begin deliberating Andy's fate. All was quiet for over an hour, and Mills thought that was a good sign. The D.A. must have agreed, because he approached the defense table with a plea bargain offer. He offered Andy a twenty-five year sentence if he would plead guilty. After discussing it, Mills and Andy rejected the offer.

The district attorney was not happy with the thought of losing, whether Andy was innocent or not, and told them that he would seek a sentence of life in prison if the jury returned with a guilty verdict.

Another slow hour passed in the quiet courtroom. Finally, the judge ordered an adjournment. He asked the defense if it wished the jury sequestered, or if it would agree to allow the jury members to go home. Andy and Mills decided that it was best to allow them to go home, so as not to anger them.

When Tom told the judge that the defense consented to the jury not being sequestered, a tall, slim man in a dark suit jumped from the spectator benches and hurried out of the courtroom. Andy asked Mills who it was, but the attorney didn't know. The man had watched the trial from the prosecution side of the courtroom, and they had assumed he was part of the prosecution team. Mills dismissed him, but Andy felt badly about the stranger's abrupt departure.

The jury was escorted back into the courtroom, given its instructions and dismissed. The woman who had given Andy an encouraging smile earlier nodded and smiled again as she passed, and a few of the others also gave him friendly looks. Their actions calmed Andy's fears, but he now felt they had made a grave mistake in not sequestering the jury. The ominous feeling grew as the night passed. He slept fitfully, with a growing certainty that something was terribly wrong.

Early the next morning he again dressed in the suit of clothes that he had worn the previous two days. He waited in the filthy cell behind the courtroom reading the names of the multitudes of men who'd etched their memories on the grimy walls. Andy hadn't been bothered by the stink and ugliness before, but now the cell seemed to vibrate with despair.

He was finally called into the courtroom and ordered to stand and face the jury. None of the jurors would look at him, and he knew, before the words were said, before anything was said, that he'd been found guilty.

How? How could they do this to him? What had happened during the night to sway the jury?

Mills had no answer for him. Something had happened after the jury had left the courtroom. Someone had gotten to them, Andy was sure of it.

The punishment phase was anticlimactic. Andy took the stand to try to convince the jury that he was not a threat to society. But he couldn't show remorse, because he knew he wasn't guilty. Mills questioned him about his plans for the future, his accomplishments.

It was futile. In less than thirty minutes, a stone-faced jury returned and sentenced Andy to spend the rest of his life in prison. As he was led away, Reese's threat echoed dully in his mind.

He'd lost.

The Liar

CHAPTER EIGHTEEN

Despair, grief and a loss greater than any he had ever known possible enveloped Andy as the metal door to the tank closed behind him. The look on his face told the other inmates all they needed to know and they left him alone as he crawled to his mattress and began the process of dealing with the reality of his sentence.

Later that week, Andy's civil attorney came to the jail to visit. Kreis had heard about Andy's sentence and was worried, since Andy hadn't called. He tried to assure his client that it wasn't as bad as it seemed; that he would be eligible for parole in seven years, with good behavior.

But the attorney really wanted to discuss his fee. It wasn't looking very good for "Tell Me Pretty Baby," and a percentage of nothing was still nothing. Kreis wanted assets he could turn into cash. He had already spent far too much time on the case with nothing to show for it, he said.

Andy told him he would sign his car over to him, along with some jewelry he no longer needed, now that he faced spending the rest of his life in prison. If it didn't hurt so badly, he might even laugh about it. There wasn't any real cash left, as everything was tied up in the record. He asked Kreis for paper and pen and made a list of property and items he would surrender as legal fees, with Kreis agreeing they would be enough to retain him through the trial. And if they should be successful, he still expected his percentage of the record. Andy wasn't in a position to argue.

Andy gave him Gina's address and phone number, writing a short note asking her to release the property. His ex-girlfriend would no doubt be glad to get rid of Andy 's things.

Kreis was now ready to discuss trial strategy. It was going to be difficult to defeat the injunction being sought by RCA and Vernon Presley against them. The plaintiffs' lawyers were expensive hired guns, and RCA was sparing no expense in its attempt to sink the record. He expressed the belief that they have even gotten to either, or even maybe to both, Judge Leftwich and the other three defendant's attorneys. The hearing was very one-sided, in his opinion. The other lawyers were doing little but tossing responsibility in Andy's lap.

Finally, the attorney arrived at his true request: he wanted Andy to release the master recording so it could be introduced as evidence. It could be the deciding factor. Also, there was a need for corroborating evidence to help prop up their case. The affidavits that were at the company's office were already before the court, but being from interested parties they didn't carry much weight. Andy asked for the list back that he had given the lawyer, and added his briefcase to the things that Gina was to release.

Andy stipulated that the briefcase and its contents were not part of any payment, and was to remain his property. The contents were to be used as evidence only, and protected at all costs. There were many valuable, mint condition Elvis records in the briefcase, recorded under the Sun label, that Andy had paid collector prices for. They had been the ones used in the comparative analyses. There were also several record labels from the fifties, also in mint condition, that were used in designing the record label for "Tell Me Pretty Baby."

The lawyer said he understood completely, and everything would be safe with him. Andy also explained what other documents were in the briefcase, but the statements by the music experts and the spectrographic analysis were the most important. Kreis said that he believed the items would be a great help in court. But what about the master tape?

That was more difficult, Andy told him. Andy had a deep emotional investment in the tape. It looked as if Don Reese had set Andy up solely to steal the tape, and Andy was lucky just to still have it. He was very reluctant to release it, even to his lawyer. Kreis assured him that the tape would be perfectly safe, and Andy finally agreed.

What else was he to do if he expected any chance of winning the fight with RCA and marketing the record? Of what good would it do him left in the bank, if he lost the court battle? He wrote a release to his bank, to let Kreis have the tape. Again, he felt he was making a very big mistake, but could see no way around it.

The next few days were a blur of activity. Andy was processed out of jail and sent to the Texas Department of Corrections. Huntsville is the prison capital of the country; the entire economy of the East Texas city is built around the many prisons there and the officials and guards residing in the area. As many industrial cities have factories every few miles, Huntsville has prisons.

It was a long and brutal bus ride to the prison, handcuffed to another inmate, leg-shackled and bouncing on metal benches, and he was glad when it was finally over. There still remained assignment and transfer to one of the many prison farms upon completion of the classification process, but that was still several weeks in the future. What Andy was glad for was some sort of movement, some action and fresh air after the months of imposed inactivity and staleness of the county jail.

Andy hunted days-old Dallas newspapers as they filtered into his cell block. They were still his best source of information. The few television stations they were allowed to watch carried mostly Houston-area news, and they were totally silent about the ongoing trial that occupied his thoughts.

Charlotte was staying in touch by letter, but the mail was slow to arrive inside the prison walls, and she didn't provide him with the legal details he hungered for. She had made it a point to be in court as often as she could, and tried to provide Andy with her observations. But there was no real information in what she told Andy, not the kind of legal intelligence he desired.

The Thanksgiving holidays came and went without notice for Andy. There was little to be thankful for that he could see. He knew life could be worse, but didn't see how. The following Wednesday, Charlotte sent him a clipping from Variety, an entertainment publication, published November 21. The article stunned Andy -- an Elvis impersonator had come forward claiming he had recorded "Tell Me Pretty Baby."

The article quoted a Maine singer, Mike Connelly, as saying he had been pressured into recording the song as a hoax, "This thing has gone on too far," said Connelly. "It's a rip-off. I didn't know when I recorded it that they were going to pull a scam like that. I want Vernon Presley to know that it's me on the record -- Mike Connelly, Elvis from good old Madison, Maine."

Andy had never heard of Mike Connelly. The fact that he claimed to have recorded the song for Cin-Kay told Andy the guy was lying. Andy himself had possession of the tape for over a year before Cin-Kay had even been contacted about acting as the record's distributor.

Connelly must have made a sweet deal with RCA, for a recording contract, maybe, Andy thought, in order to lie so outrageously. The age of the tape itself would prove it was made long before this impersonator even knew there was an Elvis Presley.

The following Monday Andy got a letter from Kreis. The attorney's letter didn't contain very much information about the legal proceedings, but did let Andy know that Kreis had picked up the items that constituted his legal fees. He had also gotten the tape from Andy's safety deposit box and would be presenting it to the court that week. He expected RCA would want to take possession of the tape for testing. The lawyer assured Andy that the tape would be safe under the exchange of evidence rule, which supposedly mandated clear, marked records of every instance the evidence changed hands. However, Andy certainly didn't like the idea of the old demo tape being in the hands of the enemy.

Kreis also told Andy about Mike Conley, introducing a new spelling of the singer's name, which would turn out to be the correct one, even though both were assumed names. RCA had declared its intention to subpoena the Elvis impersonator. The attorney explained that he thought Conley was possibly a singer known as Jimmy Ellis, a known entertainer, but Kreis wasn't sure.

Andy had heard of Ellis, and felt his lawyer was wrong. Jimmy Ellis was an Elvis sound-alike, but had music talent in his own right and had worked with Jerry Lee Lewis, Charlie Rich and with others. Ellis was currently under contract to Shelby Singleton, and not Cin-Kay.

It didn't really matter, for it was no Elvis impersonator on the record. It might not be Elvis Aaron Presley, the King, but it had been recorded in the mid-50s by someone who sat in with the Red Dots and Pete Falco and had told Pete his name was Elvis. Pete was positive it was the young man who later became the superstar, and Pete was there, he knew who he had met and played the song with in the recording studio that day long ago.

Conley was lying, and it made Andy furious. He could cause some serious problems for the record. Cin-Kay hadn't even become involved until the last minute, for distribution purposes; there was no way they could have had a hand in the old recording.

Andy spent that evening writing a letter to Kreis, explaining his thoughts on that subject. He hoped the age of the tape would quickly clear up that issue when it was admitted into evidence.

The first week of December Charlotte wrote with the news that the defense had begun presenting its case. She was excited and seemed happy with the way things had started to look positive for the record. She said Pete Falco had taken the stand and told his story about the making of the original tape, saving it all those years and then selling it to Andrew Jackson, whom he had met through his daughter's used car purchase. The plaintiff's lawyers had been unable to make him vary from his story.

Charlotte went on to tell Andy that Kreis had presented the old tape into evidence, along with the statements by the music and voice experts that could authenticate the record as being sung by Elvis. The one from Dr. Godfrey about the spectrographic analysis seemed to get everyone's attention, she wrote him. But, she said, she didn't trust Kreis.

He seemed far too eager to release the tape to RCA's attorney and, she added, she had seen him talking to several men outside the courtroom that she knew were working for the plaintiffs. One looked like a man she had seen at Andy's criminal trial, Charlotte wrote. He didn't understand who Charlotte meant, but he meant to ask her to explain when he wrote back.

Andy was given a copy of a December 1 edition of the <u>Dallas Morning News</u>. Although not containing anything new, it was still something to hold onto as hope once again wove itself into Andy's soul. Even though some of the facts in the article were a little off, Andy was glad to see the issue was still getting news coverage. He slept well that night, the first time in weeks, his hopes on the rise.

A few days later, another article appeared in the newspaper, which, while containing some new information, also worried Andy because it contained information about his trial and ensuing criminal conviction for sexual assault. He hadn't told any of the convicts he'd come to know what he was in prison for, just that he had been falsely convicted. Sex offenders receive little sympathy or friendship from other inmates, many being beaten or raped themselves. If the crime he was convicted of was general knowledge, he might have serious problems. But his attention returned to the article, and to a new twist.

"Presley suit recessed on 'dead man' question," the article began. It related a recess called because one of the defendants, Pete

Falco, had been asked if he knew the younger Presley. Attorneys representing the elder Presley and the recording company argued that since Presley was dead and could not respond to Falco's testimony, the state's "Dead Man Statute," barred the question from being asked. They also argued that if the question were allowed to be answered, it "would considerably lengthen the hearing."

Falco's attorney's responded that the statute in question did not apply and even if it did, it had been waived by Vernon Presley and RCA during the taking of depositions from their clients. Judge Snowden Leftwich had recessed the hearing, saying he needed time to research the law before ruling on the motion.

The article regurgitated the history behind "Tell Me Pretty Baby," along with a few new innuendos and allegations, one being that Andy had a sexual assault charge pending, which he knew was totally false.

Strangely, he felt better about the case, because of two facts.

First, Conley's testimony would surely be proved a lie, and the desperation behind him and whoever had paid him would be obvious.

And, Dr. Godfrey's expert opinion based upon his comparative listening and spectrographic analysis entered into evidence, would be almost impossible to refute.

Andy Meets Joe

CHAPTER NINETEEN

Andy was growing increasingly disappointed with Kreis' performance. The lawyer was making little attempt to keep Andy informed about the hearing's progress. It was Charlotte who mailed Andy newspapers clippings and did everything possible to keep him up to date.

It was from such an article, dated December 2, that Andy learned Conley had finally taken the stand to tell his story.

Conley told a packed 192nd District Court that the voice on "Tell Me Pretty Baby" was his and not Presley's. Another negative bit of testimony was reported -- an electrical engineer for Capitol Records, Joseph Kempler, claimed the tape itself appeared to be of a kind not marketed until 1957. This evidence carried enormous weight, as the tape was supposedly recorded years earlier.

Conley, who admitted that he was indeed Mike Ellis, claimed he had sung the song for his manager -- Hal Freeman in Nashville -- in June of 1978, but he did not know who had dubbed in the backup instrumentation and singing to flesh the recording out.

Conley said he had made an album in May of 1978 and had been nagging Freeman to find the album's release date. At Freeman's request, Conley said he returned to Nashville in June to record some more tunes for the album. At that time, Conley testified, Freeman had provided the lyrics to "Tell Me Pretty Baby," and Freeman and his wife sang the song to Conley to give him an idea of how the tune should go.

Freeman had suggested the song as a replacement for another song on Conley's album, Conley explained. He went on to testify that he sang it for recording purposes four or five times for the Freemans and then insisted it not be put on his album, because he thought it was "rinky-dink."

The article then turned to Kempler's testimony. Kempler, who said he received an engineering degree in Germany before World War II, said he was employed by the company that made the recording tape in question. Kempler had testified that the tape appeared to be of a type developed and distributed for field testing in 1956 and put on the market in 1957 -- three years after Falco claimed to have used the tape to record Presley's voice.

Maybe it was a good thing he wasn't there, Andy thought as he finished reading the newspaper article, for they would have had to throw him in jail for contempt after disrupting the court. No way he could sit in the courtroom and listen to such garbage from the beady-eyed Elvis impersonator and not raise a stink.

It was obvious that this Mike Conley was on RCA's payroll or had been promised some kind of favor from the recording giant if he would lie that blatantly. It was hard to believe any professional would stoop to such tactics, but if RCA had dangled a recording contract in front of Conley, Andy could understand his motives. But besides having his dates all wrong as to when the tape made its first public appearance -- which was when Andy took it to Sumet Sound well over a year before Conley claimed to have recorded it in Nashville -- the man had totally overlooked the fact that the song did not belong to Freeman, and therefore, it could not have been used on any album he might have in the works.

If it was Hal Freeman's song, and Mike Conley recorded it, then the four Dallas men had no claim to it, could not put it on the market and RCA would not be in such a tizzy. No, Andy had no trouble seeing through the smoke screen Conley had thrown up, and hoped it was clear to the judge as well.

What troubled Andy the most was the testimony by Kempler. The expert -- paid by RCA, of course -- claimed that particular type of tape was not marketed until 1957. Maybe the expert was a few years off. Maybe Falco was a few years off, and Elvis had recorded the song in 1957 in Phoenix -- against his contract -- and Pete hedged on the date some so he could retain possession of the demo tape and not be hassled by Sun Records.

Something didn't quite make sense to Andy as he read again all that was reported about the tape and RCA's making of other tapes from it. Andy paid special attention to the part where Conley said his voice was electronically inserted into the recording, and the court had listened to two tapes being played as comparison -- one a re-recording of the original and the other a recording Conley said RCA had asked him to record. Both allegedly sounded the same to the untrained ear. What it sounded like to Andy, and the thought scared him terribly, was that RCA had somehow pulled a switch of his original. He knew letting RCA take the tape was a big mistake, and he intended to raise hell with Kreis until they got to the bottom of it all. And, if his worse fears were realized, how was he ever going to get back the original tape, if it even still existed?

Andy spent the next few days seeking answers to the questions he had about the master tape. He specifically wanted to know who had possession and control of the tape now. He wrote his lawyer to find out.

Was he absolutely sure it was the same tape he retrieved from the safety deposit box? Did Kreis mark it for identification purposes in any manner?

The civil attorney never answered the letter. Nor, according to Charlotte, did Kreis make an attempt at competent representation of Andy's interests over the last few days of the hearing. It finally became apparent to Andy that his attorney had no intention of trying to win on his behalf, and was most likely collaborating with RCA to some degree. Andy had no idea what he could do to get the original tape back, especially from inside prison.

Charlotte had mentioned meeting an attorney who expressed an interest in the case, and she wanted Andy to meet him. Andy agreed, knowing it was time to seek new counsel. He wrote Charlotte and asked her to please tell the lawyer to come visit.

Andy also gave Charlotte Kreis's phone number and address, and asked her to do whatever she could to retrieve his briefcase with all its contents. Andy would write and tell the attorney that he was being dismissed, and that he was to turn over everything to Charlotte.

Andy felt he had done the right thing by sending the shifty lawyer on his way, and as it turned out, the move brought him some luck from an unexpected quarter.

A few days later he received a letter from Charlotte containing a clipping from the Dallas paper, dated December 5. Andy laughed when he read the opening. "Michael Conley lied last week when he testified he is the singer on the reputed tape of the first song recorded by the late Elvis Presley, Conley's manager testified Monday in state district court."

The article pulled no punches, or rather Hal Freeman didn't, calling Conley a "pathological liar. I think this is a cheap shot by RCA and Michael Conley Ellis ... I think they are trying to discredit the recording of 'Tell Me Pretty Baby,'" Freeman was quoted as saying.

Freeman didn't confine his comments to the courtroom. In the hallway outside, the article reported him as saying, "I think this is a very immature way for him (Conley) to act ... I think he ought to be brought back to stand trial for perjury."

But, as always, the good news was countered by some negative testimony, this time in the words of Bud Buschardt, a Dallas broadcaster and record collector, who had testified the quality of the recording was too good to have been made during 1954.

Later that week, Joe Gregory, the attorney Charlotte had met, came to the prison farm for a legal visit with Andy. Gregory told

Andy the hearing was over with and that distribution of the record had been halted. Gregory said this was only temporary, and that a trial to determine the record's authenticity had been set for March 12 of the coming year.

Gregory offered to represent Andy for a small percentage of any future proceeds from the record. Charlotte had given him all the information and documents which had been turned over to her, so he was familiar with the case. He thought be could win the case, and Andy believed he was sincere. For the first time in a long time Andy felt good about his legal representation as he bid goodbye to his new attorney.

Before he left, Gregory gave Andy more recent clippings concerning the now-over hearing. Two of the articles carried a December 6 date, and one was dated December 7. Two were from Dallas and one from Tennessee.

None of the Dallas information was news to Andy except the actual granting of the temporary injunction. He was surprised the hearing had lasted only four days. Receiving small pieces of news at a time, it had seemed to drag over several weeks.

The Tennessee paper, however, added a new twist to events. It reported that Hal Freeman had filed a $5 million damage suit against Mike Conley. Freeman claimed that Conley's "lies" had irreparably damaged Freeman's reputation and that Conley was lying in order to gain favors from RCA.

In a flurry of contradictory denials, Conley had accomplished nothing but further digging a hole for himself, a hole that Andy sat down and began to outline for his new attorney. He pointed out the discrepancies in the stories Conley had been telling, focusing on the different times Conley claimed to have dubbed his voice on different recordings of "Tell Me Pretty Baby."

It appeared to Andy that a lot of dubbing had indeed been done, but it was most likely done after RCA filed suit and it took place in their own studios. And that just so happened to be after Andy's ex-lawyer had so willingly turned over the master tape to RCA's lawyers. The thought of his tape no longer being recognizable sent a jolt through Andy.

Through all this trouble, he was still convinced that it was Elvis singing on that tape, and the idea of such a priceless recording being destroyed or altered through corporate greed, in a fit of legal maneuvering, made his heart ache. Andy felt a rush of anger trying to break through, but he told himself to stay calm.

The Professor

CHAPTER TWENTY

That winter was Andy's worse in prison. His anticipation of the forthcoming trial in March filled his dreams, as well as his every waking moment. He wanted to do something, anything, but it all seemed so hopeless.

Charlotte kept Andy sane during that time. Her visits brought joy to Andy's cheerless world. Andy knew the day would come when Charlotte would no longer be there for him, but as long as she wanted to be part of his life, he would be thankful to her.

The new year brought hopes that "Tell Me Pretty Baby" might yet reach the public as Joe Gregory, Andy's attorney, kept Andy abreast of his extensive research in preparation for the trial. It was obvious that Gregory was putting much time and effort into the case, which was amazing considering he hadn't been paid anything. His expenses were steadily growing and would escalate with the trial, yet there was no guarantee of any return unless the record went to market.

But he wasn't a fool. Before entering the deal with Andy, Gregory had consulted with recording industry attorneys who assured him that the record's potential was enormous. They estimated his five percentage points could easily be worth as much as seven or eight hundred thousand if the record was released.

But besides the money, Gregory believed in what he was fighting for. He had listened to the record, studied all the affidavits and depositions, and done more than enough research to satisfy his questions as to the authenticity of the recording. He believed it was Elvis' first. Now, he needed to convince a jury in March to see things the same way.

A law firm in Irving, Texas, was representing the other three defendants. Gregory was not receiving the fullest cooperation from either the co-defendants or their lawyers. One of the first things Gregory wanted was to find and hire the country's foremost expert in voice identification. He finally reached an agreement with the other lawyers to split the cost to hire the expert and began his search.

Gregory finally settled on Dr. Oscar Tosie, a professor at Michigan State University. Sources indicated that he was the top man in his field, and that he was constantly pushing the frontiers of voice identification. Dr. Tosie's expert testimony could not be refuted at trial. Gregory arranged to send him one of the first copies made from the original demo of "Tell Me Pretty Baby," for the professor to analyze.

The doctor's investigation and final report would take a few months to compile, and Gregory hoped it would be ready in time for trial, but requested a preliminary report. Some weeks later Dr. Tosie called Gregory and informed the lawyer that he was ninety percent sure the singer on the tape was Elvis Presley.

To be certain there would be time for Dr. Tosie to finish his report, and for him to be available to testify at the trial, Gregory filed a motion for a continuance, requesting a short delay in starting the trial.

Gregory was disappointed when Judge Leftwich denied the motion. It left Gregory wondering about the judge's impartiality. All they could do now was hope that the doctor's report was ready by the trial date, and that he could free his calendar and make it to Dallas.

But the really big break came a little over two weeks before the trial was scheduled to begin. Gregory received a telephone call from an individual who identified himself as Elvis Presley's cousin. He said that he was with Elvis when the King recorded "Tell Me Pretty Baby" in Phoenix in 1954.

This was incredible, if true. However, arrangements could not be made to get the man to Dallas before the trial. Since asking for a continuance would in all likelihood be denied, arrangements were made to take the man's deposition in time to enter it as evidence, in addition to continuing to try to get him to Dallas before March 12.

This was the best news Andy had received about the case. He just hoped everything would work out so Elvis's cousin could testify in person that the tape was indeed all it was claimed to be.

Late February, Andy was called to the administration office for a legal visit. He was shocked, then exhilarated, to see Charlotte with Gregory, then understood what was happening when Gregory said, "You remember my legal assistant, don't you, Andy?"

The smiling counsel then excused himself from the private room, telling the guard outside that his legal assistant was going to take some notes while he found some coffee. Charlotte was in Andy's arms almost before the door was closed. She covered his face with kisses, and the stolen moment was intense. The interlude was far too short, but rewarding beyond words. It was just what Andy needed to erase the pain of the last few months and to help him through the ordeal of the trial yet to be faced.

Gregory soon returned, and the moment was gone. The lawyer told Andy that the prospects weren't good for getting either Dr. Tosie or Elvis's cousin in court in time to testify. The judge simply would not entertain a motion for a continuance, but there was still hope that the depositions would be allowed in court.

It wasn't good news at all, but Gregory thought Andy needed to know. The attorney asked if there was anything Andy could think of that might help for trial. Andy was unable to think of anything, but assured him he would try to remember anything that could be of use and get a letter in the mail immediately if something came to mind.

After a warm handshake from Gregory and a tender hug from Charlotte, a guard escorted Andy back to his chilly cell after a thorough strip search. He was silent, his thoughts on Charlotte as she left the prison grounds with his attorney for their return trip back to Dallas.

Andy Meets The Judge

CHAPTER TWENTY-ONE

The first ten days of March crawled for Andy as he went about his daily prison routine. Each day was filled with thoughts of the upcoming trial, which would either allow "Tell Me Pretty Baby" to go on the market with Elvis Presley's name on the label, or mark the death of the record and all the hopes and dreams Andy had built around the recording. Finally on March 11, Andy was ordered to pack his meager possessions and report to the room where he would wait for the prison bus. It was only the first step on a long voyage ahead of him, but Andy was glad the process had finally started. At least now the waiting was over.

From the Eastham Unit Andy rode the prison bus to Huntsville once again. This time the journey was taken in a happier atmosphere. Most of the prisoners riding the bus in this direction were on their way to Huntsville to be either released, having done their time, or were on the way back to court, having won the appeal challenging their convictions and a right to a new trial.

The prisoner chained to Andy was one of those with high hopes in the latter category. The appellate court had ordered a re-trial because his trial attorney had failed to present even a semblance of a defense. The young convict claimed he didn't even know why he had been arrested when the whole nightmare began -- he had been home with his young wife and couldn't have possibly robbed the liquor store he was accused of robbing.

Andy just smiled and wished him well, remembering how his own trial had gone. They finally arrived in Huntsville and were quickly unloaded in anxious silence. Once again the shakedown and strip search took place, along with an inventory of each inmate's possessions, down to each photo and toothbrush.

Having made it this far without any problems, Andy was separated from those who were to be released and placed in a holding cell. There Andy would spend the better part of the day awaiting someone from Dallas County to pick him up. It was a relief when a deputy sheriff arrived, handcuffed him and placed him in a car. The ride back to Dallas in the back seat of the unmarked county car was long, but not boring. Andy enjoyed watching the people passing on the freeway, going on with their lives. Once, a young boy in the back of a station wagon waved at him before his mother frowningly yanked him into his seat. It made Andy smile, as few things did when he was at the prison farm in Huntsville.

The Dallas skyline finally came into sight. As the shining downtown lights filled his vision, Andy's emotions overwhelmed him, and he silently cried at the onrush of memories and lost opportunities.

He closed his eyes until he felt the car come to a stop in what he knew to be the underground garage of the Dallas County Courthouse and jail. With a deep breath he stepped out of the car as the deputy opened the door for him.

For the third time that day he was searched and his property inventoried. He was taken to a cell that smelled as if it hadn't been cleaned in years. The thin mattress on the steel bunk was uncomfortable and the sandwich he had long ago eaten was only a memory. But the day had been a long and emotionally draining one, and sleep quickly overcame him.

Hours before sunlight filtered through the dirty window on the far side of the hall across from his small cell, he awoke to the clanging of keys and breakfast. He tried to go back to sleep after eating but his anxiety wouldn't allow it. He wasn't in a large tank with other inmates, and there was no television to tell the time by. Gray light was finally beginning to light the dingy window, so he guessed they would be coming for him soon. He expected the routine to be as it had been for his criminal trial several months earlier; a deputy escorting him down to be dressed out in clothes presentable before the court, then waiting in a holding cell until the trial started.

Andy had lain back down on his bunk and dozed off when the brass keys unlocking his cell door woke him. Andy followed the guard down the hall, to a room behind the booking and property area, where he was given an out-of-style suit to wear. Andy was then taken to a small holding cell behind the courtroom where he would wait until all the forces gathered.

He didn't have long to wait. The court bailiff, a large, sour -faced man in a deputy sheriff's uniform, unlocked the holding cell and told Andy to step out. This seemed strange to Andy; he knew it was still early, and his lawyer hadn't even arrived to talk to him yet.

In a surprise, Andy was escorted to the judge's chambers, to stand before Judge Snowden Leftwich, Jr., who loomed behind a massive expanse of rare hardwoods suitable for royalty. Andy felt intimidated as the judge sat in silence in his black robe, flanked by the Stars and Stripes and the Lone Star State flag. The shelves of law books covering every wall of the room added to the imposing weight of authority.

The judge finally spoke, and his voice conveyed no compassion. He told Andy that a convicted felon would receive no respect in his courtroom, and that if Andy got out of line in any fashion, the proceedings would be stopped until Andy was physically removed for the remainder of the trial.

Andy was taken aback by the hostility in the man's eyes. He wanted to say something, anything to assert that he, too, had rights to protect in this trial, but the deputy's large hand tightening around his elbow made it clear there was no room for discussion in this chamber.

The judge went on to say that he would not allow or tolerate any contact or conversation between Andy and the media. He was contemptuously dismissed, and it was clear to him as he was escorted back to his holding cell that he was up against more that just RCA and Vernon Presley.

It was at least another hour, but felt like many more, before Andy's attorney arrived. Gregory was pleased to see Andy had made the trip in good shape, that he had been dressed in fairly presentable clothes, and that he appeared ready to get the trial underway. After the initial formalities, Andy told his counsel what had taken place earlier with the judge. Gregory was not happy to hear that Judge Leftwich had already used intimidation on his client. He was soon to learn it would become the standard course of the entire trial.

Now it was Gregory's turn to bring Andy up to date. First, the bad news. RCA had retained the law firm of John Hill of Dallas. Hill was an ex-attorney general of Texas, and his political influence with the judge was indisputable. Hill himself would not be there, but the attorneys representing the plaintiffs in court were among the best in Dallas.

It would not be easy, Gregory admitted. He told Andy that he had been unable to get either Dr. Tosie or Elvis's cousin to Dallas in time to testify. They did have Dr. Tosie's full report to introduce as evidence.

Gregory had also obtained several affidavits from people in Nashville who claimed that Conley -- aka Mike Ellis -- approached them asking that they lie to corroborate his story that it was he who had originally recorded "Tell Me Pretty Baby."

Andy felt the good news outweighed the bad, and was surprised that these music studio employees were willing to stand up to RCA. Both Andy and his attorney had high hopes that that evidence would shoot down any claim the Elvis impersonator would make when RCA placed him on the stand, which they undoubtedly would. Gregory excused himself, telling Andy that he needed to meet with the other lawyers and clients, and that he would be back for him when it came time to select the jury.

FRONT COVER RECORD JACKET

Released in 1978

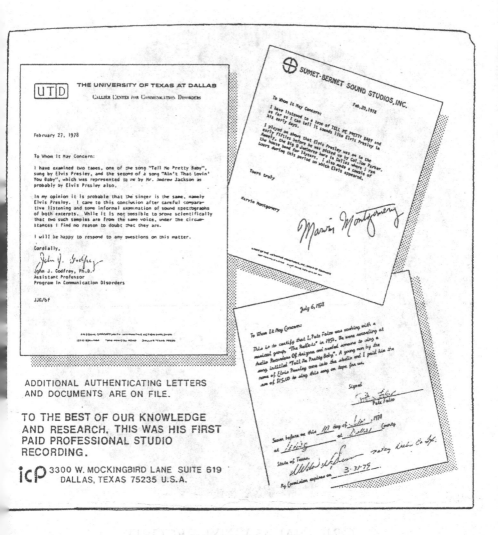

BACK COVER OF ORIGINAL RECORD JACKET

Released in 1978

ORIGINAL 45 VINYL RECORD

Released in 1978

September 6, 1978, DALLAS TIMES HERALD

Staff Photo by John Hall

Pete Falco, with what is thought to be an old recording by Elvis Presley

September 19, 1978, THE TENNESSEAN
FIRST ELIVS CUT CLAIMED

Pete Falco
Couldn't peddle Elvis

—Staff photos by Don Lottin

The pink lettering matches the pink shag upholstery of the 1950 Ford that will be used to promote the new Elvis release on Cin-Kay Records.

September 2, 1978, DALLAS TIMES HERALD

MAN SAYS IT'S HIS VOICE,

NOT ELVIS' ON RECORD

— Staff photo by Jay Dickman

Singer Mike Conley talks with lawyer outside courtroom

The Trial-March 12-22, 1979

CHAPTER TWENTY-TWO

It was close to 10 a.m. when Gregory returned, the court bailiff on his heels. Andy's attorney was smiling and energetic, eager to get on with jury selection. Even though Andy knew the crowd in the courtroom must have been large from the level of muted sound he heard through the wall, he was unprepared for the number of people filling the courtroom. He spotted Charlotte near the back, waving at him, and he returned her huge smile.

The bailiff ordered him to sit at the end of the defense table, with a deputy seated a few feet away. Gregory was next to Andy, with two other attorneys in the center of the table. Pete Falco, Don Reese and Marion Sitton were seated near the other end.

Pete gave Andy a big smile and friendly nod of his head in greeting. Marion tried to smile but was clearly too nervous, or unsure of himself, to do so. Sitton's health appeared to be failing, and Andy hoped the strain of the trial wouldn't make matters worse.

Reese, however, refused to glance in Andy's direction, and did not acknowledge his presence in any way. If Andy had still doubted that Don had anything to do with the sexual assault charges against him, Reese's actions that day removed any uncertainty.

It was beyond Andy's comprehension how anyone could do such a thing to a business partner and supposed friend, but he knew greed made men do strange and vicious things. It was ironic now, sitting in the courtroom doing battle with RCA, that Reese had still not gotten his hands on what he wanted so badly, and was sitting at the same table with the man he'd sent to prison.

The bailiff commanded all to rise, and the judge entered the suddenly hushed courtroom. Judge Leftwich was an imposing figure in his flowing black robe, and he took time to reinforce his authority by standing and piercing Andy with an icy glance. The meaning was clear: the judge would welcome the opportunity to throw Andy out of the courtroom for any reason.

With a sharp rap of his gavel Judge Leftwich called the court into session. He read aloud the allegations from RCA's suit against the defendants, giving added invective to the words, "fraud, hoax and public deception."

The judge called for voir dire to begin and the attorneys for the plaintiffs began questioning the prospective jurors. The defense counselors kept track of the answers for future reference, identifying the potential jurors by seat numbers, giving some x's and some checks.

It is an arcane process, by which attorneys for both sides try to winnow out people they think will not give the verdict each side is seeking. In this case, it was obvious that most of those in the panel were overwhelmed and excited at the prospect of becoming a juror in this case. They wanted to be part of a landmark case over an alleged Elvis Presley recording, and to listen and be close to those who had been close to the revered King.

Each of the plaintiff's lawyers seemed to have his own selection topics he felt required to ask each prospective juror. Some made no sense at all to Andy. He just couldn't see where it would matter what high school the gray-haired old lady attended, or what kind of work another woman's husband did. But, watching his attorney take hurried notes on his legal pad, apparently someone was able to make sense of the process.

The x's slowly began to outnumber the checks, though there were many with no marks at all beside their number. Andy was growing restless, and his gaze often fell upon Charlotte near the back of the room. Finally, the judge called for lunch break.

The attorneys for RCA resumed their questioning as soon as the judge called the court back into session. Only occasionally was anyone asked if he or she had any knowledge of "Tell Me Pretty Baby," or if they had ever had any contact with Elvis Presley. Anyone with knowledge of the recording in dispute was removed as most likely having already formed an opinion as to its authenticity.

There was one man in the group who was a professional musician, who said he played progressive country music in the Dallas nightclubs. Although this was exactly the type of juror Andy was hoping for, who was knowledgeable about types of music and the technical aspect of the recording industry, it was clear that the attorneys for RCA were marking him for elimination.

It was almost 4 p.m. before RCA's attorneys declared they were finished with the voir dire portion of the trial. The judge adjourned the court until 9 a.m. the following day, at which time the defense would have its turn.

That night Charlotte came to visit Andy at the jail. He had been able to get a shower and a short nap after the day's proceedings and was feeling almost human. Charlotte had news for Andy. A reporter for the Dallas Morning News, Bernie Komer, had requested an interview with Andy, but had been denied by the judge. The reporter had asked Charlotte to ask Andy if he believed he could get a fair trial. Andy told her what had happened in the judge's chambers that morning, and told her to tell Mr. Komer that there was little chance of getting a fair trial under Judge Leftwich, and that he wasn't sure what he could do about that.

Breakfast found Andy staring at the patterns on the rusted metal ceiling and thinking about what the day would bring. He was able to get a few hours sleep before the guard came to take him down to be dressed and into the holding cell. His mind was focused ahead several hours, to someone he had noticed in the courtroom but couldn't quite understand why that person was important. The face haunted him like a recurring nightmare. Something about this individual just wasn't right.

He had no idea how much time passed before Gregory arrived and passed a cup of steaming black coffee through the bars to Andy. He sipped happily as Gregory explained that today the defense would begin its questioning, and that he wanted Andy to make notes of any jurors who gave answers which, for any reason, he didn't like.

Gregory wanted Andy to be an active part of the process, not only so he would feel he was getting his day in court, but also so Andy wouldn't get restless and depressed by the long, unfamiliar process. Just before the bailiff came to escort them into the courtroom, Andy's attorney broke the news that Judge Leftwich had designated him as second counsel. That meant that most of the questioning would be done by Steven Williams, the counsel for the other defendants.

Gregory was not happy with the situation, and felt as Andy did, that he was more qualified than the other attorneys to lead the defense.

There would be many instances where Gregory wouldn't be allowed to interject himself into the proceedings, he told Andy. That was another reason for the legal pad. He asked Andy to write down any notes or questions which needed to be passed on, so the point could be made by Williams without too much delay.

The courtroom seemed even more crowded this morning than it had the day before as Andy took his seat at the defense table under the watchful eye of the guard placed near his side. Not only was every seat filled, but there were many spectators standing along the back wall, as well. His eyes fell upon Charlotte, who was seated directly behind where the last of the jury panel was seated by number.

She gave Andy a big smile, and nodded to the man sitting next to her, making a writing motion with her hand. It took a second for Andy to realize she was telling him this was the reporter she had mentioned. Komer returned Andy's smile and nod, giving Andy a thumbs-up sign that made him believe that whatever happened would not happen without the public knowing, or there at least being a public record of the trial.

The judge entered and called the court to order. Judge Leftwich briefly went over his instructions to the jury panel from the day before, then fixed Steve Williams with an icy stare and asked that the defense please not delay jury selection any longer than necessary.

The effect was immediate upon the nervous young attorney, and his response of "Yes, your honor," was an embarrassing stammer. Andy's hopes for a good day went up in smoke as he noticed Gregory cover his eyes, massage his temples and almost imperceptibly shake his head, visibly embarrassed for his co-counsel.

Williams carefully but inarticulately questioned the members of the jury panel on the things he felt were relevant to their being selected to serve on the jury. He asked some very thoughtful questions about their individual backgrounds, but Andy couldn't really see where they were all leading. There were a few times he heard an attitude come through that prompted him to mark a small "x" by that seat number on his pad.

As he listened to the answers to numerous questions, he swept the room for a face, though he didn't know the face he was looking for. It was only a hunch, but Andy believed the ominous feeling was the result of someone being there who shouldn't be.

Court was dismissed for lunch and the attorneys turned in their strike sheets. When the jury panel returned the bailiff would announce which members had made the final selection and would sit on the jury. By three that afternoon all twelve were seated in the jury box and those remaining dismissed with directions to the county clerk to pick up their fees. Those who were selected for the jury were instructed to report the next morning for the trial, which would begin promptly at 9 a.m.

Again, Charlotte visited Andy that night, as she would every night while he was in the Dallas County Jail for the civil trial. He told her about his feelings that someone was in the courtroom who shouldn't be, but she said she had noticed nothing out of the ordinary. It made him feel better to talk about it, and her reassurances that everything would be all right made it easier for him to sleep.

But his dreams were haunted by a face in the whispering crowd; narrow, with sharp, watery, eyes filled with a malicious glint. He didn't recognize it, but he knew it shouldn't be there, that whoever it belonged to was a link to something which had been troubling him. He woke with a start, the image of the thin face engraved in his mind. He knew who he would be looking for the next day, but not who he would find.

One-sided Proceedings

CHAPTER TWENTY-THREE

The <u>Dallas Times Herald</u> began its coverage of the trial March 14, 1979, with a small article headlined, "Trial begins on 'Elvis' record," in which laid out the basics of RCA's lawsuit. The article named the defendants, and noted that Andy was a convicted rapist. It gave a brief history of the preliminary hearing, along with outlining Pete Falco's story of meeting Elvis and having the King record "Tell Me Pretty Baby" for $15 measly dollars.

If word of mouth and gossip by the disappointed prospective jurors had not been enough to ensure a packed courtroom, that article in the morning edition promised a good show, with rapists, musicians, top-dollar lawyers and maybe some of the King's Memphis Mafia thrown in for good measure.

Andy had no idea the newspaper had drawn attention to him in such an ugly manner, and was surprised by the contempt in the eyes of the crowd when he was escorted into court that morning. He saw pointed fingers and heard disapproving murmurs, and guessed right -- that his conviction had been made public. He hoped the members of the jury had not been informed of this ugly fact. If they had, it would surely damage his credibility in their view and make it that much harder to win their votes.

After the obligatory nods to his fellow defendants, Andy scanned the room for the face he remembered from his dream the night before. It wasn't there, but his gaze was returned with hate and anger from every face he saw. It was unnerving, and visions of Texas lynch mobs danced through his head.

The court was called to order as Judge Leftwich entered. He quickly introduced counsel for both parties, the tone of his voice making his preference clear. He instructed Mr. Phillip Smith, lead counsel for RCA, to give his opening statements in behalf of RCA and Vernon Presley. Andy wondered why the senior Presley was included, because the man had not taken an active part in the litigation and obviously wanted nothing to do with the lawsuit.

Every eye in the courtroom was on Smith as he introduced his case and his corporate client. He also hammered to the members of the jury that he was acting on behalf of Vernon Presley, father of the late, beloved King.

After seeing the reverent look on the faces of the jury, Andy understood the constant references to Vernon Presley. It didn't matter whether the old man was present, or if he took part or merely gave his blessing. His name carried the weight of a nation's adoration for its hip-swiveling hero, and Smith was going to do his damnedest to try to convince the jury that Andy and his co -defendants were trying to mar the memory of Elvis by passing off an inferior record as the King's and making a ton of money in the process.

Smith complained that the defendants were guilty of fraud and deceptive trade practices, and if they weren't stopped right here, right now, the King's memory would be forever shamed and vulnerable to the same type of underhanded dealings. Smith was experienced, impressive, and flamboyant, and Andy prayed for a miracle, because it looked as if they would need one.

As he listened to Smith attack his company, Andy thought back to September of 1978. Just two days before the first press release in Nashville about "Tell Me Pretty Baby," Hal Freeman had contacted Andy and relayed RCA's offer of a half million dollars for exclusive rights for the song.

If it hadn't been for Don Reese refusing to sell, they would all be comfortable right now, instead of under fire in a courtroom. RCA had known about the tape for a long time, but had only decided to sue after seeing it was destined to be a hit and they didn't own it.

Andy returned to the present as Smith concluded his opening statement and the judge called upon the defendants' attorney to give his. Steven Williams nervously shuffled his notes and rose to face the jury.

His presentation was almost inaudible, and he talked to his shoes, as if they were making judgements, not the jury. His public persona left much to be desired, and he was clearly struggling with a fear of public speaking. Judge Leftwich's harsh and pitiless gaze didn't help.

Williams finally managed to tell the jury that he would prove, through, solid, scientific evidence, that the recording was authentic and recorded by Elvis Presley in 1954, in Phoenix, Arizona, backed by the Red Dots, a Phoenix band. Williams began to hit his stride as he claimed that the defense had expert testimony attesting to the identity of the singer, along with eye -witness testimony from others who had been present when the recording was made.

Williams came close to finding his dramatic self as he told the jury that the only reason RCA had brought the lawsuit was because the record was a landmark in the history of pop music, and it did not belong to the recording giant.

The record could be worth a fortune, and since RCA did not have rights to the song, the corporation wanted to assure that the fortune did not go to those who did. That, in a nutshell, was what this trial was about -- corporate greed against the determination of ordinary men to honor the memory of Elvis Presley by presenting his first record to the public.

Although Andy was surprised and happy with Williams' speech, especially after seeing how it left Judge Leftwich looking sour, he still wished it was Joe Gregory as lead counsel, and not Williams.

He was afraid that would make a crucial difference in the trial's outcome, and there was nothing to be done about it. How the situation had arisen had left him with an idea that the trial would not be fought on a fair footing. Before the trial had started, Judge Leftwich had called the defense attorneys into his chambers. He had told them that he felt the interests of the defendants in this case were identical, and he was therefore ruling that only one defense attorney would be allowed to examine the witnesses.

Gregory, who had described the meeting to Andy, said he had objected, because he had been hired by Andy to represent him, not the other defendants. The conflict of interest between the defendants, because of Andy's criminal conviction, was well established and a matter of record from the preliminary hearing.

Gregory had told the judge that as personal representative of Mr. Jackson, he intended to cross-examine or direct examine every witness that took the stand.

Judge Leftwich had made it clear that Gregory would be jailed for contempt if he attempted to examine any witness not specifically called by Gregory, and that in addition, all objections or other motions must be made through Williams, who he was designating as the sole voice for the defense.

What had made his ruling even more glaring in its prejudice was that the judge had not placed the plaintiffs under a similar restriction. In addition to Smith, RCA was being represented by David Bryant, and both were assisted by a battery of well-dressed assistants. Both men were among the most capable civil trial lawyers in the Dallas area, and thus in Texas, and they were going to be allowed to act like a legal tag-team, switching back and forth and combining their vast knowledge and experience. Even though Andy knew some of the judge's animosity came from the fact that Andy was a convicted felon, he felt the weight of the judge's prejudicial rulings had placed him under an enormous disadvantage.

The trial finally began with Smith calling the vice-president of RCA's production and development. She testified to the substance of Elvis' contractual agreements with RCA, and said she had worked with the King for many years and had never heard him mention "Tell Me Pretty Baby."

As Smith brought the woman along, it became clear his strategy was to introduce comparison recordings and use her familiarity with Elvis to discredit "Tell Me Pretty Baby." RCA, without experts, was relying on people who had known Elvis and were willing to sneer and basically say that if Elvis had recorded the song, he would have surely told them, and if he hadn't then he couldn't have recorded the song.

After laying the groundwork for comparison evidence by allowing the woman to explain her working relationship with Elvis, a procession of large speakers and electronic equipment was carried forward and placed near the jury box. As the equipment was being connected, Smith explained to the jury that they were about to hear an extensive collection of known Elvis Presley recordings, which would be followed by short tracks taken from "Tell Me Pretty Baby." The witness, being a self-described expert on Elvis' recordings, was to identify the songs for the court.

As the circus unfolded, Andy was jolted by a familiar face. One of the assistants setting up the equipment -- a tall, scarecrow-thin man with calculating eyes -- was at the plaintiff's table, talking to one of the attorneys.

It wasn't until the man stood up straight and Andy saw how tall he was that he realized he had seen him before, and why it was so out of place for him to be not only in this courtroom but so obviously working for RCA.

It was the same man who had sat through Andy's criminal trial, months earlier; the same man who, minutes after the jury had been allowed to go home before reaching a verdict, had jumped up and raced out of the courtroom.

The pieces fell together for Andy. RCA had planted a spy in the criminal courtroom to keep an eye on and, if needed, a hand in the outcome of Andy's criminal trial. Andy felt certain that he had won that night until something, or someone, had managed to influence the jury. He had believed at the time, berating himself for being so suspicious, that RCA had somehow bought the jury off. Now he felt his suspicions were confirmed.

Tugging at Gregory's elbow to get his attention, he pointed the man out. Andy tried to explain that he had seen the man at his criminal trial and believed he had tampered with the jury. Gregory looked at Andy with disbelief, but when he saw the seriousness in Andy's eyes Gregory reconsidered the possibility. As far-fetched as it sounded, it did make sense. Having Andy out of the way and making sure that a huge legal cloud was over his head would only benefit RCA in the legal battle it was even then preparing for.

Andy was asking Gregory what they could do about the situation when the man looked up and noticed Andy and his attorney watching him. Realizing that he had been spotted, he laid down the wiring he had been connecting to the table and with a quick word to RCA's legal team, he exited the courtroom as unobtrusively as possible.

Nobody else seemed to notice or pay the incident any mind. Andy watched for the man to return. Throughout the trial Andy kept watch for him, hoping they could somehow pin him down and get his name or some answers from him, but he never reappeared.

When all the equipment was finally set up, Smith asked the judge's permission to proceed. Judge Leftwich seemed skeptical, but nodded his approval. The attorney loaded a tape onto the player and pressed a button, and the silky voice that had prompted the whole affair came forth -- early, raw Elvis, in short cuts of 10 seconds or so in duration.

There was really no way to tell where one tune began or ended -- it was the King's voice in one large mosaic of sound.

It was interesting but confusing. With a flick of a switch, Smith halted the exhibition. He asked the witness, who had sat on the stand calmly throughout the setup, basking in the crowd's awe, to tell the jury what they had just heard. She rattled off several of Elvis' better-known early releases, and gave a brief history of each.

The jury was obviously impressed with her knowledge of Elvis and his music. There was no question that she already knew what songs were on the tape and their history, but the panel was fascinated with every detail. Andy felt the plaintiffs were turning the trial into a tribute to Elvis. Although he greatly admired the man and his music, Andy knew that was not what this trial was about.

Suddenly, the attorney for the plaintiffs hit the switch, but this time five seconds of "Tell Me Pretty Baby" screamed from the speakers. It didn't sound as Andy remembered, nor did the voice resemble the segments of known Elvis recordings they had been listening to.

That didn't make sense to Andy; he had played the song countless times and had it tested by experts, and in each instance the voice he'd heard was indistinguishable from that of Elvis, not this nondescript wailing.

Stopping the music, Smith again asked the witness to identify the song. She said it was unknown to her, and that she didn't believe the sound clip was recorded by Elvis Presley. From the reactions of the jury, they didn't believe it was Elvis, either. For that matter, even Andy had his doubts.

This process went on for some time. The attorney would play segments of Elvis songs, ask the witness to identify them -- which she gladly did, including anecdotes that cemented her self created status as a confidante of the late King -- and then comparing them to clips supposedly taken from "Tell Me Pretty Baby." Each time Andy heard one of the segments of his song being played, his suspicions that the segments had not been taken from the original tape grew stronger. His temper was also growing shorter, and he was on the verge of asking his attorney to object to the validity of the tape when Judge Leftwich, having grown bored with the display, called lunch recess.

Evidently Gregory had been thinking along the same lines, because just before the guard escorted Andy to the holding cell, the attorney said he would object to the evidence when the trial resumed. After eating his tasteless lunch, Andy was taken back to the courtroom and the trial picked up where it had left off, the avalanche of sound again bombarding everyone.

Although Andy knew what was coming, he was still unprepared for it. When "Tell Me Pretty Baby" next came on, before the witness could sneer that it was not being sung by Elvis, Gregory jumped to his feet and objected.

The judge's head snapped up. He had been dozing, his head on his chest, to the amusement of many in the courtroom. Frowning at the defense attorney, Judge Leftwich told Gregory that he was not lead defense counsel and therefore unauthorized to object to anything. Steve Williams then piped up, announcing that he objected to the authenticity of the sound clips that were being presented as "Tell Me Pretty Baby." With a bang of his gavel, Judge Leftwich overruled the objection. Andy's heart sank.

The charade continued for what seemed like hours. The judge finally dozed off again, as did some jury members. Finally, when a particularly loud blast of spliced and reworked recording howled from the oversized speakers, the judge snapped awake again. He ordered the tape stopped, saying that he was sick of hearing Elvis, and that he was calling the court into recess until 9 a.m. the next morning.

Andy was not the only one in the courtroom shocked by the outburst. The jury was stunned, and the attorneys for the plaintiffs pleaded with the judge to allow them to complete the examination of that witness. The judge simply told them to recall the witness the following day.

It took a minute for the jury, as well as the audience, to realize the day's proceedings were over. The guard motioned for Andy to follow him, and he was taken back to his cell. It had been a very strange day indeed.

All Glitter, No Substance

CHAPTER TWENTY-FOUR

That night, Charlotte and Andy discussed what RCA had tried to pull in the courtroom. Although she was surprised at Judge Leftwich's outburst, she had to admit she too was tired of all those song clips. She couldn't even tell what most of them were, she said. It would have been different if they could have heard the entire song.

That was the whole point, Andy explained. If allowed to hear all of "Tell Me Pretty Baby," then the jury would have been able to tell the recording wasn't the same as the original, therefore they had to keep the comparisons limited to just snatches of verse, not allowing entire songs into evidence.

The night passed all too quickly for Andy. Frustration kept him awake most of the night, and he wondered what judicial outbursts or RCA trickery he would be faced with. When he walked into the courtroom and noticed the speakers were gone, he smiled -- the day looked better already.

The female executive was once again called to the stand and asked about her association with Elvis. The jury found it all evidently very interesting, but for the wrong reasons, Andy thought. While the woman was to be admired for her business accomplishments, the trial was not about her and her closeness to the King and her memories of him. Unfortunately, the plaintiffs were turning the trial into a ceremony honoring Elvis.

When Smith announced he was done with the executive, the judge seemed ready to recess for lunch. However, after a short consultation with Gregory, Williams assured the judge that if allowed just a few minutes, the defense would quickly finish with the witness.

After being granted permission by Judge Leftwich, Williams took the floor for his first cross. He had very few questions for the witness, but they were crucial.

He first asked her if her experience with Elvis extended to the time he was under contract to Sun Records. After hesitating, she admitted that she had no personal experience with Elvis during that time, but defensively added that she knew which songs he had released under that label.

Williams then asked her to tell the jury of any personal knowledge she had of any recordings Elvis had made prior to his signing with Sun Records, late in 1954.

She could only give one answer -- that she had no knowledge whatsoever of anything Elvis may have recorded prior to signing with the legendary Sun Records. All she could do was say that she had never heard Elvis mention any recordings done prior to his time with Sun.

That was all Williams asked her, and he hardly stammered at all, though he didn't look directly at the judge when he said he was done with the witness. Andy only hoped the jury had caught the implications of the witness' admission.

After court resumed, David Bryant, the plaintiff's other attorney, introduced Vernon Presley's deposition stating that Elvis had never been to Arizona during the time the defendants claimed he had. It was not possible to cross examine Mr. Presley, of course, and Andy felt frustrated because the effect it had on the jury as it was read was unquestionable. He only could wish Mr. Presley had been there so he could have answered a few questions, mainly, wasn't it possible that a 19-year-old boy could do some traveling without his father knowing his every move?

That night, when Andy called Gregory, the attorney had some good news, although he cautioned Andy to not get too excited. Dr. Oscar Tosie, the voice identification expert from Michigan State University, had contacted Gregory and said he was arriving in Dallas the next day and would be available to testify.

Although Andy tried to stay calm, he felt a surge of excitement -- this was one of the breaks he had been hoping for. This was undoubtedly the nation's foremost expert in the field of voice identification, and he was willing to testify that he believed, almost without any doubt at all, that the singer on "Tell Me Pretty Baby," was Elvis.

But Gregory cautioned Andy to not get too excited, because they still had to get the judge to allow the doctor to testify, and that wouldn't be easy. Nevertheless, Andy's dreams that night were of records, golden records, as far as he could see.

The next morning the plaintiffs called as their first witness, Joseph Kempler, the electrical engineer for Capital Records. The plaintiffs slowly established his expertise in the highly technical field of which he was a part. His knowledge was extensive and impressive.

After RCA's attorney felt he had established himself sufficiently, he introduced the master tape into evidence. RCA had been in possession of the master tape since the preliminary hearing the previous November. A big display was made of showing the reel of tape to the jury and waving it around, shouting, "This is the very tape the defendants claim was recorded in 1954 by Elvis Aaron Presley."

After the tape was logged as an exhibit by the court clerk and entered into the record, it was handed to Kempler. He thoughtfully examined the tape and spool, as if seeing them for the first time, although when asked if he had seen them before, he answered that yes, he had.

When asked to explain to the jury, he went into detail how RCA had asked him to examine the spool and tape in order to fix the date of manufacture. He had done exactly that, he said, and had reached the conclusion that the tape could not have been used to make any recording in 1954.

Kempler explained why he did not believe that the recording was authentic, in the sense the defendants claimed it was. The tape appeared to be of a type that was not marketed until 1957, the German engineer explained. He said the tape appeared to be the kind of tape developed and distributed for field testing in 1956 and marketed in 1957. As such, he did not believe it was possible that it could have been used for any recording in 1954; it was simply too new. Under cross by Williams, his testimony did not waver.

Kempler's testimony lasted until lunch, and Andy welcomed the break from the damaging evidence presented to the jury that morning. Andy could only wish he could have gotten a good look at the tape before it had been entered into evidence. He hadn't been able to tell from a distance, but was almost certain it wasn't the same tape he had put in his safety deposit box before his arrest the year before.

The sneaky way his last attorney had so willingly turned the tape over to RCA had made him more than a little suspicious ever since it happened.

Gregory took a few minutes from his lunch period to walk back to the holding cell with Andy and his guard. When Andy was locked in the cell and the guard had gone, Gregory asked Andy what he thought of the last testimony. Andy explained his feelings about a possible switch, and Gregory said he was thinking along the same lines, especially after learning how Andy's previous attorney had been so cooperative with RCA about giving up the master tape.

When Gregory asked if Andy could positively identify the master tape, or spot a ringer, Andy answered that he could. Gregory said he was going to put Andy on the stand to testify, but would first submit a motion in limine to the court, and if granted, the motion would prevent the plaintiffs from referring to Andy's criminal conviction. There had already been enough bad publicity on that issue in the press, and there was no need to throw blood on the waters for the sharks.

When the proceedings got under way after lunch, the plaintiffs called Scottie Moore to the witness stand. He was one of Elvis' first band members and a longtime friend of the King's. Moore was currently working as a session musician in Nashville, he told the court. The jury members seemed thrilled to be in the presence of a man who had worked with and been so close to Elvis Presley.

Again, Smith managed to paint a vivid picture of the late and great superstar from the testimony of a man who knew him well. The history of his association and friendship with Elvis was presented to the jury instead of any credentials to establish his ability to identify Elvis' voice and music. He assured the attorney that he knew, as well as anyone alive, the distinctive sound of Elvis Presley's voice and the style of his music. When asked if he had heard "Tell Me Pretty Baby," he said that he had indeed listened to it, several times.

Was the voice of the singer on the recording the voice of the late Elvis Presley, the plaintiffs' attorney wanted to know? It was not, Moore told him. When asked what he personally thought of the recording, Moore told the jury that he thought "it was a bunch of crock!" That outburst seemed to effect the jury more than anything they had yet heard. Andy could only hang his head and hope for a miracle. It didn't come.

Steve Williams took the same approach with Moore that he had earlier with the RCA executive, asking what personal experience Moore had with Elvis before Elvis had actually taken up music as a vocation. The tactic backfired. Moore claimed to have known Elvis since Elvis was in high school, had begun his career as a musician at the same time as had Elvis, and they had started out, practiced and worked together in the early part of their careers. The question was a grave mistake for the defense:

Scotty Moore was adamant in his conviction that it was not Elvis singing "Tell Me Pretty Baby."

David Bryant then took the floor for the plaintiffs. He called D. J. Fontana, another of Elvis' band members during the early days of the superstar's career. Fontana's history with Elvis was much the same as Moore's, except that he hadn't known Elvis during his school years. Fontana testified that he and Elvis has been close friends both during and after their mutual musical endeavors. Fontana also claimed to have had enough experience working with Elvis to be able to identify his voice when he heard it.

Echoing Moore's testimony, to Andy's immense frustration, Fontana quietly said that he did not believe it was Elvis singing "Tell Me Pretty Baby." He didn't offer any other opinions, as had Moore, but his quiet conviction was just as damning to the defense.

Much to Andy's relief, Williams passed on questioning Fontana. The strategy could have worked in their favor, if reversed; if they would have passed on Moore and questioned Fontana, Moore's damaging testimony could have been replaced with Fontana's reticence. But it was too late for that.

As the deputy was escorting Andy from the courtroom, Gregory told him to make sure to call him at the office later that evening. Andy was curious as to what the attorney was so anxious to say.

After getting back to the cell, Andy showered and then asked the guard for permission to telephone his lawyer. After a quick check with the shift commander, Andy was escorted to a small cell containing a telephone resembling a pay telephone but lacking a change slot. There was a thick glass window to one side, from which he was observed by a jail guard, who had the option of listening to the conversation by picking up an extension. Andy picked up the receiver, pressed "0" and asked the operator to place his call.

Gregory quickly answered and accepted the call, and told Andy that Dr. Oscar Tosie had arrived and was ready to testify if the judge would allow it. If not, they were taking a deposition from Dr. Tosie to present to the jury in lieu of direct testimony.

Gregory went over the questions he was going to ask the doctor, requesting input from Andy on technical matters peculiar to the recording. After a few suggestions, Andy felt confident that they had covered the area as well as possible. He said goodbye to Gregory, and prayed that the doctor would be allowed to testify. Their defense would be much stronger with testimony from the nation's foremost expert in voice identification.

The next day began as those before it had, but it found Andy looking forward to the beginning of the defense's presentation. As he arrived at the defense table, Gregory was deep in conversation with Steve Williams. Listening to the intent exchange, he discovered they were preparing to block the testimony of Mike Conley, who had been outside the courtroom that morning.

It looked like the plaintiffs were saving their big gun for last. But, from what he had overheard between the two defense lawyers, they had a huge surprise ready that would effectively plug their opposition's pistol. Andy was beginning to look through the stack of documents Gregory and Williams had piled on the table when Judge Leftwich entered and everyone was ordered to rise.

When court was ordered to resume, Smith called as a witness a disc jockey for KRLD, a Dallas radio station. Apparently, the plaintiffs still had a few loose ends to tie up before bringing in Conley. The radio station was one of those which had received early copies of the first recordings of "Tell Me Pretty Baby," which had been released for promotional purposes. The record had received a lot of local airplay, not only from KRLD but from all the stations that had received early copies.

The dee-jay quickly recited his background as a longtime vinyl spinner. Andy was impressed with the man's history and credentials in what Andy knew was a volatile industry. The dee-jay commanded attention from the courtroom. That was, after all, what his profession was all about -- making people listen.

His voice was magnetic, and the man projected it throughout the courtroom without speaking into the microphone on the stand in front of him.

The dee-jay said that he had played the record in question on air many times, and in his opinion the voice was not that of Elvis Presley. However, just as Smith was giving an "I told you so" look to the jury, the dee-jay added that he couldn't be absolutely sure because of the age of the recording, and his comment drained the color from Smith's face.

The RCA attorney quickly asked the judge to strike the last comment as unresponsive, which drew an objection from Gregory, which drew another objection from Williams, who knew he had to cover for Gregory. The flurry of objections made the jury sit up and take notice, wondering what the fuss was all about.

The judge ordered the attorneys to approach the bench, and Andy had to strain to hear the exchange. Smith wanted the judge to order the jury to disregard the last statement by the dee-jay, and to have him answer with a yes or no. Gregory countered that the dee-jay was the plaintiff's witness, and unless he was being declared as hostile, his responsiveness was not an issue and the comment had to stand.

Williams chimed in by saying that Smith had asked for an opinion and had received one. But since Smith didn't like the opinion, he was now trying to re-ask the question in order to have the opinion disallowed.

The judge ordered them all back to their seats. After a few seconds of an attempt to look as if he was pondering the legal issues, Judge Leftwich ordered the jury to disregard the last statement from the witness. Gregory immediately stood and asked that an exception be noted from the defense, which the judge noted. After glowering at Gregory, the judge ordered Smith to proceed.

Standing in front of the witness, Smith admonished the dee-jay to limit his answers to yes or no. He asked him again if it was his professional opinion that Elvis Presley was the singer on "Tell Me Pretty Baby." The dee-jay simply said, "No."

Passing the witness to the defense, it was clear by their attitudes that the attorneys for RCA regretted not having coached this witness more thoroughly. Williams immediately attacked, and asked the dee-jay how old the recording was.

It was certainly of a fifties style and context, the dee-jay assured the attorney. But if it was that old, Williams countered, why couldn't it have been recorded by Elvis? The dee-jay said he just didn't think it was, based on all the Elvis records he had played and heard throughout his career. But, he quickly added, he could not be certain; it was just his opinion.

Then, it was certainly possible that it was in fact Elvis on the record, pressed Williams? Yes, of course, anything was possible, the dee-jay admitted. After all the plaintiffs had gone through to have that same sentiment disallowed by the judge, Williams had presented it to the jury anyway, and he was justifiably proud of his maneuvering.

Andy was sitting on the edge of his seat when Bryant stood to announce his next witness. Although he expected it, he was still shocked to hear Bryant say, "The plaintiffs will now call Michael Conley to the stand." Before the echo of his voice settled, Gregory was on his feet shouting his objection and requesting permission to approach the bench. It was quite obvious the judge was disturbed as he motioned the defense attorney forward.

With the affidavits from several Nashville recording studios in hand, Gregory strode toward the bench, determination flaming in his eyes. Bryant seemed taken aback by the objection. Frozen in mid-sentence, it took him a few moments to recover and meet Gregory at the bench.

Although the whispers couldn't be made out, the rage in Judge Leftwich's posture was unmistakable. No sooner had Gregory said, "The plaintiffs are about to knowingly present perjured testimony in this case," than the judge shouted at the bailiff to clear the jury box.

After the members of the jury had been escorted to a deliberation chamber, Judge Leftwich told Gregory, pointing a pencil directly at his face, that he had better be able to back up his claim or he would face serious consequences. Laying the affidavits out in front of the judge and the attorney for RCA, Gregory said, "I can!"

"These," he explained to the judge and to the court in general, "are sworn and notarized affidavits from several recording studio executives in the Nashville, Tennessee, area. Although each has its own particular date and details, the basis of each and everyone state that Michael Conley approached persons of those recording studios asking them to corroborate his claim of recording 'Tell Me Pretty Baby.' The first one dates from the time right after Michael Conley first announced to the press that it was he who had recorded the song, and the most recent states that Mr. Conley approached them with a financial offer only a few short weeks ago. We do not have these affiants in the courtroom to testify, as the nature of their business does not permit leaving their companies unattended, however, I will be more than happy to read the affidavits to the court if the judge so desires."

Judge Leftwich did not so desire, he told the attorney. He could read them himself. It would be he, and he alone, the judge told the attorneys arrayed in front of him, who would decide which witnesses would be allowed to testify.

After carefully inspecting the affidavits, the judge said, "These all appear to be legal and in order. However, I'm not going to allow them to be admitted into evidence unless or until Michael Conley takes the stand, and then only for the purpose of impeachment. However, Mr. Gregory, you still have not shown me, nor do these affidavits prove anything about the plaintiff's attempting to knowingly present perjured testimony."

"Your Honor," Gregory retorted, "if I may call a witness to the stand and present testimony outside the presence of the jury on this particular matter, I believe you'll find I can prove my point and substantiate my objection to the calling of Michael Conley to the witness stand." The judge nodded his head that he would agree to hear testimony without the jury present, so Gregory continued.

The witness he wished to call wasn't present, but was at his office in Dallas and available to testify. "The witness is an executive for RCA in their local office, Gregory explained, "but he will only take the stand if subpoenaed."

That was the ace in the hole Andy had been waiting to see drawn. He was leaning forward in his seat as Gregory removed a completed subpoena from his inside coat pocket and presented it to the judge.

It contained the name and business address of the RCA executive they wished to call. "It's almost lunch time anyway," the defense attorney said. "If you'll permit the court to recess for lunch a few minutes early, we can have the witness in court by the time proceedings resume if you'll sign the subpoena, Your Honor," he said as he passed the form to the judge.

His eyebrows quivering, Judge Leftwich closely inspected the subpoena, as if he suspected it would be his undoing unless he could somehow deny it. He scowled and passed the form to Bryant. The attorney for RCA scanned the form, shrugged his shoulders and passed it back. It was apparent they didn't like it, but there was nothing they could do at this point. Gregory had let them back themselves into a corner.

Signing the subpoena, the judge announced, "The court is in recess for lunch until 1 p.m. If the defense doesn't have its witness present at that time the jury will be returned and Michael Conley will be permitted to take the stand for the plaintiffs."

"Thank you, Your Honor," was all Gregory could blurt out before he was hurriedly stuffing papers into his briefcase. Andy was able to ask him if he was sure he could find the witness, and Gregory answered that yes, the man had been in his office that morning and was expecting to be subpoenaed. Despite being employed by RCA, he knew he had to respect the subpoena, and was willing to take the stand, answer a few simple questions and merely tell the truth.

This last was said over his shoulder, as Gregory hurried from the courtroom and Andy was escorted to his holding cell for what seemed like the longest two hours of his life. Finally, the bailiff came to escort him back to the courtroom, which was packed, everyone eagerly anticipating the mystery witness, except for the judge, who had not yet returned.

When he did sweep in, it was obvious to Andy that he had been told that the witness had in fact been found and was ready to testify, because the animosity on the judge's face was palpable as he frowned at the defense table. He immediately ordered the bailiff to bring in the jury.

As soon as the jury was seated, Judge Leftwich announced they would again be asked to step into the deliberation room so that the defense could present evidence in order to exclude testimony from being presented to them by the plaintiffs. It was a blatant attempt to bias the jury against the defense, and the jury members were clearly not happy as they again left the courtroom.

As soon as the jury had been escorted out, the judge ordered Gregory to call his witness. "However," he added, "you will limit your questioning to matters concerning your claim that the plaintiffs have knowledge the testimony they wish to present from Michael Conley is most likely perjury. And, keep it brief as possible; this whole thing is starting to irritate me."

After the murmurs of astonishment quieted down, Andy's attorney called his witness, who turned out to be a dapper, middle-aged gentleman who looked about keenly as he strode to the witness stand. He said his name was Wayne Edwards, and that his title was Country Music Promotion Director for RCA's Dallas office. He said that besides handling RCA's regular business and distribution in the area, he also handled artists and contracts for that part of the country. Part of his duties were to make deals for the company, he said.

What kind of deals, Gregory asked? "Well," Edwards replied, "there is a lot of talent in this area, and I have the authority to sign such people to contracts with RCA. Not only singers and bands, but song writers as well. I can make contracts with them for RCA. I'm also authorized by the company to purchase existing music to add to our catalog." He paused for a moment. "However, my primary business consists of promoting RCA material."

Andy glanced at the plaintiff's table, and the stricken looks there told him they knew exactly where Edwards was going.

Gregory continued his questioning. "Now, would you please tell the court exactly when you first became aware of the song 'Tell Me Pretty Baby' that is purported to have been recorded by Elvis Aaron Presley in Phoenix, Arizona, in 1954, before Mr. Presley ever signed with any recording company?"

It took a few moments for Edwards to answer, either from collecting his thoughts or digesting the complicated question. Clearing his throat, he finally answered. "Back in January or February of 1978, I believe it was, Mr. Jackson and Mr. Falco came to me with a cassette tape of that song which they claimed was dubbed directly from the original demo spool. They told me it was Elvis Presley and wanted me to listen to it, which I did," he told the hushed court.

Andy saw Bryant's head fall to his chest in disconsolation. Even if the rest of the court had not yet put two and two together, the plaintiff's counsel knew exactly what Edwards' words meant: that RCA had always known that Conley's claims were false.

"And what was your opinion of the recording?"

"It certainly sounded like Elvis, and I told them just that. But I also told them there just wasn't anyway to be sure, for with the right recording equipment I could sound like Elvis if I wanted to," Edwards told the court, to a general laugh.

Gregory smiled. He was enjoying Edwards' testimony, and had a right to. It was his moment. "What other experience did you have with the song and the defendants after that initial meeting where you listened to the tape, in January or February, I believe you said it was?"

"Yes," Edwards said, "it was in January or February of 1978. At that time, after Elvis' death, we, RCA, I mean, was buying up all of Elvis' music. There was quite a large battle going on in Nashville at the time with Shelby Singleton over his selling off one of Elvis' recordings from his Sun catalog, which he had purchased in 1969 from Sun Records.

"We, meaning RCA, were able to stop Mr. Singleton from doing that based on RCA's exclusive contract with Elvis for all rights to his music. After the issue in Nashville was settled I informed my colleagues there about the 'Tell Me Pretty Baby' tape, that I listened to it and I thought perhaps it was authentic.

"Shortly thereafter, I was given authorization to attempt the purchase of the recording, which I did, offering International Classic Productions $500,000 for the original recording and all rights to the song. When they refused the offer I was told to inform them that we would sue if they tried to market the record using Elvis' name in any way. They did, and we did, and here we are," he finished.

Gregory dismissed Edwards. Neither Smith nor Bryant had any questions for the record executive. It was clear they were hoping the significance of Edwards' testimony went undetected. They felt lucky the exchange hadn't been in front of the jury, for the mere fact that RCA itself had said maybe the record was Elvis and maybe it wasn't but still offered that kind of money would have made an indelible impression on the jury.

After Edwards had left the courtroom, Judge Leftwich demonstrated again his ability to astound the defense by telling Gregory that unless he could tie the testimony to his claim that RCA was knowingly going to present perjured testimony, the judge was going to allow Conley to testify.

Andy was astonished that the man had not understood the implications of the testimony he had just heard. Judge Leftwich had been there in the preliminary hearing and heard Conley testify that he had recorded "Tell Me Pretty Baby," four months after RCA's own executive claimed to have heard the tape. Andy wanted to jump up and scream at the judge to look at the dates. He may have done just that, and been thrown out of court, if Gregory hadn't responded to the judge, assuring him that he could do as he requested.

Striding to the defense table, Gregory picked up a tagged and underlined section of the transcript of the preliminary injunction hearing. Gregory also had a photocopy of the December 2 article in the Dallas Times Herald, containing Conley's picture, which reported Conley's claim that he, not Elvis, had sung the record.

With the documents in his hand, Gregory returned to the bench to present them to the judge. The attorney handed them to Judge Leftwich, who proceeded to scan them. What made the evidence so effective was that RCA had been aware of the tape several months before its star witness claimed to have recorded it. That clearly made Conley's testimony perjury, and RCA couldn't wiggle free.

The judge finished reading the documents and called Bryant to the bench, asking him what to make of the dates. When Gregory interjected that it was impossible for Conley to have recorded the record after the RCA executive had listened to it, the judge slammed his hand on the bench.

"I wasn't speaking to you," Judge Leftwich roared. "I'm speaking to the counsel for the plaintiffs. You have had your say in this matter, and now I want to hear what the plaintiffs have to say. Is that understood?"

"Clearly," Gregory told the judge. He didn't leave his position in front of the bench, however, and Andy could see Williams at the other end of the table, frozen in fearful anticipation. Not a word was murmured throughout the courtroom as everyone waited for RCA's lead counsel to make his reply, which was amazing in its brazenness when it came.

"Obviously," Bryant told the judge, "the witness we have just heard made a mistake in his reference to dates. It could clearly happen to anyone, and I'm sure the man thinks he heard the tape at that earlier time. He is simply mistaken. That's all, just had his months wrong."

With a sharp rap of his gavel, Judge Leftwich announced to the courtroom in general that the defense's objection was overruled and that he would allow the plaintiffs to call their next witness. Andy's jaw dropped in astonishment at the ruling. Gregory, who had started to walk away, spun back to face the judge with an unbelieving look on his face. He was aghast.

"Exception, Your Honor," the lawyer shouted. "Your ruling is totally contrary to the evidence. Note the defense's objection and exception to the ruling in the record. This is absurd, a travesty."

The judge hurled his yellow pencil at the defense attorney, forcing Gregory to duck to keep from being stabbed. "Anymore of that and I'll have you locked up for contempt. Do you understand me, counsel?" the judge screamed. "I'll not tolerate any questioning of the rulings made in this courtroom," he said. "Now sit down until the plaintiffs relinquish the floor."

The judge had to continually bang his gavel until the courtroom quieted down. Everyone seemed shocked by his actions. The bailiff silently walked to where the pencil was, retrieved it, carried it back and placed it at the judge's elbow.

Andy was stunned by what he had witnessed. If he had harbored any hopes at all that they could be victorious in their legal battle against the corporate giant, those hopes were now dashed to pieces. There was no way they could receive a fair trial in that man's courtroom.

The jury was called back into the courtroom, unaware of all that had taken place in their absence. When they were seated in the jury box, the judge called for proceedings to get underway. Bryant, however, stayed seated. Instead, Phillip Smith took the floor.

It was as much a shock to Andy as it was for everyone else in the room when Smith announced that they would call no further witnesses. The plaintiffs rested their case without calling Conley to the stand. It seemed like a wise move.

In light of what had happened, the possibility was clear that if Conley testified, his testimony might be ripped to shreds, if he said the wrong thing and opened the door for the defense to impeach his credibility.

As it stood, none of what had taken place had been presented to the jury, and would not figure in their decision. And, it was obvious to all that the plaintiffs were still ahead. It would be up to the defense to turn the tide, and Bryant and Smith had not wanted to give them a head start with the chancy Conley.

The Defense

CHAPTER TWENTY-FIVE

There was still enough time in the day to call a witness to the stand on behalf of the defendants, and the two attorneys decided to start with Pete Falco. Tentatively, Williams took the floor between the judge's bench and the jury box. He was nervous and there were small beads of perspiration glistening on his forehead. He kept glancing at the judge, ready to duck any projectiles thrown his direction in anger or impatience. With a quavering voice the young, inexperienced lawyer announced that they were calling Falco to the stand, and the bass player turned truck driver became a witness in his own behalf.

Andy admired Pete. He always had. The man was personable and well liked by everyone who knew him. His story was well known to Andy, having heard it told a dozen times or more. It had also been printed in several newspapers across the country when the record as first released. Andy watched the faces of the jury members as Pete was sworn in. They were attentive, but didn't seem particularly interested. Williams began by asking Falco to relate how he had come into possession of "Tell Me Pretty Baby."

It was the same story Andy had heard many times, but hearing it again brought the same small thrill, that this man had sat in on history. "It was early spring of 1954," Pete began, "and we were getting pretty hot on the local nightclub scene. I was writing most of our original stuff, and we played a lot of black blues type music, too. It was what the kids wanted to hear and what they liked to dance to. The new stuff I was writing was moving in a different direction than either western music or the blues. We had a lead singer who sounded black, though he wasn't, and his voice just wasn't right for what I wanted on three songs I had recently written. I wanted to make a demo tape, but was holding off on it till I could find a singer with the right voice.

"There was a recording studio there in Phoenix which had some new equipment. New technology for that time, anyway. It was still mono, but sounded like stereo because they could record on two separate channels onto the same tape. So anyway, we decided, that is the band, The Red Dots and me, we decided to go ahead and make the demonstration tape to see if we could maybe sell some of our music. I had made arrangements to rent the recording studio for a day later in the week, and we were playing this little place just off downtown where we were really packing them in. A lot of the kids were under age, but the guy who ran the place wouldn't let them drink, only come in and listen to the music and dance. That's when I met Elvis." The courtroom had slowly begun to settle down, and was now totally quiet. A rustle shifted through the crowd at the name.

"He was sitting up near the band, tapping his feet and singing along with us, just as if he knew all the words to every song we sung. I didn't know who he was at the time," Pete explained, "but he sure could sing. I could hear his voice even over all the instruments, and he was good. There was another boy about the same age or maybe a little younger there with him, but I never got that other boy's name. So, the next time we took a break, I went over to him and asked if he was a musician. He said, 'Yeah,' that he'd been singing for a few years and wanted to make it his living."

Bryant sensed a break and objected. "Hearsay, your honor."

"Sustained."

"Your honor," Bryant went on, "will you please instruct the jury to disregard that last statement?"

"The jury will disregard that statement," intoned Judge Leftwich. "Counsel, continue with your witness."

Williams quietly told Falco to continue his story, but to not allude to what another person may have told him.

Pete took up where he'd been cut off. "I learned he'd been singing for a few years and that's the kind of work the boy wanted to do. I found out his name was Elvis Presley and he was on his way to the West Coast to see if he could find the kind of sound he couldn't find in Mississippi or Tennessee. I could easily tell he liked our music, and I asked him to join us on our next set, which he did.

"The kid was really good and had the whole place hoppin'," Pete recalled. "Man, that kid had a voice. We were going to the recording studio the next day and I invited him to join us. We got there, to the studio the next day, a little early to set up, and we waited past time I told him we were going to start. It didn't look like he was going to show and we had already cut one of the new songs using our regular singer when the kid walks in."

Falco stopped and took a sip of water from a glass that was sitting on the rail in front of him, then continued.

"Don Reese, who was a dee-jay at the time, was with him. Don had been waiting in the parking lot 'cause he was at the club the night before and knew what our plans were. Anyway, I sure was glad to see the boy show up. That's when we recorded 'Tell Me Pretty Baby.'

"We had to do it several times before it finally sounded right. He wasn't cutting his words off after singing them, and I pulled my stool up behind him to tap him on the shoulder to signal him when to stop and start. He was trying to sing with his mouth open too much, making the words run together. We finally got it sounding the way I wanted it to, and we did the other two songs I had written. He did okay on them, but 'Tell Me Pretty Baby' was by far the best. When we finally called it a day, I gave the kid fifteen dollars, five dollars for singing each song, and he and the other boy drove away. I never saw him again after that, but I followed his career after he started to get famous. I was glad to see that he made it to his dream of being a singer," Falco finished.

He drank some more water, then told how he had tried to sell his songs, the ones Elvis had sang, but never got anywhere with them, and how he had lost the other two demo tapes in the process. "Tell Me Pretty Baby," was the only one he had left, and he had saved it as an example of his own music as much as the fact that Elvis actually had sang the words.

With Williams prompting him, Falco explained how he had made the deal with Andy, and that they had decided to produce and market the record.

He said that yes, he knew what Elvis had looked like during the 50s, and he was sure it was the same young man who had sang with the Red Dots in the spring of 1954.

Cross-examination by Smith only brought out more details in Pete's testimony, totally failing to sway him from his quiet conviction that Elvis had recorded "Tell Me Pretty Baby," and that it had been indelibly burned into his memory.

Andy thought the jury believed him. He certainly did, even if it had cost him everything he held dear, including his freedom.

Falco was dismissed, with the option to recall if needed, and Pete took his seat at the defense table. He was obviously drained by his time on the witness stand, but they all assured him that he'd done a fine job. The judge called a recess for the evening after Pete took his seat, and with a few good-byes Andy was taken back to his cell. His mind would keep him busy that night, going over the details of the day, and before he knew it, he drifted to sleep.

He was awake and waiting for the deputy. He felt rested and pleased with Falco's testimony, and thought that if the other defendants were as credible, they stood a good chance of winning.

Soon, Gregory came to greet him good morning with another strong cup of coffee. He told Andy that they would most likely get to his testimony that day, but it would be after lunch. The plan was to put Reese and Marion on next, then Andy and Dr. Godfrey in the afternoon.

They would finish their defense the next day with Dr. Tosie, whom they still believed would be allowed to testify; the members of the Red Dots and two more men who were close to Elvis and his music in the early days and believed that "Tell Me Pretty Baby" had in fact been recorded by the King.

With closing arguments and jury deliberations, they were looking at two more days, Gregory said. The bailiff came and called them to the courtroom, and in a few minutes the judge and jury arrived also.

Steven Williams, his ego boosted by his success with Falco, confidently called Reese to the stand. As Don gave his oath to tell the truth, Andy wished he could ask the man a few questions himself. Was Don really behind Andy's criminal conviction, and just what was it Don intended to do with the original tape if he had gotten his hands on it?

Don wouldn't talk to Andy or to Andy's attorney, about anything, so those were questions that Andy would never know the answer to.

After identifying his connection with International Classis Productions as an investor and percentage partner, he was asked to explain his relationship with Pete Falco and how he became involved in the recording of "Tell Me Pretty Baby." Reese began by relating how he'd been a dee-jay in Phoenix in the early 50s, and he'd known Pete as a bass player and song writer for the Red Dots, a local band that was getting some attention, especially with teenagers.

He said the band had moved away from country and western, and were experimenting with the newer, louder music now called rock and roll. Reese said he'd liked their sound and would catch the band whenever possible. That's when he saw Elvis.

"It was 1954, the early part when the nights were still known to get cool. I was at this little club that the Red Dots were playing at and when they started their last set of the night a young man got up from the audience to sing with them. He was really good and the crowd loved him.

"Being a dee-jay, I was interested in what the public wanted and this new sound seemed to be the coming thing. I found out later that Pete Falco had invited the boy to sing with them, and I was introduced to him. I found out his name was Elvis Presley and I had no reason to doubt that, yet the name meant nothing to me at the time.

"I didn't hear the name again until about a year later when Elvis started making a reputation for himself. Anyway, I was there when Pete invited the young man to come to the recording studio the next morning to sit in with them to record a demo tape of some of Pete's songs. I didn't have anything else to do that next morning, so I made it a point to be at the studio."

Reese stopped and looked at the jury. They were paying attention to him, almost like they'd been listening to Falco. It was the magic of the King, still alive in a Dallas courtroom.

"I was outside for a long time and it didn't look like the boy was going to show up. I really wasn't interested in watching the Red Dots cut a demo unless the new kid was with them. I had heard them lots of times before and knew Pete Falco personally, so that was no big deal for me. I was just about ready to leave when this hot rod comes roaring into the parking lot and the young man was riding as a passenger. He got out and the other boy stayed in the car.

"I followed him in and watched him record three songs with the Red Dots. Pete gave the boy some money and the boys left. I never saw them again in person after that but, when I saw pictures of Elvis later on, it was the same young man I had met in the club that night and watched record 'Tell Me Pretty Baby,'" Reese told the jury.

Was there any doubt in his mind that the young man he saw record the song in question was anyone other than Elvis Aaron Presley, Williams asked? "Not to my belief," Don answered. "His face, his voice, everything about him was just like the Elvis we all know looked and sounded when he was young."

Williams turned, a pleased look on his face. He'd done well leading Reese, and he passed him to RCA's attorneys.

Bryant started for the plaintiffs. He couldn't get Don to change his basic story, but got some of Don's motives out and made them seem reason enough to lie for.

Don admitted that yes, he saw an opportunity to make some big money. He was, after all, in the business and knew the profits which could be made on a new name after it shoots to the top. He admitted to unsuccessfully trying to buy the recording from Falco over the years. He had only been able to buy into the song as a small percentage holder and a working partner when Pete had finally decided to let go of the old tape, he told Bryant.

Reese said he'd been managing an ice cream parlor in Dallas when he first met Andy and heard there was a possibility of marketing a record. That was his entire story: no scam, no hoax, no intent to defraud, only business and the hopes of getting this rare recording before the public after all these years. He was dismissed from the stand.

The attorney for RCA had been able to chip away some of the polish from Reese's testimony, but hadn't broken his basic position that it was the King who had recorded "Tell Me Pretty Baby." Gregory was threatened by Judge Leftwich when he stood to object to a certain line of questioning from Bryant, being told he would be placed in jail for contempt if he again interjected himself into the proceedings. The jury seemed confused by the judge's anger, for they had missed the judicial display the day before.

Marion Sitton was called to testify, and undid all the good of the two previous witnesses. The elderly businessman had not been well and looked pale and weak. He had no personal experience with either Presley or the recording, and his testimony was limited to the business aspects of the partnership.

It was a mistake to call him to the stand, and that was soon obvious. He admitted to coming into the partnership to capitalize on the possible profits. Yes, he had heard the tape, but was not a music expert and could not say for sure if Elvis was singing. He did, however, testify that he had been shown affidavits by Pete and Reese attesting to the fact that they had met Elvis and knew of the recording, and had made his decision on the best available evidence, including scientific evidence.

Smith showed Sitton no mercy. He immediately attacked his credibility as a witness, accusing him of perpetuating a scheme to market a product he himself had not and could not verify as authentic. By the time Smith released the shaking witness, he had all but admitted the whole thing was a hoax and the only reason he was in it was for the huge profits that could be made if they were successful. Andy only hoped that the jury was able to see how Marion had been manipulated by the artful attorney into agreeing to such outrageous notions.

The judge called for noon recess after Sitton returned to his seat at the defense table. Andy heard Reese calling Marion every name he could think of as he was being led from the courtroom by his guard. Sitton did not return after lunch, nor for the rest of the trial. That was the last time Andy ever saw his old partner.

The butterflies in his stomach had grown teeth by the time Andy was again seated at the defense table and the court called to order. He wasn't surprised to see that Sitton wasn't at the table with the others, but was astonished when Reese spoke to him.

"Don't you screw up, too," Reese growled at him. "I've got too much riding on this to lose it all now." It was easy to see what Don's priorities were, and Andy ignored him.

Quickly, Gregory told him to take it easy and just answer the questions he was asked, not to stray or get off the topic, and please not to say anything that the plaintiff's attorneys could use against him when they cross-examined. The motion in limine had been granted, so there would be no questioning about his criminal conviction, Andy was told, and he was admonished to not mention it or he would get ripped to shreds. Andy assured his attorney he was ready and wouldn't do anything stupid.

"The defense will now call Andrew Jackson to the stand," Gregory announced. The bailiff stepped to Andy's side to escort him to the witness stand. As Andy took the high seat in front of the microphone, he scanned the seemingly endless depths of the courtroom. He felt every eye drilling through him, straight to his heart. He searched the faces of the jury, hoping to find a smile or some friendly encouragement. None was there.

When Gregory asked him to state his name for the record, Andy's throat constricted in fear and nervousness. For a moment he thought he couldn't get through it, but after he spoke his name, the bands of tension loosened. Gregory was skilled, and knew just how to put a witness at ease.

He began by asking Andy a few questions regarding his background in the music publishing business, and led from there to the first, fateful meeting with Shanti Falco, how she had come into his dealership in Grand Prairie and been fascinated by the records on his wall.

She had bought a car, he said, and had promised to introduce Andy to her father, a truck driver who had once been a musician and happened to have an old tape the girl claimed had Elvis Presley singing on it.

That, of course, brought immediate objections from Bryant and Smith, who both jumped to their feet and yelled, "Hearsay, your Honor!" And, of course, Judge Leftwich sustained their objections in a bored voice, ordering Andy to not give testimony as to what someone else had said. It was all frustrating, but Gregory was prepared.

In a well-prepared show, Gregory got Andy's testimony before the jury and entered into the record without having to back up and start over.

"Yes," Andy answered; he had been led to believe that Pete Falco was in possession of a tape containing the voice of the late Elvis Presley. Until that time, when such information was relayed to him by a third party, he had no such idea the tape existed. "Yes," Andy answered again; he was skeptical of the claim, but wanted to check it out. Once over that hurdle, Gregory was able to proceed to questions Andy could answer directly because they involved his direct involvement.

Had Andy made contact with Pete Falco in order to examine the tape? "Yes," Andy told the jury. He had met with Falco at the man's home and inspected and listened to the tape which was quite old and seemed to be all that Falco claimed it was.

Andy outlined his efforts to authenticate the demo tape before he agreed to buy it. He told of taking the tape to a music studio in Dallas and having several experts listen to it, and that each had stated his belief that the singer was Elvis, in his early years.

Again, Bryant and Smith objected to Andy's allusion to other opinions, and again the judge backed them and instructed the jury to disregard Andy's reference to other experts and their opinions. But Gregory had made his point -- Andy had in fact authenticated the tape.

Gregory then introduced the third partner into the story, asking Andy what he had done next. Andy told of going to the ice cream parlor where Reese was working as a manager, and how Reese had told him basically the same story that Falco had. Andy said he had no reason to doubt what two people had told him independent of each other, and that those two opinions -- two men immersed in the music industry, with knowledge of the King recording a forgotten masterpiece -- convinced him to purchase the tape.

He told of his plans to market the tape, but how his first attempt failed due to lack of sufficient capital. Despite the failure he continued trying to authenticate the record by other means. He told of contacting Dr. John Godfrey of the University of Texas at Dallas, who was a speech pathologist and an expert in the field of voice identification.

Andy told of asking the professor to examine the tape and give his professional opinion whether or not the singer was Presley. This was in early 1978, Andy explained. Gregory hurriedly cautioned him not to explain the doctor's findings, but to tell the jury what he did after receiving those conclusions.

Andy took the lead from his attorney, and said, "Based upon Dr. Godfrey's report, and the two affidavits from Mr. Falco and Mr. Reese, I set out to find investing partners and start up International Classic Productions, whose first project would be the production and marketing of 'Tell Me Pretty Baby.'"

Andy continued his story, saying he and his partners had professionally reproduced the original tape on several cassettes which were used in the promotion of the record. They were introduced to Hal Freeman in Nashville, who agreed to handle distribution. He said that the operation was beginning to look like a success, with the record beginning to get airplay and orders beginning to pile up, when RCA filed its lawsuit.

"RCA had been contacted early on and had heard the tape, but wouldn't say one way or the other if they believed it was sung by Elvis, even though they offered half a million dollars to buy it from us," Andy said.

RCA's attorneys immediately objected, each on different grounds, and Judge Leftwich quickly sustained their objections without specifying which he was upholding. Andy's patience was growing short at the judge's obvious bias, but there was little he could do to change it.

"What did you do with the original master tape after you had the professional working copies made?" Gregory asked.

"I placed it in my safety deposit box at the bank," Andy answered, "and there it remained until I released it to the attorney who represented me in the preliminary hearing on this matter. That attorney wanted to let the attorneys for the plaintiff examine it," Andy said, with a glower for Bryant and Smith, who smugly eyed him in return. "I didn't like the idea. I haven't seen the tape since I put it in the safety box last September, even though it's entered in evidence here," Andy said.

Walking to the evidence table, Gregory asked the court's permission to present the exhibit to the witness for identification.

Judge Leftwich grudgingly granted the request, as there was no legal way he could refuse. Andy owned the tape, after all. Andy noticed the nervousness on the RCA lawyers' faces and began to worry as Gregory carried the tape to him, which was tagged and in a plastic bag.

"You are the legal owner of this tape, whoever the singer may be, is that not correct, Mr. Jackson?" Gregory asked.

"Yes, I am," Andy replied as he took the spool.

"Please examine it if you will, and tell the court if this is the same tape you last saw in September of last year when you locked it up in your safety deposit box, Mr. Jackson," the attorney said.

Andy carefully studied the tape, and felt himself grow faint as what he'd suspected was proved right. "This is not the same tape!"

A howl rose from the plaintiffs. "Objection! Your Honor, this witness is attacking the credibility of my clients as well as this court when in fact it is the defendants' credibility which is in question in this trial."

Gregory quickly rebutted. "Your Honor, the witness has not attacked the credibility of anyone or of this court. He was simply asked to identify material evidence which belongs to him, and he stated he could not identify it as such. Now, if the court cannot see fit to allow us to pursue this line of questioning, I must move for a mistrial."

Judge Leftwich was visibly upset. Taken aback by the quiet authority showed by Gregory, the judge thought for a moment, then rapped his gavel and announced he would allow the questioning to continue.

Andy felt that his ruling would have been different if the jury had not been present. Gregory had laid a neat trap, using the presence and scrutiny of those in the courtroom to hold the trial in legal balance. The observers were only so gullible, and their fascination with the old tape -- the focus of so much antagonism and contempt -- had enabled Gregory to draw a line that the judge was unwilling to cross.

Judge Leftwich's face was red, and the attorneys for RCA in a lather, consulting each other and their assistants, angry at being unable to control the flow of evidence for the first time in the trial.

"Would you tell the jury why you cannot identify this tape as the same one you purchased from Mr. Falco and placed in your safety deposit box last September," Gregory repeated.

"I can't tell about the tape, of course," Andy said. "But the spool isn't the same one. It looks similar, but it's not exactly the same color and it's not as heavy. But mainly, it doesn't have the marks I know were on it when I got it from Pete. There were several scratches on it, near the center of the hub area, where it locked onto the tape player Pete had. I remember the marks, from where the latch on the drive would catch the spool when it was played.

"It was my prized possession, and I knew every mark and scratch on it. This is not the same tape," Andy told the jury, as he looked into each of their eyes.

The implications were tremendous, but to Andy the only thing that mattered was that somehow he had lost the master tape. How could he ever find it and get it back? Did it still exist, and if so, who had it? He wanted to bury his face in his hands and cry even as he gave the fake tape back to Gregory.

"At this point, the defense would object to the validity of this exhibit and request a formal investigation into the chain of custody of the evidence," Gregory told the judge, who was having none of it.

"The chain of custody of this exhibit is not a question for this court or jury," the judge stated. "The tape was delivered to the plaintiffs by the previous attorney for Mr. Jackson for examination. And as such, has been under this court's control ever since. The tape is the same one which was originally presented during the preliminary injunction hearing and will be accepted as such by this jury. So ruled!

"If your client has any problems with the authenticity of the tape, I suggest he take it up with his former counsel," the judge snidely added. He had, by judicial authority, sidestepped any implications that RCA had switched the tape, and placed any possible blame back on the defense.

Although not entirely unlikely, Andy doubted his last lawyer had anything to do with substituting the tape. Not without RCA's help, anyway. When he got out of prison, Andy told himself, he would take the tape to a laboratory and have it tested, getting to the bottom of that on his own if necessary. At least they still had the cassettes recorded from the original, and the records that had been pressed from it, to fall back on.

After a few questions allowing Andy to assert that he believed Elvis was truly singing on "Tell Me Pretty Baby," and that he in no way intended a scam or hoax, Gregory passed Andy to the plaintiffs.

Bryant approached the witness stand and immediately set upon Andy. "You say you had no intentions of pulling a hoax or scam on the public when you and your partners tried to market this record using Elvis Presley's name shortly after his death, but you can't expect the jury to believe that. You are quite a con man, aren't you, Jackson?"

Shocked by the vehemence in the lawyer's tone, Andy didn't even answer before Bryant accused him more directly.

"Are you not currently under indictment for robbery and have you not a long history of theft charges in Dallas County?"

Andy was astonished, as were most of the people in the courtroom, who immediately began to whisper with one another. Before Andy could blurt out a denial, his attorney objected loudly and approached the bench, demanding to know what Bryant was referring to. Not only had the court granted the motion in limine, Gregory said, which barred the plaintiffs from making any reference to the crime Andy had been convicted of, this particular accusation was absurd and had no basis in fact. Bryant countered that the witness had opened the door to the question of his credibility, and that the plaintiffs were currently in possession of Jackson's criminal file, which showed he was a thief and a robber.

Gregory demanded proof, and requested a hearing be held outside the presence of the jury. If the plaintiffs were able to prove what they claimed, the line of questioning would continue. If they couldn't, Gregory wanted the jury ordered to disregard any comments intended to discredit the witness or his honesty and an apology offered to Mr. Jackson.

The judge, having faith in RCA's claim, ordered the jury to the jury room while evidence supporting RCA's charges was presented. Andy felt 12 sets of eyes boring into him as the jury stalked out. He had no idea what Bryant was talking about, but knew the jury was holding him responsible anyway.

After the twelve jurors were out of the courtroom, the judge ordered Bryant to present any evidence concerning Andy's criminal activities, other than the case he had been convicted for and was barred from discussion by the motion in limine. Andy flinched as the judge announced, at the top of his voice, the basis of his criminal conviction. While the jury was out of hearing, the courtroom was still packed with spectators, most of whom were looking at him with contempt.

Bryant hurried to the plaintiff's table, and was handed a thick file by an assistant. "Here," he triumphantly cried, "here is the criminal file of Andrew Jackson, showing a long history of arrests and convictions for thefts, robberies, larcenies and con games. An indictment has been issued on this latest robbery case, as you can see here," Bryant added, pointing out each claim to the judge.

"May I inspect the file, please?" Gregory asked. Slowly, one by one, he read the papers, laying them aside in front of the judge as he did so.

"There is no social security number, no date of birth or any other specific identification contained in any of these," Gregory said, amazed by the audacity of RCA's attorneys. "How can you claim this is the same Andrew Jackson?"

"Unless you can prove it's not," the judge said, "I'm going to assume it is and let the questioning continue. We all know your client has been in trouble with the law before, on much worse charges than what is currently being presented to the court. You should feel lucky I didn't allow evidence of his sexual assault conviction be placed before the jury. If you have nothing else to say, we will now continue."

"Ten minutes, your Honor," Gregory responded, quickly buying time. "Just give me ten minutes to check out these charges and indictments down in the District Clerk's office, and we can clear this up, I'm sure. You've allowed the plaintiffs to introduce surprise evidence, and the law requires that I have a reasonable opportunity to rebut that evidence."

Again, Gregory's legal reasoning caught the judge off guard, but he evidently believed Gregory could do little to disprove the charges. "I'll give you ten minutes, Mr. Gregory, but not one second more. If you're not back in this courtroom when I call it back into session, we will proceed without you. Is that understood?"

With a nod of his head, Gregory acknowledged the ultimatum. "This court's in recess for ten minutes," the judge announced.

Snatching up the top few charges in the thick file, Gregory ran out of the courtroom, barely ahead of the crowd swarming to the snack machines and bathrooms. Finding the elevator doors closed, he headed for the stairway, and ran down three flights of stairs, skipping every other step.

Luckily, he bounced out of the stairwell in front of the District Clerk's office, but no one was at the counter. Before he could catch his breath to ask for help, one of the nearby clerks called to see if she could be of any help.

Stretching the truth only slightly, Gregory explained, "I'm Mr. Jackson's lawyer and we're upstairs in court right now. I'm trying to defend him, and we need the full files on these two cases," he told the woman as he handed her the charge sheets. "The judge only gave me ten minutes. If you'll please let me just borrow the files, I'll return them to you later this afternoon, when we're out of court."

She looked doubtful, but the obvious desperation in his voice and his honest face won her over. "Oh, all right," she said. "But you get these right back to me before you leave the court today, you hear?"

She went straight to the file, which was indexed in some arcane system known only to the file clerks. She looked for an agonizingly long minute, and returned with the files. With a murmured "Thank you, thank you," Gregory bolted for the door.

His good luck continued. The elevator door was open when he stepped into the hall. Jumping ahead of two startled couples, Gregory quickly punched the button for the correct floor. A glance at his watch showed him he was out of time. Although the ride lasted only a moment, it gave him time to find what he needed in the files.

Still reading when he stepped off the elevator and into the hall, he closed the file and straightened his tie before entering the courtroom. The judge was just taking his seat and calling the court into session.

"Well, glad you could join us, counsel," the judge remarked sarcastically. "Are you ready to proceed, or do you have something else to put before this court?"

"I do indeed have something to put before this court, your Honor," Gregory calmly announced, much to Andy's relief. He'd been squirming on the stand while Gregory ran downstairs, and didn't think he could have endured much more of the hate-filled glares aimed his way. His ugly suit was damp with nervous sweat, and he had finished the pitcher of water sitting in front of him.

"May it please the court," Gregory said. "I have here the full file on Andrew L. Jackson, in these two criminal cases that the attorney for the plaintiffs claim were committed by my client, and I ask that the court review the details concerning the identification of the perpetrator," he said as he dropped the case files on the judge's desk.

"You'll clearly see that those charges indicate the thief and robber to be a person by the name of Andrew Leroy Jackson, a black man at least a full decade younger than this man on the stand." Taking a deep breath, and fixing Bryant with a scornful smile, Gregory said, "Now, unless my esteemed opponent can convince the court that my client is a young black man by the name of Leroy, I suggest he withdraw from the line of questioning that he was attempting earlier."

It took the judge only a few minutes to scan the files and see that Gregory had indeed located the proper files, which presented conclusive evidence that Andy was not the con man they were implying he was.

Regardless, no one offered an apology or excuse. There was little doubt they knew full well they had had the wrong man's files, just as it was clear they were hoping to get away with it. The judge called for the bailiff to bring the jury back.

When they were all seated, he told them they were to disregard the questions put to the witness earlier concerning any pending robbery indictments. He also instructed them to not consider any implications about Mr. Jackson being a con man outside the pretext and substance of this trial. At his wording, Andy almost yelled, and his attorney just threw up his hands. But they had won a minor skirmish.

Judge Leftwich ordered Bryant to continue his cross, and warned the RCA attorney to stick to matters that were relevant to the lawsuit. Again, Andy was forced to go over every detail of his association with his partners, his knowledge of the recording itself and all the authentication he sought on it, and all his attempts to produce and market "Tell Me Pretty Baby."

Andy's head ached by the time Bryant was through grilling him, and he was happy to hear the judge call the court adjourned for the day. Gregory congratulated him on a job well done as he was led away from the defense table and out of the courtroom.

Andy wished he could have spoken to Gregory and to Charlotte, but it had been a long day and he was glad it was finally over. He'd felt humiliated on the stand, but had answered every question truthfully. If he thought of anything he really needed to ask Gregory, he would call him. At that moment, all he wanted was to be alone.

It's Elvis

CHAPTER TWENTY-SIX

It wasn't until Andy returned to his cell and had some dinner that he realized it was Friday and he would be sitting there all weekend with nothing to do. At that moment, however, all he wanted was to wash away the day's anxieties and rest. He asked the guard if he could make a telephone call before going to the shower.

He called Charlotte. Explaining how worn out he was, Andy asked her to wait until Saturday to visit. The weekend visits would allow them more time, he said, and he was just too tired to have a meaningful conversation. She readily agreed. She said she was also feeling the strain of the long week, and wanted to get some rest. He was glad she understood, because he did not want to disappoint her.

He woke for breakfast, then slept until lunch, after which he washed as well as he could in the small sink. He was restless. The uncertainty fostered by the trial had exhausted him, and the unfairness of Judge Leftwich had him uncertain as to what chances they had.

He made a conscious effort to clear his mind when he was told his visitor had arrived. Charlotte looked rested and lovely, sitting behind the security screen in the visitation room, and Andy was pleased to see her. She told him how well she thought he'd done on the witness stand, and how she believed his testimony had proved to the jury that there was no scam intended.

He certainly hoped she was right, but told her they were up against more than met the eye of the courtroom audience. Andy asked if she'd talked with Gregory. She said she had, and that Andy needed to call him. They were going to present their scientific evidence on Monday, and Gregory was evidently expecting trouble putting Dr. Tosie on the stand.

Andy didn't know what good he could do, but said he'd call his attorney that evening. The rest of the visit was spent in quiet conversation and light flirtation. Andy knew her promises of love were conditional upon his freedom, but she made him feel better, and he was grateful that she had the courage to face the contempt of the courtroom audience, as well as take the time to visit him and show her concern.

A few hours after supper, a jailer took Andy to make his phone call. Gregory answered on the second ring and greeted Andy warmly. Yes, he had asked Charlotte to have him call, but it wasn't of grave importance. He just wanted to tell Andy he thought he had done a fine job on the witness stand. It was a pretty slick move the plaintiffs had pulled in order to discredit him and confuse the issue, and they were lucky to have countered RCA. Andy told him it wasn't luck; it was having a good lawyer.

"I don't know how good you're going to think I am on Monday," Gregory said. "I'm going to try to put Dr. Tosie on the stand, but I'm expecting a major battle. That's what I wanted to talk to you about, Andy.

"We already have Dr. Godfrey, and I don't believe they have grounds to limit his testimony. I wanted to know if you feel confident enough with Dr. Godfrey's opinion to forego an attempt to include Dr. Tosie."

Gregory explained his reasoning. "We could try to get them both on, of course. But RCA has filed a motion to exclude Dr. Tosie's testimony on the basis of a conference between your previous attorney, RCA's lawyers and Judge Leftwich in his chambers. The judge said he wanted no surprises in this case, and of course he was talking about surprises from us. Evidently, they've taken that untranscribed conference as the endpoint for declaring witnesses even though we've named Dr. Tosie in the interrogatories.

"Now, if we call him, they'll object," Gregory continued. "There will be another hearing outside the presence of the jury on whether or not to allow him to testify. The jury is already mad at us about the Mike Ellis thing, and will only get madder. I want you to think about it, but I'll do what you want me to."

Andy could see his lawyer's point, and considered the matter for a few minutes. "I want you to try to put them both on the stand," Andy finally said. "Call Dr. Godfrey first, so we'll have his testimony firmly planted before trying to call Dr. Tosie. If RCA objects, I know you'll do the best you can against them and the judge to get his testimony before the jury. All we can do is put as much in front of them as possible and hope it sinks in.

"Tell me," Andy asked, "if we don't get to put Dr. Tosie on the stand, will they let his deposition be read before the court and admitted into the record?"

"That will be entirely up to the judge," Gregory said. Without saying more, Gregory had told Andy what he wanted to know -- Judge Leftwich could slam the door on Tosie's testimony. After a few encouraging words, they said goodbye.

Sunday crawled by. Andy exercised, running in place until he couldn't stand. He couldn't seem to find the optimism he'd felt before. He wanted it to be over, but in a strange way was afraid what Monday would bring, and it would all come too soon.

It did. Andy felt as if he had just fallen asleep when the clanging of trays woke him. The meager meal left him empty, even though he ate every bite. He washed his face and shaved as best as he could, without the benefit of a mirror.

Not for the last time, he marveled at the inconsistency of jails. He was given a razor, but not a mirror to use while shaving. Many things inside the walls made no sense, but few could be questioned.

Feeling lucky not to have butchered himself, Andy was slicking down his hair when the deputy came to escort him downstairs. There were still a few hours before court was called, and Andy dreaded the wait in the holding cell after he was dressed out.

At least they gave him a decent suit, he told himself. Wearing the street clothes, he sat by himself in the holding cell, listening to the early morning sounds of the old courthouse as the building came to life.

Half asleep, he was startled when Gregory came in through the side door. Gregory was in a cheerful mood, which made Andy feel better. The two men went over the defense strategy of what would most likely be the last day of evidence. They wanted to stay on track, not letting the plaintiffs distract the jury from the real issue: was it or wasn't it Elvis Presley singing "Tell Me Pretty Baby?" Anything else, any success that RCA had in shifting that focus would only be bad for the defense.

The bailiff finally came to get him, accompanied by the deputy, who was never more than a quick lunge away from Andy whenever he was in the courtroom. Chains and handcuffs are not allowed in most 20th century U.S. courtrooms, due to the adverse effects they have upon a jury, and heavily armed guards standing around tend to intimidate potential witnesses from testifying.

As a result, it is extremely close supervision that is relied upon to deter a prisoner's escape, and it usually proves highly effective.

"All rise," the bailiff intoned, announcing Judge Leftwich's entrance. Everyone silently stood as the judge entered, black robes flowing, a scowl on his face.

Andy knew it wouldn't be a good day for the defense. When the judge was in a bad mood, it was always the defense that received the blunt end of his wrath.

Gregory quietly announced that the defense was calling Dr. John Godfrey to the stand, and the elegantly dressed professor walked in, was seated and sworn in.

Gregory quickly established Godfrey's credentials, letting the doctor reel off his impressive list of education and scientific accomplishments. Although Andy had met the distinguished scholar, he was impressed anew and hoped the jury would give the doctor's testimony the weight it deserved.

Dr. Godfrey related how he had met Andy, and the dates clearly demonstrated the wise decision RCA had made in not putting Michael Conley on the stand. According to Conley, he had recorded "Tell Me Pretty Baby" more than eight months after Andy met and handed the original master tape to Dr. Godfrey for him to test.

The doctor explained how Andy had brought him the original tape, along with several old Elvis records to make comparisons with. He was not, of course, claiming to do blind research in that he knew the identity of the subject; his agreement was to either confirm or deny the voice match, if one existed, between the singer on "Tell Me Pretty Baby" and the Elvis records.

"Did you, by scientific analysis, and by virtue of your extensive experience and training in the field of voice and speech therapy and identification, reach a conclusion?" Gregory asked.

Without hesitation Dr. Godfrey stated that he had.

"And who, in your opinion, was the singer on the original master tape of 'Tell Me Pretty Baby' that Andrew Jackson brought you for analysis?" the defense lawyer asked.

"It was quite conclusive. In my professional opinion, it was Elvis Presley singing the song," the doctor replied. When asked how he came to that conclusion, Dr. Godfrey went into great detail on the scientific procedures he used to identify speech and voice patterns.

"Naturally," he concluded, "there is no way to be absolutely certain who recorded the tape I was brought by Mr. Jackson. But, by using every means possible in the field of voice and speech analysis, the voice of the singer on the tape in question, and the voice of Elvis Presley as recorded on his known records, were the same."

With the clarity and confidence of that statement still echoing in the jury's minds, Gregory passed the witness to RCA. Smith took his best shot, demanding to hear in detail every process the doctor used and what percent of accuracy the test results could provide. Dr. Godfrey held firm; that it was his expert opinion that the singing voice on the disputed tape was the same voice singing on other, recognized Presley classics. Certain patterns, he said, could not be duplicated by even the best impersonators, and those voice patterns matched the patterns generated on known recordings by Elvis Presley.

Yes, he admitted, there was a margin for error. Even the best equipment was subject to mechanical difficulties and frequency variations. "I can only guarantee seventy to eighty percent accuracy," the doctor stated. That was all RCA's attorney could coax from Dr. Godfrey, and he would have to be satisfied with that concession.

As the judge thanked the doctor and dismissed him, Andy thought that his testimony had gone over well. It was only to be expected that no test could guarantee total accuracy, and even then there was still the problem with the jury believing whoever was presenting the testimony. Dr. Godfrey had impressed the jury with his accomplishments and presentation, and they had gotten his expert opinion before the jury, which was the important thing. If they could only add to it with Dr. Tosie, the jury would have little choice but to agree with them, because RCA had not been able to find experts willing to say the voice on "Tell Me Pretty Baby" was definitely not Elvis.

"The defense will now call Dr. Oscar Tosie to the stand," Gregory announced.

Bryant was on his feet before the last word had left Gregory's lips. "Objection, your Honor," he shouted. "The plaintiffs have prepared a motion to exclude Dr. Oscar Tosie's testimony, and we request the court rule on that motion outside the presence of the jury," Bryant shouted, in a flourish of animated theatrics.

"The court will hear the motion to exclude testimony," Judge Leftwich announced, in a tone that left no doubt as to his pleasure at seeing the defense's strategy foiled. "Bailiff, remove the jury."

Bryant was handing copies of his motion to the judge and Gregory before the last jury member had straggled out. Gregory was expecting the maneuver, but sat anyway at the defense table to study the document.

Perhaps it wouldn't be in proper order and he could contest it on technical grounds. But they weren't going to be that lucky; John Hill's team of lawyers were exacting in their pursuit of legal excellence and high fees. The motion was legitimate.

The judge evidently agreed. "The plaintiff's motion is in order and is based upon my ruling during the preliminary hearing for temporary injunction. Unless you can present evidence or argument as to why I should not, the court intends to grant this motion," Judge Leftwich told Gregory.

Gregory gave it his best shot. "Your Honor, nowhere in the record of this preliminary hearing is there any reference to the basis on which this motion rests. And," he added, "Dr. Tosie was named as one of our expert witnesses and his report tendered to the plaintiffs during pre-trial discovery. Our witness was disclosed during interrogatory process; this is not a surprise witness!

"I have a transcript of the preliminary hearing record available if your Honor would like to point out the ruling to which he is referring. I certainly haven't been able to find it."

"The ruling referred to was made in-chambers and is not part of the transcript, Mr. Gregory." Gregory knew it before the judge said it, but wanted the judge to say so for the trial record. The judge continued, "if you had diligently communicated with the co-defendants in this case, you would have known I would not allow any surprises to be brought in this trial. That matter is settled and closed. As for your answers to the interrogatories being timely filed, they were.

"However, in light of the prior ruling, your submissions will not stand. No other interrogatories have been served upon you, requiring that you name your expert witnesses. Therefore, any new expert witnesses after the time of the temporary restraining order will not be permitted by this court. The plaintiff's motion to exclude Dr. Oscar Tosie's testimony is granted," the judge ordered.

"But, your Honor, this is totally unfair," Gregory began, before Judge Leftwich slammed his gavel and emphasized his anger, leaning forward and shouting, "Mr. Gregory, I've warned you before about questioning the procedures of my court. One more such incident and you'll be conducting your defense from the inside of a jail cell. Is that understood, counsel?"

Gregory nodded, too frustrated and angry to speak. Andy looked to Williams for some sort of help, but the young co-counsel was cowering in his seat.

Taking a deep breath, Gregory regained his composure enough to find his voice. "The defense would tender a formal bill of exception to the court's ruling and ask that Dr. Oscar Tosie be placed on the stand, in complete accordance with the Texas Rules of Court, to give his testimony to the substance of the evidence he would have presented to the jury, had this Honorable Court allowed it. This is requested in order that the matter be preserved for appellate review," he finished.

His legal footing was secure, and the judge had not expected this type of attack. The attorney had made a legitimate request, and there was little the judge could do but grant it. Otherwise, the appellate court would surely overturn any favorable ruling for the plaintiffs.

He grudgingly allowed Dr. Tosie's testimony entered into the record, but it still wouldn't be placed before the jury as evidence to be weighed in its decision-making process.

He evidently intended to do all he could to influence the outcome of this trial, but wouldn't go beyond certain limits if they would guarantee a reversal.

"Bill of exception noted and the witness will be allowed to testify for this specific purpose only," the judge rules. "You may now call your witness, but keep it brief, counsel. I'm sure the jury is growing impatient, and we don't need to waste time on testimony they won't hear."

Dr. Oscar Tosie, Professor of voice identification from Michigan State University, walked into the courtroom and onto the stand. After giving his oath, he stated his credentials and calmly asserted that he had consulted to both the Central Intelligence Agency and the Federal Bureau of Investigation, along with authoring dozens of papers on the subject.

He had, he told the court, compared known recordings by Elvis Presley through both spectrographic and comparative analysis. The results, he said, left him 90 percent certain that the voice on the tape which had been submitted to him as "Tell Me Pretty Baby" was that of Elvis Presley as compared to his known recordings.

After thanking the professor for his trouble, Gregory dismissed him from the stand. It was doubtful if anyone could have been more credible on the subject of voice identification, and it was a damaging blow to the defense that it had not been allowed to follow Dr. Godfrey with Dr. Tosie.

Making one last effort to get Tosie's testimony before the jury, Gregory approached the bench. "Your Honor," he cautiously said, "I have here the sworn deposition of Dr. Oscar Tosie, stating basically what you just heard. I request that this document be tendered to the jury and entered as evidence."

"Request denied," snapped Judge Leftwich. "Bailiff, bring the jury back into the court so we can get on with this trial now," he said.

As the jury filed back in, Andy wondered what the outcome of the trial might be if the jury were able to hear and see the entire proceedings that had taken place -- the judge's fits and hurling of his pencil; the calm contempt of Gregory when he proved RCA had tried to plant another Andrew Jackson's crimes on Andy; the professional and dignified testimony of Dr. Tosie.

Williams rose to call the next witness for the defense. Falco had managed to locate the old Red Dots, and had brought them to Dallas to testify. Since they were present when the record was made, the judge couldn't bar their testimony. Andy hoped

Williams could pull off their questioning without letting Judge Leftwich browbeat him too badly.

The drummer was the first member of the Red Dots to be called to the stand. It was obvious by the cracking of Williams' voice that he was nervous, but it was also apparent that he was determined to do a good job. Leading the drummer through his history, Williams elicited his recollections about the tape's recording.

The drummer's story was similar to Falco's, except that he could not swear that he had heard the young man who sat in with the band introduce himself as Elvis Presley. He stated that Falco had done most of the talking with the boy, but that the physical resemblance to Elvis, as the world would come to know him, was unmistakable.

His last statement earned quick objection from Bryant, followed by an equally quick statement from Judge Leftwich to the jury to disregard.

Trying to avoid a confrontation with the judge, Williams moved to more factual grounds. The drummer stated that yes, he remembered the day the Red Dots recorded "Tell Me Pretty Baby," and yes, a young man who was passing through town sat in with the band and sang on the record. Pete had paid the man $15 to sing with them. There was little else he could tell the jury, just that he was there; the recording took place with a young man he saw only the night before performing the vocals. Satisfied, Williams turned him over to RCA.

Bryant immediately tried to discredit the drummer by asking him what percentage of the profits of "Tell Me Pretty Baby" he was receiving if the record reached the market. For the first time in the trial, the high-powered attorney had calculated badly. The drummer stated quietly that he had no claims whatsoever on the song. The band had never had a contract, nor had they done any recordings for sale. The original demo had been made to promote Pete Falco's songwriting, and it belonged to Pete Falco to do with as he pleased. He had merely come to tell the truth and help out a friend.

After a few more questions intended more to save face -- and to not leave the jury with the memory of the drummer's answer embarrassing the plaintiffs -- Bryant dismissed him.

Judge Leftwich helped the plaintiff's cause by immediately calling the court into recess for lunch, destroying what momentum the defense had built. Andy was hurried off to his cell, where he gulped his food and washed it down with tap water just before he was called back into court.

The saxophone player was next, and the courtroom stirred in sympathy when he was led to the stand. Blind and wearing dark glasses, the tall, gray-haired musician tapped one side of the aisle as the bailiff guided him by his elbow.

As he gave his oath, his humble but assured demeanor left no doubt in Andy's mind that his honesty was beyond reproach.

His voice was deep and carried throughout the courtroom, even though he spoke softly and carefully. It was he and Pete who started the band, he said, and they had known each other for years before. He said he remembered the night in question very well.

It was he who had noticed the boy at the club and then pointed him out to Falco, he said, the night before they had recorded three songs written by Pete.

"That young fellow sure could sing," he told a rapt jury. He knew the boy's name was Elvis, because he had talked with him on both occasions that the boy had sung with the band; on stage that night and in the recording studio. He hadn't heard the singer's last name, but had no doubt at all as to his identity. He quietly explained that it had been the most memorable experience of his life.

It was impossible to miss the respect the jury had for the blind musician, and RCA's lawyers wisely declined to cross examine him. As the magnificent old gentleman tapped his way out of the courtroom, Andy's hopes once again rose.

Williams then called the man who'd played rhythm guitar for the Red Dots in 1954. He had been the youngest of the group, and was still in the music business, playing guitar in a country and western band that had gained acclaim in Arizona.

His testimony was similar to the drummers in that, while he couldn't testify to having heard the singer name himself, he could swear that a young man had climbed onto the stage and sang with the band one night, then recorded with them the next morning and then disappeared.

It was when he said that he later found out that the man was Elvis Presley that he ran into trouble. Bryant followed his well-worn script, objecting and requesting the jury be instructed to disregard what the guitar player had said as hearsay evidence.

"It's not hearsay evidence, your Honor," the musician surprised everyone by saying, directing his comments to the astonished judge. "I've met Elvis a couple other times, when he was performing in Vegas, and he remembered me. We didn't talk about the songs he sang for us, just how far we, especially him, had come since those days. He probably didn't even remember the name of the song then, considering all the records he'd made and all. But it was him, you bet. I recognized him and he recognized me," the guitar player insisted.

For a moment the judge seemed unsure how to deal with this bit of unsolicited honesty, but quickly decided on intimidation. "You will refrain from addressing the court unless asked a direct question," he thundered. "Nor will you be allowed to give testimony concerning Elvis Presley recognizing you. Unless you can truthfully state that the young man you claim recorded the song with you and your music group in 1954, in Phoenix, Arizona, introduced himself to you personally as Elvis Presley at that time, your testimony to that effect cannot be accepted in this court. Is that understood?"

The witness nodded, that he did indeed understand, and the judge then instructed the jury to disregard any of the man's off-the-cuff testimony linking Elvis to "Tell Me Pretty Baby."

Williams tried to rehabilitate the witness, but it was no use. From that point forward, the guitar player's answers amounted to, "I don't really know how to answer that," or "I can't say for sure." Williams finally gave up in frustration and passed the witness, but he was no help to them. He had been intimidated into uncooperativeness by the judge's assault on his ability to distinguish fact from fallacy. He was soon dismissed.

The next witness for the defense was the Red Dots' lead guitar player. He'd evidently lived the musician's stereotypical life in the fast lane, because he looked old and wasted, with rheumy eyes, stained fingers and a constant trembling.

In comparison to the other band members, his memory had failed him almost completely, and he was unable to confirm any of their claims. Andy suspected he had been a heavy drinker or drug user for years. There was little he could add to the evidence, and Williams quickly passed him to the plaintiffs, who quickly dismissed him.

"Your Honor," Williams said, "I'd like to pass the next two witnesses to my co-counsel, Mr. Gregory." Judge Leftwich looked at the plaintiffs' counsel. "Is there any objection, Mr. Bryant?" Looking uncertain at first, Bryant slowly nodded his head and simply stated, "No objection, Your Honor."

Williams sat down like a deflated balloon. Andy was extremely pleased with this unexpected turn of events, which could very well turn this trial in a positive direction.

Both witnesses to testify for the defense had been in the music business for years, especially Marvin "Smokey" Montgomery. Their credibility was beyond reproach.

Gregory had a genuine expression of satisfaction as he rose from his seat. Looking straight at Judge Leftwich he stated, "Your Honor, the defense will now call Mr. Leo Teel to the stand."

Gregory definitely had the attention of the court as Mr. Teel took the stand. After taking the oath and stating his name, Mr. Gregory asked, "Sir, would you tell the ladies and gentlemen of the jury how you're employed?"

"I'm self-employed. I have my own recording studio, located in Grand Prairie."

"How long have you been self-employed?"

"I've been in the music industry since the mid-40s." "I've been a musician, music historian and sound engineer for many years. I'm knowledgeable of all the techniques used in the recording of music."

Gregory asked, "Have you ever met or worked with Elvis Presley?"

"Yes sir. I've worked with Elvis on shows in the '50s."

Gregory paused to let the jury ponder that statement. He could sense from their faces that they were interested in this witness' testimony.

As Gregory waved a hand in Andy's direction, he asked if Teel knew Andrew Jackson. Teel said, "Well, yes and no."

"Could you clarify that statement, Mr. Teel?"

"Yes, sir. I believe it was in June of '77 that Mr. Jackson first came to my place of business to inquire about some recording equipment."

"And, do you know why Mr. Jackson was interested in recording equipment?"

"Mr. Jackson was building a recording studio at his place of business on East Main Street in Grand Prairie, only six blocks from my business location. He wanted to know if I could give him a cost-estimate to equip his studio."

"So, what you're saying is that you didn't socially know Mr. Jackson? Is that correct?"

"Yes, sir. That's correct."

"Did you ever have occasion to meet Mr. Jackson again?"

"Yes, sir, I did."

"Please tell the jury when, where and what the reason was for that particular with Mr. Jackson?"

"Well, I believe it was in February or early March of '78 that Mr. Jackson came to my business and asked if I would have time to listen to a 15 rpm master tape and tell him who I thought was the singer on the tape."

"Did he tell you in advance who he thought that singer might be on the master tape he brought you?"

"No, sir, he did not."

"And, were you able to form a professional opinion of who the voice was on the master tape?"

"Yes, sir, I was. After running the tape through a couple of times on my equipment, I told Mr. Jackson that in my opinion the singer was Elvis Presley."

Gregory then asked, "Did you happen to know the name of the song on the tape you thought was Elvis?"

"No, sir. Not until after I gave my opinion did Mr. Jackson inform me that the title of the song was "Tell Me Pretty Baby."

"No more questions of this witness," said Gregory.

Leftwich glanced at the clock. "We'll take a fifteen minute recess," he said. "And then Mr. Bryant can begin cross-examination." Gregory noticed David Bryant as he rolled his eyes and looked away as though he could care less about the testimony Gregory had just presented the jury.

Exactly fifteen minutes later Judge Leftwich entered, called the court to order, and asked for the jury. Gregory studied their face as they marched in but couldn't tell what kind of impression Mr. Teel may have made on them.

Leftwich glanced over at the plaintiffs' table and asked, "Mr. Bryant, are you ready for cross-examination of this witness?" Bryant replied, "We have no questions for this witness." As Leftwich excused Mr. Teel Gregory thought he saw a hint of shock in his expression. The judge then looked over at Joe Gregory. "Mr. Gregory, do you wish to call another witness?" The atmosphere suddenly changed as everyone directed their attention to Gregory.

"Yes, Your Honor. The defense will now call Marvin "Smokey" Montgomery."

"Good afternoon, sir," Gregory said to Montgomery, who had just taken the oath, and was seated in the witness stand.

"Would you tell the jury how you're employed, sir?"

"I'm self-employed. I'm a co-owner of Sumit Sound Recording Studios here in Dallas since the early '60s."

"And how long have you been in the music industry?"

"My music career actually started in 1934."

"Would you please tell the jury what you do?"

"Yes, sir. I'm a musician, arranger, songwriter and record producer."

"Would you mind giving the jury a brief overview of your music career?"

"Well, it's quite extensive, but I'll try to be brief as possible. I started playing the banjo in 1922. My music career started in 1934, as I stated already, and eventually I joined the 'Light Crust Doughboys' in 1935. I've played for seven presidents, including Franklin Delano Roosevelt. I've also appeared with the 'Light Crust Doughboys' in two Gene Autry movies, including 'Oh Susanna.' I've written and produced numerous songs and have had various hit records over the years. I also ran the house band in the early '50s at the Big D Jamboree. I'm also a music historian."

Bryant was impassive, tapping a pencil on his table. Judge Leftwich appeared to be almost asleep, but all of a sudden looked-up and said, "All right counsel, let's wind this up, it's getting late."

"Yes, sir," said Gregory.

"Mr. Montgomery, have you ever been associated with Elvis Aaron Presley during your music career?"

"Yes, sir, I have."

"Would you please tell the jury when you first met Elvis Presley?"

"It was at the Jamboree in the early '50s. Elvis was trying to get started as a singer and was on our show two or three times. Between performances he'd take a nap, and I'd have to get him up when it was time for him to go back on."

"How long have you known Mr. Jackson?"

"I've known Mr. Jackson since 1968."

"Would you describe for the jury how you met?"

"I first met Mr. Jackson at the old Sumit Sound business address on Greenville Avenue back in the summer of 1968, as I recall. Mr. Jackson was looking for a music arranger to help him produce some children songs."

"And, from that first meeting with Mr. Jackson, did y'all establish a working arrangement that has lasted all these years?"

"Yes, sir, we did."

"Please tell us more about that."

"I arranged all of Mr. Jackson's songs. I helped produce them and played various instruments in most of his recorded songs."

Gregory then asked, "On February 20, 1978, did you sign a letter attesting to the fact that you had listened to a tape of 'Tell Me Pretty Baby,' and as far as you could tell it sounded like Elvis Presley in his early days?"

"Yes, sir, I did."

"Mr. Montgomery, is it still your professional opinion today as you sit before this jury that the voice on the master tape embodied with the song entitled, 'Tell Me Pretty Baby,' is the voice of Elvis Aaron Presley?"

"Yes, sir! My opinion remains the same!"

The jury seemed to hang on to every word out of Montgomery's mouth. They quickly recognized this man knew his business in the music industry and he was no doubt a legend in his own right.

The RCA lawyers seemed fascinated with this testimony also, and wisely declined cross-examination.

As Smokey Montgomery walked past Andy leaving the courtroom, Andy's hopes soared to the highest heavens. Andy respected his old and faithful friend, one of the greatest musicians to ever play a banjo, and a true American treasure.

Gregory announced that the defense would rest. Judge Leftwich, looking slightly bemused, said, "All right. No more witnesses." The judge then offered a quick statement to the jury before recessing for the day.

"Ladies and gentlemen of the jury, all the witness testimony that will be presented in this matter has been placed before you. It is your duty to consider it, believe or not believe it or any part thereof. You have yet to hear summations from the lawyers.

"It's getting late and we will take up that part of the trial beginning in the morning. At that time the attorneys for both sides will sum up their cases for you, and then you will be asked to deliberate on the facts you have heard in this trial and return a decision."

Stopping for a moment, the judge looked at the jury and out over the courtroom, deciding on what to say next.

"We are nearing the end of this lengthy trial, and I thank you for your patience. I know it has been difficult at times, for it has been quite trying on me as well.

"Your real work is yet ahead of you, so rest well tonight and come back in the morning ready to give this matter your fullest attention. I'll see all of you in the morning at 9 a.m. This court is now adjourned until that time," he concluded and then quickly left, a flurry of robe behind him.

The deputy allowed Andy to sit and talk with his lawyer until the courtroom was clear. Gregory told him it was impossible to make a call as to what the jury might do, but the last two witnesses certainly seemed to have made a great impact upon them. The defense had given it their best shot, considering the tremendous judicial restrictions they had been under. It appeared that closing arguments would make or break them.

He looked over at Williams as he said this, and it was clear -- Gregory wished it were he giving the summation for the defense, rather than Steven Williams.

Andy did, too.

The Verdict

CHAPTER TWENTY-SEVEN

Andy relived the trial a hundred times that night. He went over each witnesses' testimony, every piece of evidence, reviewed every question and remembered every answer in an attempt to convince himself that there was a chance the jury would believe them, or that Williams could somehow give such an impassioned, brilliant summation that the panel would say yes, of course it was Elvis, and send RCA cowering back to Nashville in defeat.

And at 3 a.m., unable to either sleep or believe he and his co-defendants would win their case, Andrew Jackson prayed. Not simply for victory, but for redemption -- for the chance to retain some of his dignity; for Pete Falco and his daughter to win some financial security. He prayed for the Red Dots to be vindicated, and for Joe Gregory's perseverance, Charlotte's faith and Williams' determination to be rewarded.

His prayers sustained him through the morning's dismal events. Sitting in the same dingy suit he'd worn the previous day, he listened as Williams tried to persuade the jury to believe in the small bit of scientific evidence they'd been able to slip past the cunning judge.

But just when it seemed Williams was making an impression, just when he had stopped stammering and was talking with confidence and animation, Judge Leftwich pounced.

Williams and Gregory had decided that they needed to bring up the possibility that the original tape -- introduced into evidence and from which all other copies stemmed -- was not the true master tape, as Andy had testified to. If they could get the jury to believe that; if the seed of doubt could be planted that there was no possible way to decide if it was Elvis singing on the tape because RCA had switched tapes: well, it was a shot.

But when Williams fired, RCA fired back. Bryant objected, Judge Leftwich sustained and mercilessly berated Williams, who promptly went into a shell. They had expected an objection, but had depended on Williams somehow continuing and finding a way around the walls erected by RCA and protected by the judge. But Williams was simply too inexperienced, too timid, too easily intimidated.

Judge Leftwich had picked well when he appointed the young attorney as lead defense counsel. Hounded by Judge Leftwich, Williams retired, leaving the floor to David Bryant, who proceeded to earn his surely astronomical fees.

Bryant fed the spark flickering in the celebrity conscious jury by referring to Elvis and Vernon Presley again and again. Bryant said he had met Elvis' dearest and closest friends, and they had all told him that "Tell Me Pretty Baby" was a hoax, a fraud, a sham unworthy to be associated with the greatest singer America had produced.

You have heard the tape, Bryant whispered to the jury, and you are intelligent, and you are worthy, and you can surely see for yourselves that the recording these con men have tried to use to make a quick buck is fake, and if left to sit on the shelves under the King's face, will bring dishonor on the King's true art. And worse, he whispered, it would devalue his legacy.

It was emotion and celebrity against science and blue-collar anonymity, and the defendants never had a chance. After a 3-hour deliberation, the jury returned its verdict.

Although he'd expected the worst, the words still struck Andy with terrible force, each a blow that knocked another chip from his dreams.

"We, the jury, find that the recording 'Tell Me Pretty Baby,' owned and distributed by International Classic Productions, was not sung by Elvis Aaron Presely," the foreperson read from her verdict sheet.

"Furthermore, we find that International Classic Productions shall desist and refrain from marketing, selling or otherwise transferring, or causing to be sold, marketed or otherwise transferred, directly or indirectly, any copy of 'Tell Me Pretty Baby' as a performance of Elvis Presley."

The judge quickly called the case closed, and with a sharp rap of his gavel, ordered the temporary injunction to remain in effect until he could sign a permanent one.

Andy slowly left the courtroom in a daze, and the deputy placed him into the holding cell to await the jailer to escort him upstairs. It had happened so fast. Surely with the last two witnesses their case had been more convincing than that, wasn't it? How could they have so easily deemed them all a bunch of liars, Andy asked himself as the jail guard took him from the holding cell upstairs.

He told the guard that as soon as his lawyer had time to get back to his office, he needed to make a telephone call. It was unnecessary. Andy had barely had time to light a cigarette before the guard returned with the news that his lawyer was waiting to see him. It was a relief that Gregory had taken the initiative, for Andy truly didn't know what to do next.

After a few consoling words, the counselor told Andy he felt there were numerous grounds for appeal, and he would be contacting the other defendants with a request that they share the costs. If they agreed, he would get the paperwork under way.

Gregory had not been paid a dime for his services, his only compensation being a hoped-for percentage of the profits of the record, if it was eventually released. He had covered expenses out of his pocket, but said he could no longer afford to do that.

There was another option. If the other defendants refused to help, Andy could appeal as an indigent, Gregory said. In such a case he would be appealing in his own capacity, not as a member of International Classic Productions. It was a last resort, and entailed much paperwork, but it was an option they would resort to if all other avenues failed.

Andy left their final meeting in the Dallas County Jail feeling that all hope was not yet lost. It would be an uphill battle, but it had been all along.

After showering and a meager supper, Andy was called out and escorted to the visitation room, where Charlotte was waiting. Andy told her he would most likely be leaving the next day to return to prison, since the county had no reason to keep him. He hated leaving because he knew she wouldn't be able to visit as often.

She promised to travel the few hundred miles when she could, and said she would write as often as possible. Her words helped, but he knew it wouldn't be the same as getting to visit several times a week. Andy also told her, just before the visit ended, that he intended to appeal the verdict, and that the battle wasn't over yet.

Somehow, his words sounded hollow as they echoed off the drab steel walls.

Epilogue

His return to Huntsville was long and bitter. He watched the world pass by the barred windows and breathed the fresh air, knowing it would be his last glimpse of the free world for a long time. Andy said little to the young man who was chained to him, instead keeping his head against the window for most of the long ride south.

His stay at the Diagnostic Unit was short, as he had already passed through the testing and classification process. He was soon back on the Eastham Unit, working at his old job.

It took a week for his mail to catch up to him, and it contained a letter from Charlotte, who enclosed a clipping describing the trial's end. The article started starkly and contained a few surprises.

"It's not Elvis."

"After 10 days of testimony and more than three hours of deliberation, a six-man, six-woman jury told state District Judge Snowden Leftwich that the performer singing on the record 'Tell Me Pretty Baby' is not the late Elvis Presley."

"The jury's decision that the song was recorded by someone other than the late, great rock star means the judge will sign early next week a permanent injunction prohibiting Dallas-based International Classic Productions from selling any more of its 'Tell Me Pretty Baby' records.

"Don Reese, the owner of International Classic Productions, estimates his company is left with 'thousands' of copies of the record. He insisted Friday that 'Tell Me Pretty Baby' is authentic

Presley and said he planned to appeal the verdict. Friday Reese also claimed the judge had not treated his side fairly in court.

"'We were not allowed to present evidence that would have proved beyond a shadow of a doubt that was Elvis Presley' said Reese. Reese said his attorneys were not allowed to present testimony from a Michigan State University voice expert who was '90 percent positive' the voice on the record is that of Presley."

Andy was not surprised to see the one-sided report. At least someone had been able to add another perspective of the trial's unfairness. And, since it was Don making the comments, Andy wasn't too put off, and indeed had to laugh at Don's claim that he was the owner of International Classic Productions.

It was so like Reese to make such a claim, knowing he owned far less percentage of the company than either Andy or Pete Falco. What worried Andy was that Don might try to use that same claim in the future for his own purposes, perhaps, even, trying to legally gain possession of the original tape. Andy reminded himself to do something about that possibility at the first opportunity.

That opportunity was not long in coming, as Joe Gregory came to Eastham for a visit that week. Andy was glad to see his former attorney and was surprised by the visit. Andy told him of his concerns over Don claiming to be the owner of the company. His lawyer told him not to worry, that if there was ever any question as to the ownership of International Classis Productions, they all had copies of the contract, which would be the final arbiter in such a disagreement.

Gregory had some good news for Andy. He had filed a motion for a new trial the day after Andy had left the county jail. The basis for the request was the fact that during the jury's deliberations, the jury had sent several notes to Judge Leftwich, requesting clearer instructions on assorted legal points.

In each instance, the judge refused to clarify his instructions, responding that the jury would have to do its best with the instructions he had already given them. Nor had the judge allowed him, or Steven Williams, to provide the information to the jury. Once Gregory had the chance to talk with the individual members of the jury and found out they were willing to testify on the matter at a hearing, he decided to file the motion requesting a new trial, Gregory told Andy.

He also had the notice of appeal ready, if they needed it. But, Gregory said, the appeal would wait until the matter of a new trial was decided. The bad news was that the decision whether or not to grant the new trial was in the hands of Judge Leftwich.

As Andy expected, the judge was not going to willingly open the gate to any action that might help Andy. Three months later, Gregory wrote and said his motion for a new trial had been overruled by operation of law, a fancy way of saying the judge had merely let the time limits for a new trial expire, thus effectively killing any chance to pursue it.

In the same letter, Gregory told Andy that he would soon file the notice of appeal. However, along with the notice of appeal, they would also be required to post a surety bond in the amount of $8,000. Because none of the other defendants were willing to put up anything for the appeal, it was all left up to Andy, who, of course, had no assets left.

In a bit of good news, Gregory told Andy that he was allowed to file an affidavit of inability to pay the costs of an appeal. It was a process allowing indigent persons equal access to the courts, and was a mechanism used by prisoners fighting prison conditions and other legal matters from their prison cells, or simply by poor people who could not afford to pay the costs of court proceedings.

The next day, Andy was in the administration offices of the Eastham Unit, getting the warden to notarize his affidavit of indigence. He had been up most of the night preparing the new document, because it had to be filed with the court by July 19.

While in the assistant warden's office, Andy asked to see the mailroom supervisor in order to weigh the legal documents and find out the correct postage. He intended to send it certified mail, but had no idea how much the extra postage would cost him.

Andy's request to see the mailroom officer was denied, and he was told to "guess" at the amount of postage required. That night, Andy collected a little over two dollars in stamps, more than enough to cover the required postage for the four-page legal document. He stamped the envelope, included a note to the mail officer requesting the parcel be sent certified mail if the postage was sufficient, and if not, to please mail it first class.

Andy marked the parcel, "Urgent," and made sure the note let the mailroom office know that the package had to be in the Dallas court by July 19. He placed it in the mailbox the morning of July 14.

The evening of July 18, the legal parcel was handed back to Andy, marked to the effect that it was $0.41 short of the postage necessary for certified mail. Andy was stunned. Here it was the day before the affidavit was due, and it had yet to be given to the U.S. Postal Service.

The mailroom officer had completely ignored his instructions to send the parcel first class if the postage was insufficient to send it certified mail. Andy couldn't understand why a package marked "Urgent" and "Legal" was held for five full days in the unit mailroom. Andy could only assume the action was deliberate, as the Texas Department of Corrections was notorious for interfering with prisoners' legal mail.

In a panic, Andy borrowed the additional postage and mailed the package on July 19. He could only hope the early date of notarization and the timely postmark would be enough to save him, and get the affidavit accepted by the court. Weeks later, he was notified by the court clerk that his affidavit had been received and filed July 23. It did not take long for RCA to see through this legal loophole, and the company's lawyers filed a contest to Andy's affidavit of inability to pay costs, which was accepted and filed by the court clerk on July 29. Evidently, someone in the Dallas court was quietly looking out for the record company's interests, and had notified RCA of Andy's intent, as there was no legal reason for them to be notified.

On August 1, Andy received a letter from Judge Leftwich, stating that, "The Court is setting a hearing on the contest for August 17, 1979. And, the Court feels that it is doing a useless thing by these hearing, for unless Mr. Jackson can somehow convince the Court prior to such hearing that his affidavit in lieu of cost bond is timely filed within the law, this Court has no intention of wasting the assets of Dallas County, and the state of Texas, to bring Mr. Jackson to this Court for such hearing."

Andy quickly drafted and mailed a response, explaining the facts leading to the late filing of the affidavit. Surprisingly, the judge accepted Andy's letter and construed it as a motion in response to the judge's letter demanding Andy to show cause.

The judge replied, on August 9, saying that, "Unless you can show me some way that I can get around your late filing, and it would certainly seem unlikely that you can, there is no reason for me to hear the contest on your pauper's oath in lieu of cost bond, nor to bring you here for such purpose."

Totally bewildered by the judge's reasoning, Andy sat down with some of the prisoners who were well-versed in the law -- called "writ writers" in prison -- and explained to them his predicament.

The convicts empathized with Andy's situation, for one of them knew Judge Leftwich through his reputation as irrational and unpredictable. All they could suggest was to file a proper legal motion, asking that the hearing be reset, and ask for more time so he could show good cause as to why the court should accept his affidavit. One of them agreed to help and he and Andy went right to work in the prison law library.

In less than a week the motion was completed and mailed. Andy had done what the judge had told him was unlikely for him to do; that is, show a legal and procedural means by which the judge could get around the late filing of the affidavit. Andy had diligently researched the law, and he had put together an impressive and properly argued legal motion.

On August 14, the judge responded. "The Court has decided that it was unnecessary to reset the hearing on your motion and contest of your affidavit in lieu of cost bond in view of the replies filed in connection with such motion."

Andy translated the convoluted legalese to mean that the attorneys for the plaintiffs had filed replies convincing the judge to find in their favor. Andy wondered how much cash was involved in those convincing replies.

The letter continued. "The Court adds that there is evidence that you did not actually post your affidavit in lieu of cost bond until July 19, 1979. Among other matters, there is the fact that your motion to reset reached here in less than 24 hours, while your letter motion, which you say was posted in the same manner with the U.S. Mail on July 19, not only did not reach this Court on the 20th or 21st of July, but arrived on July 23, 1979." The judge was using the prompt delivery of one motion to dismiss the late arrival of another. He also enclosed his official order overruling Andy's motions and his right to appeal.

The judge was not finished. He had also attached an Intervener's Motion to Dismiss, the judge's Order to Overrule Andy's affidavit of inability to pay cost, and the plaintiff's response to his motion to reset. In each instance, the judge had ruled against Andy and for the plaintiffs.

After all was said and done, the unit mailroom's negligence had resulted in Judge Leftwich's order denying Andy's right to appeal. His last hope was gone. His hopes and dreams of winning the right to market "Tell Me Pretty Baby" lay finally and irrevocably smashed.

The middle of the next week, Gregory wrote Andy and voiced his regrets over the way things had turned out. They had done the best they could, Gregory said, but it was like trying to fight a brick wall with Judge Leftwich sitting on the bench. They never had a chance, the lawyer realized. If there was ever anything he could do to help, Gregory said to let him know. With that, Gregory bade Andy luck and said goodbye.

As time passed, Andy adopted a more fatalistic attitude, not accepting events but adapting to them, and to the institutional grind. As he knew would happen, Charlotte totally stopped visiting and then writing. He'd resigned himself to the certainty of that, and although hurt by it, knew that anyone would be hard pressed to maintain a relationship in prison unless they had been legally married for years and had years of shared history.

He haunted the legal library, knowing that he needed to be ready in case a legal avenue presented itself and a chance arose to speed his release or market "Tell Me Pretty Baby."

He learned the long reach of those set against him when he finally took it upon himself to begin gathering his scattered possessions, which had been taken by Judge Leftwich's court as evidence and left there by Andy in hopes of using them in an appeal.

Andy contacted the Dallas court clerk to ascertain the whereabouts of the original tape and how to have it returned to him. Andy waited months, but he was never answered.

He refused to quit. He was certain that the tape he had seen in the Dallas courtroom was not the same one he had locked in his safety deposit box the morning before his arrest on the trumped-up sexual assault charges. But, if he could get the tape which was presented as evidence during trial and prove it was a substitute or had been tampered with, he believed he had a chance of recovering the true original master tape.

Andy was able to contact a Dallas lawyer who agreed to help search for the missing tape. Attorney David Botsford, being nearby, undertook the laborious and dirty job of rummaging through the Dallas County Clerk's storage warehouse for the elusive reel. He eventually located the case files in the archives, and made a diligent search, but the master tape was not found.

In 1988, Andy filed several motions with the Dallas courts requesting the release and return of the master tape. The courts never responded to any of those motions.

Andy did not stop trying to contact the court clerk, or anyone who could point him in one direction or another. In April of 1994, he asked the Dallas clerk to supply him with a cost list for the Statement of Facts and list of exhibits on file in the matter of

RCA v. Jackson. He hoped that the master tape would somehow appear on the list of exhibits, and he also wanted the Statement of Facts in order to again try, somehow, to appeal the jury's decision of 15 years earlier.

Andy finally received a reply to his inquiry about the price of the trial records, and it shocked him, even after all the years fighting RCA and Judge Leftwich and recognizing the lengths they'd go to in order to keep the record off the market.

The return address on the letter was that of the Dallas County District Clerk's office, but the handwritten letter enclosed had no letterhead or signature. It said that the exhibits he requested had been destroyed. Furthermore, the court reporter's notes had never been transcribed, so a Statement of Facts had never been prepared. The notes were the property of the court reporter, not the clerk's office, and there was no record available that would indicate who that court reporter had been.

Those notes, along with the exhibits of the trial, had most likely been destroyed. Andy's final hopes of retrieving "Tell Me Pretty Baby" by tracking down the master tape were ground to dust, just as thoroughly as had been his hopes of trying to market the record.

Andy still believes that "Tell Me pretty Baby" is authentic Elvis Presley and dates the true birth of rock and roll. While it is possible that Andy was the target of a scam, used to perpetuate a hoax; with the scientific testing that the tape was subjected to, that possibility is a faint one. Today, more sophisticated equipment exists to test and establish the identity of the vocalist on the record, and Andy would welcome such scientific inquiry. But now, the question that remains, of course, is the location of the original master tape of the studio session that resulted in this book -- which was written to reveal to the public the secrets behind the recording and attempted marketing of "Tell Me Pretty Baby."

This story ends in an ironic twist, one prompted by an off-hand comment made by none other than Judge Leftwich, who after dismissing the jury that day, said to Andy, completely off the record, "Mr. Jackson, you still own the rights to the song. Should you wish to sell the record someday, you may consider using the name 'Mystery Artist' or 'Mystery Singer' in place of Elvis' name. Who knows, you might be able to sell a few records like that," the judge concluded with a sarcastic smirk as he stepped down from the bench.

Andrew Jackson now intends to do exactly as the judge suggested so many years ago. Not so much that it is sound business advice, but because it is the only method left to reproduce "Tell Me Pretty Baby," and give Elvis fans the opportunity to be transported back into the magical realm of this historical recording event -- without further court intervention.

Due to the nature of the original records produced in vinyl, with the advancement of technology today, "Tell Me Pretty Baby" will be transferred from a pristine first generation record without loosing any quality of sound.

And now, after a quarter of a century, fans will have an opportunity to purchase the new collector's edition of "Tell Me Pretty Baby;" soon to be released as a single CD crediting "Mystery Artist."

Maybe this time, at long last, fans can decide for themselves just who it was that strolled into a small Phoenix recording studio in early 1954, for a rendezvous with destiny.

Incidentally; according to Broadcast Music, Inc. (BMI) of Nashville, Tennessee, the original recording is still getting airplay in Canada and Scandinavia, and was used for the segment introduction theme -- "Is It Elvis' Lost Record" -- on The Drew Carey show in early 1991, and again in 2001.

In addition, the record received heavy media coverage in the European community and was used in a TV documentary in Finland in 1996.

Evidently, there are those who recognize and give credence to the "timeless voice," Elvis or whoever this mystery artist may be that caused a storm of action and reaction around the world during the '70s.

I personally believe that if Elvis had been alive during all these years of controversy surrounding this recording, he would have come forward one way or the other. Don't you?

ANDREW JACKSON
2009
"I'm thrilled to be able to add 'Tell Me Pretty Baby' to my collection."
Dick Clark American Bandstand

To add "Tell Me Pretty Baby" to your own collection, go to our website: www.internationalclassicproductions.com

APPENDIX

A true and correct copy of the oral deposition of Joe D. Gregory, Andrew Jackson's trial lawyer, is included in this Appendix. It is included because it was a primary source for the facts used by the author to write this book.

Mr. Gregory was privy to, and indeed a victim of the vile judicial proceedings and the judge presiding over those proceedings. The sworn testimony of Mr. Gregory lends credence to and is part of the historic events leading to the writing of this book.

* * * * * * * *

ORAL DEPOSITION OF
JOE D. GREGORY

Vernon Presley & RCA Corporation v. Andrew Jackson

APPEARANCES

FOR THE PLAINTIFF:
MR. THOMAS J. BEVANS
ATTORNEY AT LAW
440 Louisiana, Suite 475
Houston, Texas 77002

FOR THE DEFENDANTS:
ANTHONY J. NELSON
Assistant Attorney General
P. O. Box 12548
Austin, Texas 78711-2548

Also Present: Rusty Hubbarth

JOE D. GREGORY,
the witness hereinbefore named, being first duly cautioned and, sworn in
the above cause, testified under oath as follows:

EXAMINATION

BY MR. BEVANS:

Q.   Mr. Gregory, my name is Tom Bevans. I'm an attorney that's
been hired by Andrew Lee Jackson in the cause entitled Andrew Lee Jackson
Versus E. J. Estelle et al Cause Number TY-79-416.

Would you please tell us your education, sir?

A.   I have a law degree from Baylor University. I have a bachelor
of arts degree from University of Texas at Arlington, and, of course, high
school education.

Q.   What year did you graduate from law school?

A.   In 1974, received my degree cum laude.

Q.   Cum laude?

A.   Right.

Q.   Did you have any other honors while you were there at
Baylor Law School?

A.   Numerous honors. I can't tell you what they specifically are.
I graduated first in my class at Baylor.

Q.   You were admitted to the Texas Bar that year?

A.   October of 1974, I believe.

Q.   And since that time, what is the nature and extent of your
practice?

A.   For approximately the first year and a half, I practiced with
an insurance defense firm in Dallas, Burford, Ryburn & Ford, and since that
time have been engaged in private practice in a firm that I was senior partner
of ever since then.

Q.   And the name of that firm?

A.   Well, it's changed over the years. It was initially Gregory,
Sargeant & Gregory, and that's (spelling) S A R G E A N T. Then it became
Sibley, Gregory, Sargeant & Gregory, and then in I would say approximately
1976 or 1977--I can't recall exactly--it became Gregory & Gregory, which it
has been up to. the current date.

Q.   The other Gregory is your brother?

A.   Yes.

Q.   Okay. And your practice, is that civil?

A.   Yes, strictly civil.

Q.   Defense or plaintiff or both?

A.   At the current time, it probably is made up of I would say ninety percent a plaintiff's civil practice, ten percent involving business litigation for business clients, and as far as my practice is concerned, it's been that way probably for the past four years, and prior to then was a little bit heavier on the business practice.

Q. Are you board certified in any area?

A. No, I'm not.

Q. When did you meet Andrew Lee Jackson?

A. I can't tell you the specific date. I don't know that I can even tell you the particular year that I met him. In point of fact, I believe the first indication that I or first contact I had from him was in a telephone call, where he called me inquiring about whether or not I would be interested in representing him.

Q. Okay. Was your first representation in the cause Dallas County Cause 78-10402, RCA and Vernon Presley Versus Andrew Lee Jackson?

A. I'm not sure about the cause number. I couldn't tell you the -- about the cause number.

Q. No. Is that the first one you ever represented him?

A. Yes. That's the only time. I've only had something to do with Andrew Lee Jackson in that one case arid that one case alone.

Q. Okay. Do you recall the trial dates on that?

A. No, sir, I do not. I know it was a fairly lengthy trial.

Q. When you say lengthy, what --

A. My memory seems to tell me that the trial lasted in excess of a month, but I cannot give you any specific dates or anything in connection with the particular trial.

Like I say, my file was destroyed. Our office practice is to keep our file for about six years, and then we go through the particular files. I had no knowledge that this particular action was pending until after it -- you know, after it was too late to preserve the particular file.

Q. Okay. I could be wrong, but I think somewhere I read that the actual trial dates were March 12th through March 22nd of 1979 or '78. Does that sound about right?

A. I could not answer that question. Like I say, my memory tells me that it was a lengthy trial. I know that it seemed to be very lengthy for me at that time. It could have been two weeks.

Q. Going back to your practice in the period ' 78, '79. was that mainly plaintiff --

A. I did at that time probably I had this is just a ballpark estimate, somewhere between thirty and forty percent of my practice was made up of a practice involving business litigation and/or business clients in addition to the plaintiff's practice that I did at that time.

Q.   Do you recall the principal issues in that Dallas case?

A.   Yes.

Q.   Okay. Would you enumerate those for us, please, sir?

A.   Well, I think the principle issue was whether or not the song, quote, Tell Me Pretty Baby was recorded by Elvis Presley.

Q.   Any other secondary issues or --

A.   I think if we would have received a response from the jury that that was or if -- if we had convinced them it was sung by Elvis Presley, then we would have won that lawsuit, so I can't think of any -- you know, there may have been some issues concerning whether or not the contract that RCA had with Elvis Presley did or did not affect our right to use his name. There were some collateral issues such as that, but this particular recording of Tell Me Pretty Baby predated the point in time that RCA had their, quote, contract.

So, you know, but the threshold question concerning whether or not it was or was not Elvis Presley that recorded the song had to be found in our favor before we could ever get to the other issues concerning whether or not any particular agreements with RCA would in turn affect our right to advertise or sell that particular letter. I say "us." I mean the clients, to sell the particular recording as a recording by Elvis Presley.

Q.   So the -- identifying the artist would impact on all subsequent issues.

A.   Yes.

Q.   The judge in that case, was Snowden M. Leftwich?

A.   Snowden Leftwich, yes.

Q.   Okay. Did you find any judicial error, as far as you're concerned, in this case, and would you enumerate them?

A.   Well, I felt like there were numerous errors committed by Judge Leftwich in that particular case. I'll have to kind of regress a little bit.

At the time that I was employed by Mr. Andrew Lee Jackson, there were several other individuals. One of them was a gentleman by the name of Don Reese, if my memory serves me correctly; another gentleman by the name of Pete Falco, who was supposedly the individual that recorded the song with Elvis Presley, and there could have been another individual whose name escapes me, may or may not have been been the third individual, but they had this -- this particular agreement between themselves, some type of a partnership agreement or whatever where that they were sharing in certain percentages of the revenues that might be generated in connection with sale of the recording.

Mr. Jackson, of course, was at that time in jail. He had no

funds to hire me, and what I then in turn did, with Mr. Jackson's consent, is set down with the attorneys who were representing Mr. Reese and Mr. Falco. They were at one time representing Mr. Jackson, but they felt like there was a conflict; therefore, they told Mr. Jackson find an attorney.

He had contacted me. I sat down with him. We entered into an agreement where that any fees or anything that I earned would be coming to the law firm in the form of a percentage of the revenues generated on the song.

I made it a condition of my employment in connection with that because I knew I would have to withstand certain expense in connection with the litigation. Before I signed an agreement, I made it a condition that the other attorneys, Mr. Dennis Brewer's firm was the one that was involved out of Irving, that they, together with me, determine who was, quote, the foremost expert in voice identification.

I agreed to withstand half the expense of getting him to listen to and study the tape to determine whether or not he felt like it was or was not Elvis Presley. I wanted that determination for my benefit because I felt like the law firm of Gregory & Gregory would have to expend a sizable amount of money in connection with trying the case, and the hope at that time was that we could get that opinion back soon enough where that I could then file a motion for continuance and get Judge Leftwich to continue the case.

The results of the test came back positive, that a professor and gentleman by the name of Dr. Oscar Tosie out of Michigan State University indicated that it was his opinion that it was, in fact, Elvis Presley who was the recording artist.

I accepted the employment, approached Judge Leftwich with what I thought to be good, solid, firm grounds because there was a conflict of interest between Mr. Jackson and the other clients that Mr. Brewer represented.

We were within something like forty-five days or so prior to trial. Judge Leftwich denied the continuance. That was one point that I felt like was there. Whether or not that was reversible might be a question.

The other point that where I believe Judge Leftwich committed error, the attorneys for RCA, Hughes & Hill, they had served interrogatories on all of the parties defendant in this particular case where that the answers were due something like within thirty days of trial, in that time frame. One of the questions that they asked, of course, was for us to identify our expert witnesses.

At that time, we had Dr. Oscar Tosie, not only his name but, memory tells me, his report. We tendered the report to the attorneys for RCA -- pardon me, for RCA in a timely fashion in accordance with the interrogatories. R -- RCA then filed a motion to exclude Dr. Tosie's testimony on the basis that there had allegedly been a conference between the then attorneys for the RCA and the then attorneys for Andrew Jackson, Mr. Reese, and Mr. Falco in chambers where the judge had announced, quote, there will be no surprises in this case, gentlemen.

Judge Leftwich conducted a hearing on the motion to exclude Dr. Tosie's testimony. He ruled that even though we had answered the interrogatories timely, there had been no other interrogatory served on us requiring us to name the experts. He held that this untranscribed conference in chambers at the time of the temporary restraining order hearing on the temporary injunction, whenever he announced, quote, there will be no surprises, that that was sufficient grounds for him to prevent us from presenting the expert witness testimony of Dr. Tosie.

Now, the reason why the -- what Dr. Tosie had done, he had himself compared certain known recordings by Elvis Presley through both -- I think they call it spectrographic analysis and also through a procedure whereby he took certain excerpts from certain songs and did what was then recognized as a reliable test within that area, the test being a comparative analysis by a group of individuals, and the number, it seems to me like there was thirty or forty individuals that actually sat down and listened to these comparative tapes that he had done and came up with a percentage likelihood that it was Elvis Presley.

His own personal opinion, he came to the conclusion that he was ninety percent sure it was Elvis Presley based on the study, that he had done, which was supposedly a well-recognized manner in which you determine the -- the speaker, or the artist in this case. Memory tells me that his testimony was seventy, eighty percent sure that the artist was Elvis Presley.

That entire testimony was excluded by Dr. Tosie. During the trial, in light of the rules that then existed, we presented in the way of a formal bill of exception, we went ahead and brought Dr. Tosie to Dallas during trial and let him take the witness stand and testify what he would have testified had the judge allowed him to, so we had the error preserved for the appellate court to look at.

Another what I thought was, quote, reversible error on on Judge Leftwich's part involved his ruling at the beginning of trial. He felt like that the interest of each of the parties defendant in this particular case was identical, and, therefore, he ruled that only one attorney for the defense would be allowed to cross-examine or conduct direct examination of a witness that took the stand. I objected to it, indicated to The Court that, you know, I had been hired by Andrew Lee Jackson himself individually as his attorney, that the defense was seeking attorneys fees as well as other matters of affirmative relief from him, in addition to seeking a restraining order, and as his attorney, I intended on cross-examining or direct examining each and every witness that went on the witness stand.

Judge Leftwich let me understand that I would be placed in jail if I attempted to examine any of these particular witnesses, and so he made the defense select between myself, as an attorney solely representing Andrew Lee Jackson, and the other attorneys who represented Mr. Falco and Mr. Reese between who was going to cross-examine or who was going to direct examine a particular witness. That was another error I felt like was, quite, reversible.

The only other error that comes to mind in connection with this lawsuit involves some excluded evidence in connection with the conduct of this trial early on before they had a temporary injunction hearing. We had the -- of course, the testimony transcribed at the temporary injunction hearing. I was not a party -- or I say a party. I was not involved in the case at that time, but the attorney for RCA, their lead counsel, whose name escapes me -- I can remember David Bryant, but I cannot remember the other lawyer's name -- had examined an officer from RCA.

This particular officer had indicated that early on when Mr. Reese and Mr. Jackson and Mr. Falco were first starting up trying to promote and sell this record, they had approached him in hopes that they could make some type of agreement with RCA, and they had let this particular officer, located in the Dallas-Fort Worth area, listen to the recording. The particular officer, you know, I think they may have delivered in fact a tape to him of the recording. That deposition was taken by RCA themselves before the hearing, the temporary injunction hearing.

At the temporary injunction hearing, RCA placed on the witness stand Johnnie Herra, or I believe it was Johnnie Herra, some Elvis impersonator who got on the witness stand and they elicited testimony from him that he had recorded that song some time after the officer from RCA had listened to it, which, you know, those facts had to be known by the attorney because the attorney took the deposition.

They had to know that this Elvis Presley impersonator that they got put on the witness stand at the temporary injunction hearing was committing perjury because it would have been impossible for him to have recorded it at a date after the RCA officer listened to it, a physical impossibility.

I had briefs prepared, presented to Judge Leftwich. Whenever I called the attorney for RCA to the witness stand to prove that he had knowingly presented perjured testimony, Judge Leftwich excluded it, and, in the process of the formal bill when we were presenting it, literally threw a pencil at me from the bench that I had to duck to keep from stabbing me.

Now, there were numerous other errors in connection with the particular case, but those four, the last three of which I mentioned, I believe, were, quote, truly reversible or the only thing that comes to mind for me at this point.

Q. Now, did he show any prejudice as opposed to error, or was his prejudice encased in the error?

A. Oh, I think probably one of the points of error that we would have prepared in a brief would have been just the fundamental unfairness that we were approached with in this particular case, you know. I think during the course of the trial I was threatened numerous times out of the presence of the jury to put me in jail because I did not agree with the procedures that The Court was trying to conduct the trial, and -- and, you know, at this point I can't remember.

My memory seems to tell me that Judge Leftwich would not allow but one person on the defense to even urge any objections, and I think probably numerous times during the trial, I would try to object, and the judge would tell me to sit down, that I was not the attorney that was objecting while this witness was testifying because Mr. -- oh, the attorney representing Dennis -- out of Dennis Brewer's firm, who was representing the other parties defendant, had examined; therefore, if he examined, he had to make the objection. He would not let me object on behalf of Mr. Jackson to testimony that was going on.

I'm sure that would have been a point in conjunction with the others, otherwise, you know, numerous objections frivolous sustained by The Court. I'm sure just a point of error would have been addressed to just the total unfairness of the proceedings by Snowden Leftwich.

Q. Was enough of this done before the jury where it possibly would have had an influence on the outcome of the jury decision?

A. No question about it.

Q. In your mind --

A. Yes.

Q. -- there's no question?

A. Yes.

Yes.

THE WITNESS: Off the record.

(Discussion held off the record.)

Q. (By MR. BEVANS) Was there some testimony to the effect that the -- the physical tape itself was not, quote, manufactured or in use?

MR. NELSON: Let me interrupt for a second because I want to get it on the record. We're reserving all objections to the time of trial; is that correct?

MR. BEVANS: Okay.

MR. NELSON: I just want to get it on the record. That's the agreement.

MR. BEVANS: Okay.

Q.   (By MR. BEVANS)   Was there any testimony to the effect that the physical tape itself was not manufactured or used until after 1954?

A. Well, what occurred was there was testimony to the effect that the particular tape and possibly even the cylinder, I guess, or whatever you call it, --

Q.   We're talking about --

A.   -- that it was recorded on, one or the other, was not, quote, manufactured until after 1954 or whenever it was the recording was supposed to be recorded.

Now, that particular testimony, you know, that was the testimony that was even presented at the temporary hearing. Now, the way the course of this discovery went in connection with this particular lawsuit was the original, what I'll call the master tape, the master tape had been delivered by an attorney at one time who represented one of the parties. It may have been even Andrew Jackson before I came -- came on board representing him. He delivered this tape to RCA.

All right. Now, the particular tape that was placed in evidence, it was not, quote, represented by us to be the master tape because we did not believe it to be the master tape, and whenever I use the term "we," please appreciate I'm talking about my client.

As it turned out, initially, whenever they received the tape from Mr. Falco -- he was the one that had it and had had possession of it for years and years. Mr. Falco carried the tape to a recording studio and had a small cassette like you see in these cassette recorders, a copy of that master tape done.

That master -- that copy of that cassette tape was preserved. The master tape in turn by this other attorney was delivered to RCA. When it came back to us, of course, there was no, I guess, identifying markings on it, but we had it run through a spectrograph at Collier Speech & Hearing Center in Dallas, and as it turned out, the tape that was delivered to us back by RCA in fact was not the master tape.

We felt like -- I felt like during the trial we proved scientifically that RCA had done a tape switch in that trial. And the reason why is because there was -- on the little cassette tape -- there was not any echo on the recording. The master tape or the alleged master tape that was delivered back to R C -- by RCA to the parties defendant contained echo on it.

Now, the testimony was presented by a recording expert and also by the gentleman that was with Collier's Speech and Therapy Clinic over in Dallas, and it was to the effect that you cannot take away sounds off a recording because when you do, you bank it out, at least technology at that time. And, therefore, as far as which came first, which was a parent, which was a child, the little cassette tape had to be a generation prior to the alleged master RCA had at one time in its possession because the RCA tape had sound on it, in other words echo, that the little cassette tape did not have. So to lead to the conclusion, it was our position, which we urged to the jury, that RCA had actually, whenever they got possession of this tape, did a switch on the tape.

And at the same time, it had been discovered, quote, that the recording studio in Phoenix, Arizona did not have, quote, an echo chamber at that time. They did not have what they call electronic echo that they add to recordings nowadays, and their expert witness testified that this could not have been recorded in that studio because they didn't have electronic echo, and this was electronic echo on the master. He also testified that it couldn't even be an echo created within a chamber because they did not have an echo chamber at that recording studio.

The only problem with that was is that we had a little cassette tape that did not have any echo on it which proved, quote, scientifically that the -- that this tape was of a younger generation -- older generation than would be the, quote, master tape.

I hope that was understandable.

Q.   Yes. The outcome of the trial was in favor of RCA?

A.   Yes.

Q.   Did you poll the jury?

A.   Yes, and I believe it was unanimous.

Q.   Did they give you any reason for their findings?

A.   I spoke with several of the jurors after the trial was over with. All of the jurors seemed to be impressed with the fact that RCA brought in to testify numerous of the -- I say numerous. I think there were two individuals who had been with Elvis Presley's first band. These two individuals took the witness stand. They were now session musicians in Nashville.

They took the witness stand and testified that it was not -- they listened to it in front of the jury and said: That's not Elvis Presley; there's no question about it. And numerous of the jurors even when trial was over, you know, wanted to visit with these individuals because they had touched Elvis Presley, and so the indication that I got from the jurors is they felt, like that if anybody should know whether or not that song was or was not Elvis Presley, it should be the individuals that played with him during the mid 1950s.

Q.   But these people were musicians, not voice experts, right?

A.   That's right. That's right.

Q.   On losing the trial, you filed a motion for new trial?

A.   Yes.

Q.   Was there -- it was denied?

A.   Yes.

Q.   What was the reason?

A.   Reason for the denial?

Q.   Yeah.

A.   I don't know that any particular reason was stated by Judge Leftwich other than to deny the motion for a new trial.

Q.   Okay. Would you explain the appeal -- let me ask you another question before. You mentioned before there were two other defendants. Did they attempt to perfect an appeal?

A.   Yes. We filed -- the motion for new trial was filed on behalf of all parties defendant. I believe, if I'm correct, that both myself, law firm of Gregory & Gregory, and Dennis Brewer's law firm out of Irving jointly filed a motion for new trial, so you know they -- they actually participated in the filing, also.

Q.   Did they file an appeal?

A.   No.

Q.   So you and Jackson attempted to appeal, right?

A.   Yes, if I can explain.

Q.   Yes, please do.

A.   What occurred in connection with the appeal was that I think my law firm -- my law firm had already spent in the course of some forty-five days, memory tells me, somewhere in the approximate neighborhood of fifteen thousand dollars in expenses. It could have been several thousand more. It could have been a few thousand less, but I know the expense was in excess of, say, twelve thousand. It could have been as much as eighteen, nineteen thousand.

At that point in time, I was unwilling, due to the length of the trial and the anticipated cost from the court reporter -- we got an estimate from the court reporter as to what the cost, of appeal would be. I was unwilling to expend any further funds in connection with the thing due to the limited amount that our firm was to receive on the percentage of revenues generated.

I attempted to locate other individuals that would take a small percentage of any future revenues in connection with contributing -- I believe fifty thousand dollars is what they were going to contribute towards expenses on appeal and then expenses in connection with a retrial of the lawsuit.

Mr. Jackson had -- had just a small percentage, so he was unable to really give up too much. He indicated a willingness to give up some at that time. I tried to get Mr. Falco and Mr. Reese and the law firm of Dennis Brewer to give up some percentages where I could try to raise some revenues to take care of the cost of appeal, could not get an agreement made because Mr. Reese and Mr. Falco were unwilling and thought that they would ultimately get me to pay the cost of appeal. I was unwilling to do so whenever it became apparent to me that there were no funds available and what small percentage that Mr. Jackson had was not sufficient to go out and peddle and generate enough funds to be able to finance the appeal.

I either spoke with Andrew on the phone or I sent him a letter or something indicating to him that his only option then would be to file a pauper's affidavit and, in fact, prepared some pauper's affidavits and the necessary materials, sent it to him down in the penitentiary to complete, sign and all, and get back to me for filing, and my memory tells me that it didn't get back in time to do the filing.

Whenever it did get there, it was filed, but I think it was summarily denied by Judge Leftwich possibly because it was lately filed or whatever. I know there was objections filed by both the court reporter and the defendants and everything else in connection with that pauper's affidavit.

Q.   So you didn't actually prepare any appeal papers.

A.   The only thing I indicated to -- no, I did not. I did not -- by "appeal papers," what are you speaking of? Now, the notice of appeal, you know, all the predicate steps were laid with the exception of securing the record and, you know, getting the court reporter to prepare all the papers.

Q.   Yeah.

A.   Everything was done up to the point in time where that the -- you know, the appeal bond or the cost bond, you know, to take care of the transcript and the statement of facts, whenever it came time to post the necessary security to get those things done, it became apparent that Mr. Jackson, himself being in the penitentiary, could not -- had no funds nor any means through which they could be, you know, that could be posted. I attempted an investigation in connection with what he had to determine whether in fact he was indigent.

Q.   Other than the judicial errors which you have already related, what would your appeal have been based on?

A.   Well, I think -- you know, I think I've already outlined for you the primary four points. Fifth point if you talk about, you know, there would be a direct relationship to examining a witness that takes on the witness stand and being able to preserve error during the trial by being able to object. That would be five fundamental points. There were some additional points I'm sure that would have been brought up. Primarily, you know, fundamental unfairness during the trial.

One other point comes to mind now that set here and talk about it. You know, there was some evidence that was primarily evidence that Judge Leftwich let come in during the trial. It related to the rule against piling an inference on an inference -- let me finish my question.

Q.   I'm sorry.

A.   What -- in fact, it was some of these early band members that had been playing with Elvis Presley, during the temporary hearing without objection, had been allowed to testify that, quote, normally, whenever they were traveling around with Elvis Presley on his tours and during his early days, whenever they started to enter a town, Elvis Presley always mentioned whether or not he had been there before, and, quote, since Mr. Presley had never mentioned being in Phoenix before whenever they went to Phoenix some years after this recording was allegedly recorded, that meant he had never been there before; but that is absurdly inadmissible because it does involve piling an inference upon an inference, and, you know, I think I had briefs prepared and everything in connection with that submitted to the judge indicating that it was, quote, not only piling an inference on an inference, it also constituted a rank hearsay.

So that would be possibly the only other point that I can think of. I'm sure probably the brief itself would have contained as high as twenty points of error in connection with the appeal because the trial was riddled with error by the trial court.

Q.   What were your chances of winning on appeal based on your professional experience?

A.   Nothing is ever a hundred percent. Okay? I've been involved in -- I've tried many, many cases, some large, some small, over fifteen years of practice almost, and I cannot remember a case that I've ever had in the past -- some of them have been reversed, both -- I've tried cases in-- in or been involved -- I can't say tried. I appealed a case out of Judge Mahon's court, federal court in Fort Worth, that was reversed.

Comparing this case -- the points of error in this case to that case where it was reversed by the Fifth Circuit, hands down, this case would have been reversed any time before that one. Of all the cases that I can remember ever being involved in trying, I think the chances of getting a reversal for appeal were stronger in this case than any case I ever was involved in on appeal.

Q.   Was there ever any money -- money amounts attached to Jackson's loss?

A.   You'll have to rephrase or repeat because I don't understand your question.

Q.   Did Jackson --

MR. NELSON: Can we take about a five-minute break?

MR. BEVANS: Yeah.

(Recess held.)

Q.   (By MR. BEVANS) Earlier, you talked about percentages of what you would get out. What are we talking about dollar figure as a possible loss in losing the -- in losing the lawsuit and losing the appeal? What dollar amount would you place on that loss?

A.   We visited at that time whenever I was in negotiations prior to agreeing to represent Mr. Jackson. We contacted -- and I say we. I can't tell who it was, whether it was me or someone else, contacted some individuals to find out what the potential was for in particular recording to see what type of revenues it would generate. I cannot remember the specifics, but I know that I felt like the percentage that our firm was getting, you know, I'm just sorry. For the life of me, I cannot tell you what that percentage was or what percentage our firm was going to get off the thing. I know our percentage was somewhere -- I can't -- under oath, I couldn't swear what the percentage was or even --

MR. NELSON: Establish a dollar figure of the loss?

A.   give you a range, but I know as far as our percentage was concerned, it was approximately the same amount that Mr. Jackson had. Okay? We may have had -- well, I think we had a few points more than Mr. Jackson had as a matter of fact, but based on our evaluation of the situation, it would have been worth several hundred thousand dollars, you know, seems to me like three or four hundred thousand that we thought we would receive, minimum, in terms of revenues generated in connection with sale of the record.

Then we had the sale of the, quote, sheet music that was attached to it that we felt like we would make, you know, thousands of dollars on. That number I can't tell you. I don't know whether we were talking about our part ten thousand or our part fifty thousand.

And then there was also revenues that we thought we would create in connection with trying to, you know, do a movie rights or whatever, because if in fact it had turned out that the thing was Elvis Presley and all, this -- Mr. Falco was a very lovable individual that we thought could be presented, and all of that was all tied together into the agreement where that we would receive revenues in connection with sale of the record, in connection with sale of any sheet music, in connection with the sale of any type of spin-off advertisements in connection with that and also in connection with the movie rights or any type of books that were sold or anything else on this particular incident that occurred in 1954, '53, whenever it was. I felt total that my firm potentially could have received seven, eight hundred thousand in connection with it, but that was to be real -- you know, that was hopes.

Q.   (By MR. BEVANS)   You felt that Jackson was a good businessman.

A.   I never did develop an opinion about that.

Q.   I mean the whole deal had potential.

A.   Well, I don't think Mr. Jackson -- I don't think Mr. Jackson was in control as far as business is concerned. Mr. Jackson would not have been in control. If the lawsuit had been successful, Mr. Jackson would not -- he would merely participate in a share of the revenues, and I'm sure out of those revenues the expenses would have been deducted, but Mr. Jackson would have had a voice in what was done, but he would not have been in control, but whether or not he was a good businessman or not, I don't know.

MR. BEVANS: I have nothing further at this time.

EXAMINATION BY MR. NELSON:

Q.   Mr. Gregory, my name is Tony Nelson, and I represent the defendants in this case. The defendants who are left in this case are Jack Garner, and I believe -- lost my list of all the rest of my defendants, but I believe Jack Garner and two other employees or former employees of the TDC, Mr. Brinkman and a Mr. Gomez. I believe those are the three remaining defendants. I'm going to probably skip around a bit, so forgive me if I do.

The first question I have for you, Mr. Gregory is on what date, if you recall, did you receive -- well, let me ask you this. Did you ever receive a package from Mr. Jackson containing his pauper's affidavit to be filed?

A.   Do you want to repeat your question? Are you saying what date, or are you asking --

Q.   I changed the question. Did you ever receive a correspondence or a package from Mr. Jackson containing his pauper's affidavit to be filed for the appeal of the Presley Versus Jackson litigation?

A.   The main thing I can tell you is my best memory tells me that I did receive some affidavit, but they were late. Okay. In other words, it was not in a timely fashion, but --

Q.   So you do recall having received it, though. The answer to the question of do you recall having received it is yes?

A.   I think that's correct, yes.

Q.   Okay. Do you recall the date on which you received that?

A.   No, I do not, other than I can put it in terms of a reference point. I know that during that period of time, our -- you know, our appellate time tables had changed, but I know that the date that I did receive something back from him which I had prepared and sent to him, it was late as far as the date when the pauper's affidavit was supposed to be filed under the rules.

Q.   All right, sir. Do you recall how many days late it was, or approximately?

A.   No, I don't. I'm sorry. I mean, it was more than a day or two. It could have been -- I would say it could have been five days; it could have been two weeks. Okay. That's the best I can do for you.

Q.   All right, sir. Do you recall how many pages were in that document that was sent back to you?

A.   No, sir. I'm sorry. I don't.

Q.   Do you have a rough estimate, sir?

A.   No.

Q.   From your knowledge of what was required to be filed at that time -- well, strike that.

Do you recall if the documents that you received back contained more than the pauper's affidavit that was required to be filed with The Court?

A.   I'm sorry. I don't know that, either. I know that there could have been numerous documents, all of which were prepared so that they would satisfy the particular steps in connection with the -- the appeal. Had it been in fact granted, the pauper's affidavit granted, I don't think that it necessarily -- the paperwork would necessarily have tied Mr. Andrew Lee Jackson to me as his attorney on appeal, so there could have been numerous other documents pro se prepared.

Q.   What is your recollection, sir, of what was required in 1979 to perfect appeal by way of pauper's affidavit? What is your recollection?

A.   That fact I cannot -- you know -- you know, the only way I could answer that question would be to look at the particular rules. I don't have any of that stuff committed to memory.

Q.   Would you --

A.   I know there has to be a pauper's oath in essence indicating that you do not have sufficient funds to -- to, you know, pay the cost on appeal.

Q.   All right, sir. And that document still does exist more or less in the present form today; is that correct?

A.   I think there is still a pauper's affidavit, yes.

Q.   And the pauper's affidavit, at least in its present form, is only a one- or two-page document; is that correct?

A.   Sir, primarily, you know, I don't -- well, you know, I think that would depend upon the particular individual that drafted the particular affidavit.

Q.   All right, sir. Would you agree with me that, generally, all that is necessitated is a very basic statement that sets forth that this individual is indigent and unable to pay the costs of perfecting appeal?

A.   I'd say basically that is the particular -- that is the substance of the contents. There may very well be other requirements as far as the contents of the particular affidavit, and it's been my practice whenever I prepare such an affidavit to get the specific rule down and look at the specific rule and prepare the affidavit, or whatever, strictly in accordance with the rule.

Q.   All ·right, sir. And you did in this case prepare the affidavit for Mr. Jackson to complete?

A.   My memory tells me that I did prepare the affidavit, or it could have been contained within the contents of my letter. I told him what type of an affidavit had to be prepared. You know, I can't answer you honestly one way or the other. I know that either a letter or something was sent to Mr. Jackson communicating to him what he was required to do because I knew at that point that it appeared as if that we would not be able to come up with sufficient funds to be able to perfect the appeal --

Q.   All right, sir.

A.   -- as far as cost on appeal. So whether or not I prepared the instrument, sent it to him, or sent him a letter that had included within it the document, I would think that my practice probably would be to prepare the necessary paperwork and send it to him, but I can't tell you honestly at this point in time whether I did or didn't.

Q.   All right, sir. But you would say that that would be your general practice or would have been your general practice at that time?

A.   I think so yes.

Q.   Is it fair to say, also, that it would have been your general practice not to have prepared a document that contained unnecessary or superfluous information, in other words, that you would have probably just prepared a basic affidavit that would have contained what was required under the statute? If I understood your earlier testimony, you would have prepared a document that met the statutory requirements, and pretty much that would be it. Is that a fair statement?

A.   I believe that's a fair statement, yes, sir.

Q.   All right, sir. And, again, and I don't mean to be redundant, but is there anything in your recollection of what the statute required at that time regarding a pauper's affidavit that would indicate to you that such a document would be a lengthy document, in other words, in excess of five or six pages?

A.   I can't answer that question unless I had the specific rule in front of me.

Q.   All right, sir.

MR. NELSON: We can go off the record for just a second.

(Discussion held off the record.)

MR. NELSON: I'm going to --

THE WITNESS: You got a copy of the rule?

MR. NELSON: Yes, sir.

THE WITNESS: Okay. Off the record.

(Discussion held off the record.)

Q.   (By MR. NELSON) Mr. Gregory, I'm handing you what I've marked as Defendant's Exhibit Number 1 for purposes of this deposition, and I'm going to represent to you that that's a copy of the 1979 Texas Rules of Civil Procedure and specific a copy of Texas Rules of Civil Procedure Number 355, and, if you will, read that rule, and I think you will agree with me that that specific rule covers filing of an affidavit in lieu of cost bond; is that correct?

(Witness reviews document.)

THE WITNESS: Either read the question back or repeat it, one of the two.

MR. NELSON: I'll just let the reporter read the question back, if you don't mind.

(Record read back.)

A.   That's what the rule provides, sir.

Q.   (By MR. NELSON) Okay, sir. Have you had the opportunity now to read the rule?

A.   Yes.

Q.   Okay, sir. Would you agree with me that there is nothing in that rule that would require a lengthy affidavit to be filed by an individual who was filing an affidavit in lieu of cost bond?

A.   As far as the particular affidavit itself, without consideration to other documents that have to be filed in connection with an appeal, the answer to your question is yes, I agree.

Q.   Okay, sir. So you would agree with me that the actual

affidavit -- and I'm only speaking and addressing the affidavit itself by the requirements of the rule that was in effect at that time. Assuming that what I have given you is an accurate representation of that rule, an accurate copy of that rule, there's nothing in that rule that requires any sort of a lengthy document to be filed with The Court; is that correct?

A.   In order to perfect the appeal?

Q.   Yes, sir.

A.   In order to perfect the appeal, there are numerous other documents that have to be prepared.

Q.   I understand there's numerous other documents, but we're specifically only addressing the affidavit, the requirement of the affidavit in lieu of cost bond.

A.   Okay. As far as the affidavit itself, without consideration for the other documents that have to be filed --

Q.   Yes, sir.

A.   -- at or about the same time, the affidavit itself could be a single-page instrument, yes.

Q.   All right, sir. Thank you very much. Now I'm going to hand you what I'm going to mark for purposes of this deposition as Defendant's Exhibit 2, and I will represent to you that I've handed you a copy of the 1979 version of Rule 356, excuse me, of the Texas Rules of Civil Procedure; is that correct?

A.   Correct.

Q.   And that rule sets out the time limits -- I'm not referring to the rule by its limits proper name, but it sets out the time limits for filing of appeal and perfecting appeal; is that correct?

A.   Appears to.

Q.   Okay. And, if you will, read that over, briefly, or take as much time as you need to, but just read it over, sir.

(Witness reviews document.)

A.   All right.

Q.   (By MR. NELSON) All right, sir. Would you agree with me -- what is the time frame that's set out under the rule for filing of affidavit in lieu of cost bond?

A.   Pauper's affidavit, twenty days after rendition of the judgment or order overruling motion for new trial.

Q.   All right, sir. Thank you.

A.   Or after the motion for new trial overruled by operation of law.

Q.   By operation of law. All right, sir.

MR. NELSON: If there are no objections, I'll

move at this time to have those two exhibits attached to the deposition.

MR. BEVANS: Fine.

MR. NELSON: All right, sir.

Q. (By MR. NELSON) Now, I believe it was your testimony that you don't have any recollection of when you received the affidavit from Mr. Jackson other than it was late; is that correct?

A. I recall that it was beyond the time limits within which it was supposed to be filed --

Q. All right, sir.

A. -- under the rules.

Q. Okay. Same rules that we just were making reference to; is that correct?

A. Assuming those to be the rules in effect at that time, that's correct.

Q. All right, sir. Do you have any recollection of when you, either through telephone conversation or written correspondence, contacted Mr. Jackson to inform him of what he needed to do to assist in perfecting the appeal?

A. The only way I can answer that is in terms of sequence of events that occurred. Okay?

Q. All right. That's fine.

A. All right. The judgment was ultimately signed, and even prior to that date, it became apparent that we would need to appeal this particular case, and I felt like there were grounds to appeal; and immediately after the verdict, I started trying to work towards trying to generate some funds and, in fact, before Mr. Jackson ever went back to the penitentiary, had a meeting with him, discussed with him whether or not he had anything that he could use to pay that I could sell or I could do anything with to get the appeal -- get the necessary funds raised for the appeal.

When it became apparent that I could not do that, then I started working towards trying to get the individuals Mr. Falco, Mr. Reese, and Mr. Brewer's office and everybody else involved in trying to see what we could do to generate the funds. Neither Mr. Falco nor Mr. Reese indicated that they had – that they had any funds, so and, and of course, at that point in time, we had like -- I think the rules used to provide that your first motion had to be filed within ten days, and then you could file an amended motion within thirty days or something like this. But there was an actual hearing on the motion for new trial toward the latter stages of when you could have the hearing before it was overruled by operation of law.

Q. Let me stop you.

A. We had the hearing. Now, --

Q.   Okay.

A.   -- it didn't take over, say, two to three weeks, maybe thirty days at the most for it to be determined that no one had funds. All right?

Q.   If I could, I would like to interrupt you, if you will, and I'll let you get right back. I wanted to make sure I'm clear on a point.

A.   Okay.

Q.   The hearing for a motion on new trial took place before the motion was overruled?

A.   By operation of law.

Q.   By operation of law?

A.   I believe that's correct, --

Q.   Do you recall --

A.   -- and I could be --

Q.   -- about the time frame?

A.   (Witness shakes head.)

Q.   All right, sir. I'm sorry for interrupting you.

A.   Seems like we did have a hearing because one of the points there was something about some – you know, I know I spoke with numerous of the jurors to find out whether or not there was any juror misconduct in connection with the thing.

Q.   All right, sir.

A.   We secured some affidavits from certain of the jurors concerning certain conduct. I don't know that that was strong enough. There was a question concerning whether or not what occurred -- which I can't remember right now -- was or was not reversible error in connection with that. I hope I'm not getting that point confused with another case. But there was a hearing, and we tried to place one of the jurors on the witness stand to testify concerning what activity went on during the jury room, during their deliberations.

Q.   All right, sir. You can continue, if you remember your train of thought, on the rest of your response if you wish.

A.   Okay. Trying to shortly state the response, it became apparent within I would say even before the hearing on the motion for new trial that it was going to be difficult to raise the funds, and none of the parties nor, for the small percentage that I was getting, was I willing. I even tried myself to get these – Mr. Falco and Mr. Reese and Mr. Brewer's firm to give up some of the percentage points that they had. If they would given my firm the percentage points, my firm would have paid the cost of appeal in order to appeal the case. That would not be done. Then that's where the fifty thousand came in.

I said: Okay. Then if you won't do that for me in exchange for my firm taking care of the cost appeal, give me --- seems to me like I was saying five percent. Give me five percent and let me go out here because I've got an individual that will pay fifty thousand dollars for five percent of the future revenues, and in turn, I will use that fifty thousand to finance the appeal and also give us some funds where we can try a better case the second time around. I would say probably at least two weeks, possibly three to four weeks would have been the date when I sent to Mr. Jackson the necessary paperwork so he could get a pauper --

Q.   I'm sorry. Two weeks prior to what?

A.   The deadline for when it was to be posted.

Q.   All right, sir.

A.   I would say in the neighborhood of, well, I think I could definitely say not less than seven days.

Q.   All right, sir.

A.   Okay. Not less than seven days. He had it at least seven days prior to the date when it was due to be filed in the court. Could have been as much as fourteen days.

Q.   All right, sir.

MR. NELSON: Now, Mr. Bevans, I believe you have agreed that you will produce, along with a number of other exhibits that have been -- all the other exhibits that have been listed in the pretrial order, Exhibits A through R, that you will provide to defendants within the next day or so.

MR. BEVANS: (Nods head.)

MR NELSON: And included amongst those is a letter which is purported to be from Mr. Gregory dated 7-10-79; is that right?

MR. BEVANS: That's in the time frame.

Q.   (By MR. NELSON) Mr. Gregory, would you say that it was foreseeable to you prior to the motion for new trial being overruled by operation of law that it was either going to be denied by The Court or just not ruled on by The Court? In other words was it foreseeable to you that you weren't going to prevail on your motion for new trial?

A.   Oh, yeah. I think that we knew that the probabilities were that we were not going to prevail --

Q.   Fairly early on?

A.   -- on motion for new trial. Well, I don't know what you mean by fairly early on.

Q.   Well, let's say more than thirty days prior to the ninety days that you have before it's overruled by operation of law.

A.   Well, you always hope as an attorney that you can convince a trial judge that he made a mistake.

Q.   Understood.

A.   Okay. And, you know, I don't know if there was no order entered overruling the motion for new trial. My memory tells me we still had an order. Now, it may have been an order was not signed; therefore, it was overruled by operation of law since there was no order entered even though we had the hearing.

Q.   Is your recollection of that hearing that it was a favorable one for you, that the judge was leaning in your direction, or do you have any recollection in that regard?

A.   I don't remember. I think the primary reason why we had -- you know wanted to make sure we had the hearing is because we had the potential juror misconduct in the trial. Now, I really don't recall that that -- that that -- that particular point would have been a strong one on appeal.

Q.   All right, sir.

A.   So it was primarily a function of us just wanting to make sure that we preserved that as another appellate point.

Q.   All right. As I just said, Mr. Bevans has marked as an exhibit in his pretrial order a letter from you on the 10th.

A.   On the 10th of?

Q.   July.

A.   Okay.

Q.   1979.

A.   To Mr. Jackson.

Q.   Do you have any reason to dispute that that is when you would have written him and that is the manner in which you contacted Mr. Jackson?

A.   You know, I can't say that -- you know, I know Mr. Jackson had a girlfriend that I was also communicating with. At that time, she would come by the office. She was making trips down to the penitentiary to see Mr. Jackson. I don't recall her name, but whether or not it was mailed to him or given to her to hand deliver to him or whether or not there had been any other materials sent him before that date, I don't know unless I looked at the file, but if there's a date on the letter, I'm not going to argue with the date because I don't ever recall an instance whenever I dated a letter other than a date it was mailed.

Q.   All right, sir. And if I were to represent to you that the file in this case indicates that the motion for new trial was overruled by operation of law on June 29th, 1979, do you have any reason to dispute that?

A.   No reason to dispute it if that's what the record reflects.

Q.   All right, sir. And I'm going to show you what I'm going to mark as Defendant's Exhibit 3 for purposes of this deposition, which is copy of the complaint filed by Mr. Jackson in this cause that we're here on today, TY-79-416, and I'm going to refer you to page number four of that complaint and paragraph two.

A.   Paragraph two?

Q.   Yes, sir. Second full paragraph and ask you to read that.

          (Witness reviews document.)

A.   Okay.

Q.   (By MR. NELSON) All right, sir. And you'll agree – I'll let you pass it to Mr. Bevans. He might want to examine it after you're done. You'll agree with me that there in the complaint, Mr. Jackson represents that as of July 6th of 1979, I believe it is, that he had not had any contact with -- he doesn't name you, but he says he had not had any contact with the attorney who represented his interests, and that is yourself; is that not correct?

A.   What's your question? Repeat the question, please.

Q.   My question is -- let me break it down.

A.   I don't know that I necessarily agree.

Q.   I had a compound interest -- compound question here.

          You were the attorney who represented Mr. Jackson's interest in the Presley Versus Jackson lawsuit; is that correct?

A.   As far as I know and believe, yes.

Q.   And you were the only attorney who represented his interests in that lawsuit; is that correct?

A.   As far as I know and believe, yes.

Q.   Now, that paragraph -- in that paragraph of the complaint, Mr. Jackson indicates that as of, I believe, on or about July 6th, 1979, he had not had any contact with the attorney who represented his interests in this lawsuit or anyone else. Is that what the paragraph states?

A.   The paragraph states what it states.

Q.   Okay. But you would agree with me that's a rough paraphrase of what the paragraph represents?

A.   The paragraph states: Because I was not at the hearing on Defendants' motion for new trial, I don't know when said motion was filed and I was not notified of any proceedings or the status of said cause by the attorney that represented my interest, or anyone else.

Q.   Okay?

A.   Now, finally, I wrote to one of the other defendants on or about July 6th and asked him to please request attorney Joe Gregory to bring me up to date concerning said cause.

          Now, that's what it says plus two other sentences.

Q.   Okay, sir. Would you say the representations made there within Defendant's Exhibit 3 are untrue?

A.   I don't know. You know, because I don't know after -- after we had the you know, there would -- there would have been no particular reason other than trying to communicate and indicate to Mr. Jackson, like I say, some seven days to two weeks prior to the time when the pauper's affidavit was required to be filed that I made Mr. Jackson aware of the fact that it was going to be necessary to get it filed because we couldn't get the funds generated nor would anybody give up the interest in order to do it.

Q.   Yes, sir.

A.   Now, as to whether or not prior to that date I had stayed in daily contact with Mr. Jackson, I would say no, I didn't.

Q.   Okay, sir.

A.   Whether or not I sent him letters or copies of letters and stuff like this, I don't remember.

Q.   All right, sir. And you said you had no reason to dispute the July 10th dating of the letter to Mr. Jackson. Now, I'm sorry --

A.   If the letter is dated July 10th, I'm sure -- and it's on my letterhead, it was probably sent out July the 10th or --

Q.   I haven't seen the letter --

A.   -- or given to his girlfriend to carry it down.

Q.   I have not seen the letter, sir. Mr. Bevans is going to provide that to us. And that letter -- and it's been represented to me that that letter was the document that informed Mr. Jackson of his need to file a pauper's affidavit with The Court by July 19th of 1979. If that letter does in fact state that when it's produced to me by Mr. Bevans, do you have any reason to dispute that that was the content of that letter?

A.   I can't answer that.

Q.   I know it's a bit unfair to you because I don't have the letter to produce. I apologize.

A.   The letter says what it says. Now, if the question is whether or not that was the contact where I informed him that he had to file the affidavit, I can't swear to you that. I know that I was -- his little girlfriend was coming by talking to us, okay, and she was going down and seeing Andrew as often as she could go see him, and I'm sure I was communicating with her in connection with what -- what was going on --

Q.   All right, sir.

A.   -- through phone calls, and right now, I couldn't tell you whether or not I ever got a phone call from Andrew. I know I received a phone call at some time in the past from Andrew Jackson --

Q.   Okay, sir.

A.   -- while he's been at the penitentiary. Whether or not it was during that time frame or some other time frame, I don't know.

Q.   All right. Let me pose you a hypothetical question. If under Rule 356, as I handed to you Defendant's Exhibit 2 of the Rules of Civil Procedure -- Texas Rules of Civil Procedure that were -- excuse me, that were in effect in 1979, an individual had twenty days within which to file his pauper's affidavit in lieu of cost bond, --

A.   Uh-huh.

Q.   -- would you agree with me that not knowing that he had twenty days to file it well, strike that.

If an individual has twenty days to file a cost bond under the applicable Rules of Civil Procedure and does not know of that deadline or have knowledge of that deadline until after the elapse of ten days of that twenty-day period, would you agree with me that that could hamper or interfere with his ability to perfect his appeal within the time prescribed by the rules? question clear enough?

A.   I think the only thing you did is you said cost bond, and you meant to say affidavit.

Q.   I'm sorry, affidavit in lieu of cost.

A.   You know, if the – you know, assuming a reasonable period of time within which the mail goes, you know, I mail stuff from here and to – and it's to all over the country the next day. I can't even tell you in this particular instance whether or not on that particular occasion the letter was not hand delivered by the girlfriend. I don't know. I don't know whether it would have been hand delivered or mailed, but assuming a reasonable period of being transported and assuming that the affidavit is just merely a single page type affidavit, there should be no problem whatsoever in getting an affidavit back within nine days and getting it filed.

Q.   All right, sir. But you would agree with me that it would put more time pressure, would make it a more time-pressured situation, would you not?

A.   Well, in my practice, I think about time pressure as being whenever I have something here that I need from -- from another state to be filed within two or three days, and if that's true, then I usually use Federal Express or Fax --

Q.   All right, sir.

A.   -- to get it done.

Q.   You were --

A.   If you calculate three days at the most from the 10th, okay, that's 11th, 12th, 13th. He gets it the 13th. He turns around and mails it' back to me even the 15th or 16th. I get it the 19th and file it.

Q.   All right, sir.

A.   You know there's two days there that are completely gone if it takes three days, and to my memory, back during that period of time, you know, three days -- three days under our Rules of Civil Procedure were in effect at that time. If you send somebody a notice, then it's going to be presumed by the law that they get it in three days, the third day.

Q.   All right, sir.

A.   So if it was mailed the 10th, then it should have been to Mr. Jackson the 13th, and if Mr. Jackson could have waited until the 16th, one, two, three days or longer to get it back, . . .

Q.   Okay, sir. You were aware of when this affidavit was due in court, correct?

A.   At that time, I'm sure I was. At this time right now, of my own independent recollection, I don't know.

Q.   You don't have independent recollection today of what that date was, but --

A.   No, sir.

Q.   -- at that time, you were aware; is that correct?

A. Yes, sir, I'm sure I was.

Q.   Is it a fair statement to say that you would have been awaiting a response from Mr. Jackson on this case?

A.   Well, I can tell you like this. I know that at that point in time based on what I had already expended in funds in connection with the trial in bringing witnesses from Michigan and all over the country and bringing other expert witnesses, I wasn't going to spend any more money unless they gave me more interest in connection with the lawsuit.

So in terms of waiting, you know, once I got -- once I got to the point where that I knew that I was not going to put in any further funds or anything in connection with the interest and was not going to pay the cost of appeal, as far as I was concerned, had Mr. Jackson gotten back the pauper's affidavit and it would have been timely filed and assuming Judge Leftwich would not have overruled it and denied it to him, then Mr. Jackson would have been free to retain any attorney, so I don't know what you mean by your question is it fair to say I was waiting.

I don't know that you can say I was waiting or not. As far as I knew, Mr.. Jackson could have went to another attorney and got it back. I think I probably indicated to him that if he would get it back to me, I would file it or he could file it directly with The Court, either one.

Q.   All right. Well, was there anything from your experience with Mr. Jackson at that point with this litigation in the Presley Versus Jackson lawsuit that indicated to you that he wasn't serious about this case?

A.   No, there wasn't anything. He was totally serious about it.

Q.   1 mean, it would be fair to say that he was committed to the case; is that correct?

A.   Sure, sure.

Q.   And also fair to say that from that, you expected him to get it back to you, probably.

A.   Well, you know, I don't know unless I looked at the contents of the letter.

Q.   All right.

A.   Now, I don't know whether -- you know, memory seems to tell me that not only had his girlfriend been talking to him, it's possible that Mr. Reese or Mr. Falco had went down to the penitentiary and talked to him during that time frame, too. But my belief was that all of the parties defendant wanted me to appeal the case as opposed to Mr. Brewer's office or any other attorney. They wanted me to handle the case from that point forward. The particular problem was they couldn't get Mr. Brewer's office to shake loose any of the percentage that they had.

Q.   All right, sir. Now, again, I apologize to you that I can't present you with the letter, but I don't have it to present to you at this point. If I represented to you -- and Mr. Bevans can correct me if I'm wrong about the content of the letter -- that the letter informed Mr. Jackson that if he would get it back to you by the 19th, it would be filed --

A.   Uh-huh.

Q.   -- if the letter did state that, then would it be fair to say in light of what you knew about Mr. Jackson's commitment to this action that you expected a response from him or would have expected a response from him?

A.   I'm sure that's correct.

Q.   Okay. Was there anything that indicated to you that he was unhappy with your representation in the seeking representation by another attorney?

A.   Not that I'm aware of.

Q.   So as far as you knew, he was satisfied with your representation?

A.   As far as I know and believe.

Q.   And if you were willing to, he would have certainly been agreeable to your representing him?

A.   I think that's correct.

Q.   Okay, sir. Now, I believe early on you testified that this whole file was destroyed. Can you be more specific --

A.   Well,--

Q.   -- regarding that?

A.   Well, you know, currently in my office I probably have four hundred active files, somewhere between four and five hundred active files. I have a thriving practice where I close several hundred files each year some of which are long enough to stack from here to that wall, and after a period of six years, a file -- it is our business practice to go through those particular files, pullout ones like probate -- will files are kept in a separate place -- but files like that are pulled and destroyed.

Q.   Okay, sir.

A.   And so in this particular case, I can't tell you the particular date that it was done, but I know sometime, you know, it seems to me even after I received correspondence from Mr. Jackson indicating -- I didn't know this lawsuit was going on, this one, and I received a letter to requesting that I prepare some kind of affidavit or something.

Q.   All right, sir.

A.   And I think the file was even gone at that point in time, or I couldn't find it at that point in time, one of the two, but I have searched, and I can't find it now. It's gone.

Q.   And -- well, will -- let me ask you two questions. So you don't believe that you varied from your practice of, give or take a couple of months or a year, maybe, that you destroyed this file six years or so after the case was tried and completed.

A.   Well, it's usually six years from the date the file was closed. Our practice is -- we have computers, and our practice is to put all of our closed files on computer so we can find the particular file number. They're numbered sequentially. Number one file was closed back in 1974, and then at some point in time, I know we started our numbering system again, but they're just stacked in one right after another, and annually, based on the closing date of that particular file, they are disposed of.

And the way our closed file systems work, we have some identify we have the name of the client, some identifier on it that indicates what type file it was where we do not have to go back in and look at each file to say no, I don't want to dispose of this one; pull this one out.

Q.   All right, sir. Would your computer file indicate as to when the Jackson -- Presley Versus Jackson file was closed?

A.   I don't think so.

Q.   Did you not have computer at that time or --

A.   Well, we got --

Q.   -- what would be the reason? Why do you think that your computer file would not indicate --

A.   Number one, we got a new computer system that we did not transfer a lot of the records in connection with it. Now we have a networked system. The other filing system at one time was on a card system where everything was alphabetized. Some of those files went into the computer, were put on the computer. I guess I could check to determine with the most recent listing we have. After so many years, you don't keep printing out, okay, a hard copy of what's on the computer.

Q.   Uh-huh.

A.   Usually, the hard copy of what is printed is files that we have still in our closed files.

Q.   All right, sir.

A.   In other words, the past six years worth of files, all right?

Q.   All right, sir.

A.   They're all printed and alphabetized so we can go directly to the name of the client, then go the file and close file and retrieve it.

Q.   Okay, sir.

A.   And as to all files that have been destroyed, usually the computer records are deleted --

Q.   Okay, sir.

A.   -- because there's no sense in keeping a computer record of a file that's been destroyed that you don't have.

Q.   Okay, sir. If your computer file were to indicate when this case was closed, or -- well, strike that.

A.   Let me say it to you like this. I know as we sit here that the computer file will not reflect the particular date Andrew Lee Jackson's file was closed, the Presley matter, primarily because it is -- it is in excess of six years old. It was not the character or type of file that we would keep, and, therefore, it is not on the computer files, --

Q.   All right, sir.

A.   -- period. Now, what I thought was on occasion -- I know that Mr. Jackson's file was a very large file, all right, and seems to me like it was separately boxed, all right, in these file boxes that you get from the office supply. And I thought perhaps that it might have been kept, so I looked myself personally in some places around my home. I have a large storage building that was built back behind my home where I have some files in large boxes that I kept, and I went to those boxes because it is, and it's not there. There is nothing even on the computer that will reflect where it is.

Q.   All right, sir. Would you -- is there any record keeping mechanism or record whatsoever that you have possession, control, or custody of that would indicate when this file was closed?

A.   No, sir, I'm sorry, there is not.

Q.   All right, sir. probably obviates the need for the next question, but do you have any of the envelopes --

 A. (Witness shakes head.)

 Q. -- that you either sent documents to Mr. Jackson or received documents from Mr. Jackson?

 A. The only thing that I might possibly have would be something within -- within a general file that related to the affidavit that I -- that I sent to him.

 Q. All right, sir.

 A. I might have a letter that I received from him, but it's stuck in a general -- I've got a general file that's my JDG file, my initials, general file. But it would take probably to go through those darn things to find them, unless you could give me a --

 Q. Are you willing to agree to supply that to Mr. Bevans without the necessity of a subpoena?

 A. If you want to pay somebody to look through those files, I'll be more than happy to grant you access to them, sir, to look through those general files that, you know, contain -- and you can look to your heart's content.

 Q. All right. And without that, we would need to subpoena. Is that basically --

 A. What I'm saying is I'm willing to produce them for you in connection with producing all of those records, and you can look through them to see if you can find it. I don't even know that it's there.

 Q. All right, sir.

 A. Okay.

 Q. Okay. That's a fair response. As I said, I'm going to skip around.

     THE WITNESS: Let's go off the record a second.

     MR. NELSON: Okay.

     (Discussion held off the record.)

     (Recess held.)

     (Record read back.)

 Q. (By MR. NELSON) Mr. Gregory, you testified that there was interrogatories that were answered on behalf of Mr. Jackson in a timely fashion identifying Mr. -- Dr. Tosie, I believe as your expert witness; is that correct?

 A. Mine along with the other parties defendant, yes.

 Q. All right, sir. And that the judge excluded Dr. Tosie on the basis of, you said, no surprises, his conference in chambers, not transcribed conference in chambers where he said that there would be no surprises and excluded him on that basis.

A.   The statement was made that, quote -- we even tendered Dr. Tosie for their deposition, had arrangements for them to take his deposition on very short notice.

Q.   Was his deposition taken?

A.   They elected not to take his deposition. They elected to proceed with their motion. The judge's ruling was that during the -- after the temporary -- the hearing on the temporary injunction, he announced in chambers, gentlemen there will be no surprises. There had been no interrogatories served on any of the parties defendant up until that point in time that requested the names of their experts.

Q.   All right, sir.

A.   Then we got served with – there was a set sent, and the answers were timely filed.

Q.   All right, sir.

A.   And they claimed that it was too close to the trial date for them to prepare to rebut anything our expert said.

Q.   Had there been a pretrial order required by Judge Leftwich in this case?

A.   None.

Q.   That was a no?

A.   No, not to my knowledge.

Q.   Okay. So no pretrial was filed. Do you have any recollection of the testimony of Dr. Tosie being excluded on the basis that it lacked scientific reliability?

A.   No. Absolutely no.

Q.   So if – if Mr. Bryant were to – strike that.

So the sole basis, as you recall, for Dr. Tosie being excluded was this off-the-record, in-chambers conferences where the judge announced there would be no surprises and considered this evidently a surprise and excluded this testimony; --

A.   That's correct.

Q.   -- is that correct? Okay, sir. Now, you also spoke of the difference between the cassette and the master tape. The cassette, that was, I take it, copied from the master; is that correct?

A.   The cassette tape itself did not have echo.

Q.   I understand that.

A.   All right. Now, it -- now, who copied it, no one could say because the only thing that was known then, the supposed master that came from RCA had echo on it, that means it could not have been --

MR. NELSON: Let me interrupt you on this one and object as nonresponsive.

Q.   (By MR. NELSON) Was the cassette -- and I'll ask you, if you can, to answer this yes or no. Was the cassette copied from the master tape, the original master tape that you purport to be the original master?

A.   Could we go off the record for a minute, and then I can explain to you why I can't answer that?

MR. NELSON: Sure.

(Discussion held off the record.)

Q.   (By MR. NELSON) If you can answer yes or no, was the cassette that you spoke of earlier and testified about earlier copied from the original master tape or an authentic derivative thereof? Yes or no, if you can answer it.

A.   It had to be copied from -- yes.

Q.   Okay.

A.   Had to be.

Q.   Was that cassette ever introduced into evidence at the trial

A.   Yes.

Q.   -- in this cause?

A.   Yes.

Q.   Was it?

A.   It was.

Q.   Was it ever played for the jury?

A.   I'm sure it was, yes.

Q.   Okay. Were you --

A.   Let me -- let me back up and say this. I don't know -- the tape -- you know, the quality of the cassette tape itself was probably not as good as a more sophisticated recording tape. Okay? The prime importance about it was is that it had been checked through spectrographic analysis as well as through voice identification experts and individuals that were experts within the recording industry, and there was an indication that that cassette tape did not have echo on it; therefore, the cassette tape was copied from a tape that did not have echo. It could not have been a copy of the, quote, master RCA returned.

Q.   Now, I have limited knowledge of recording technology, but from my own experiences, will you agree with me that when you record from a recording of a recording of a recording of a recording and so forth, that with each subsequent recording, you lose sound quality?

A.   Depends on what you mean by sound quality. I know that you cannot record from a tape and erase sound from that tape because if you erase sound -- if you try to erase a sound, you're going to completely blank the tape, with technology that existed at that time. In other words, you can't take echo off a tape, period. You can't do it, or you couldn't do it at that time

226

I was made to understand and do believe.

Q.   Okay, sir. Now, but you did just state and I believe testified that the cassette that you believe to have been a derivation of the original master was played for the jury during the course of this trial.

A.   Whether or not the entire tape was played for them or not, I couldn't tell you other than whether excerpts were played or just small portions of it. I would think it probably was, but me telling you that I remember the specified instance of it being played, I do know the experts examined it.

Q.   Would you say, sir, that a sufficient I know portion of the tape was played for the jury to be able to make a judgment as to whether or not that was a tape of Elvis Presley? that yes or no.

A.   Well let me say to you like this. If -- just to answer your question, the significance of the tape -- the cassette tape would be of a lower quality, sound quality and everything else, than the master tape itself. Both of them, the voice of the singer sounded the same. Okay? So if you were going to just strictly from a layman's standpoint try to do it, you would want to use the master that had the echo on it. That's not the significant point of the existence of the tape.

Q.   Okay, sir.

A.   Theoretically, if the master tape that RCA introduced in evidence, if it was the --

MR. NELSON: I'm going to interrupt you and object as nonresponsive.

A.   Let me finish my response because I do believe it is responsive. Theoretically, if the master tape that they introduced was in fact the master, then it is a physical impossibility for the cassette tape to have existed because it couldn't exist.

MR. NELSON: I'm going to object as nonresponsive.

Q.   (By MR. 'NELSON) My question was: Was a sufficient portion of the cassette played to allow -- in your opinion to allow a jury to determine if the voice was that of Elvis Aaron Presley, yes or no?

A.   I don't know. I don't know.

Q.   All right. Thank you. But it was at least in part played during the course of the trial to the best that you recall?

A.   I would think that it would be, but I really can't answer the question whether it was or wasn't. If it was played, it wasn't played for the purpose of allowing the jury to try to determine who the singer was.

Q.   All right. Now Mr. Gregory, you said your out-of-pocket costs in this case were at least twelve thousand dollars?

A.   All I can do is give --

Q.   I understand, a ballpark.

A.   I even tried to look because our tax records, we keep them for six years, too, and then they're gone and destroyed.

Q.   Your estimate would be in the area of twelve thousand dollars?

A.   I would say twelve to eighteen.

Q.   All right. And I believe it was also your testimony that your firm's share, your firm's fee out of --

A.   We had a contingent interest.

Q.   On a contingent interest, I understand, would have been in the ballpark of eight hundred -- seven to eight hundred thousand dollars?

A.   You know, that's assuming that everything goes good. Okay? In other words, the song does -- they say that the song could easily sell two million records, okay, if it actually was identified to Elvis Presley, whether we could advertise it as such, figuring what the standard revenues were, whatever the percentage royalty was customary on a record like that, you know, calculating all that together, in point of fact, in this particular case the record had been stamped itself. There was not a recording, you know, any label like Sun or RCA or anybody that put it out, so, therefore, the -- the revenues generated in connection with the sale would have been larger than what was customary --

Q.   Right.

A.   because they were printing it themselves. Then there was some royalties that you could get in connection with sheet music, et cetera, et cetera.

Now, lumping all that together, I know that my thoughts and dreams at that time were that I could -- you know, that our law firm could wind up with the interest they had making in compensation of a half a million dollars. I know it was at least that much.

Q.   Okay. We'll accept that number, in excess of a half million dollars, and you would agree with me, would you not, that based on your business assessment of this venture, that that would be a conservative estimate; is that correct?

A.   Well, I don't know whether you can say conservative or liberal because I don't understand your question from that standpoint.

Q.   Well, not from a -- certainly not from a political standpoint. Conservative from the standpoint of a low-ball figure as to what you could reasonably expect, if everything went reasonably well with this venture, for your firm to collect as its contingency fee.

A.   It was a gamble is the only thing I can tell you. It was a gamble.

Now, I thought it was a -- at the time I initially got involved in the lawsuit, I thought it was a good gamble.

Q.   All right, sir.

A.   Especially in light of the fact that I was able to get an opinion of, quote, the foremost voice identification expert in this country that it was Elvis Presley.

Q.   All right, sir. In that you mentioned that, at one point you testified, I believe, that Dr. Tosie was ninety percent sure. Then you said Dr. Tosie was seventy to eighty percent sure.

A.   No, no. Dr. Tosie himself --

Q.   What percentage was his estimation of the --

A.   Okay.

Q.   -- identification?

A.   His, Dr. Tosie's, opinion was that he personally, based upon his analysis himself, was ninety percent sure. Now, at the same time, he had a computer analysis that was done. He also – he also had a test that is used in kidnapping cases, was used in kidnapping cases at that time, was used by Dr. Tosie whenever he testified whenever the Shah of Iran tapes were identified. Dr. Tosie was one of the expert witnesses in that case.

It is a comparative analysis by a group of individuals that are skilled within not only recording, but also speech therapists and things like this, where he had them do this, quote, empirical analysis, and that is where the seventy percent positive, thirty percent negative comes from in terms of whether or not that --

Q.   All right, sir.

A.   -- testing determined whether or not it was in fact Elvis Presley.

Q.   Okay.

A.   So to answer your question, Dr. Tosie did not say ninety and seventy. Dr. Tosie, based on the spectrographic analysis, his computer analysis, said he's ninety percent sure. The other testing that he did and the results of that testing came in at around seventy percent.

Q.   All right, sir. So depending on which test you use, there's a thirty to ten percent variance; is that correct?

A.   We presented the case in terms of Dr. Tosie based on then accepted procedures for identifying a speaker on a recording in kidnapping cases and other type cases. He testified that he was ninety percent sure. That was part of the bill. That was a bill itself.

MR. NELSON: All right. I'm going to object at this point as nonresponsive, and I'll ask the question again, and I'll ask you to answer it, if you can, as yes or no.

Based on what testing you used, whether it be Dr. Tosie's spectrograph testing or the other testing that you mentioned, there's a thirty to ten percent variance; is that correct? Yes or no, if you can.

A.   Your question is stated incorrectly because Dr. Tosie's opinion that he was ninety percent sure is not based strictly on spectrographic analysis, so I cannot answer your question either yes or no.

Q.   (By MR. NELSON) All right. I'll rephrase it again. Dr. Tosie's opinion, on whatever basis that you understood his opinion to be based on --

A.   Okay.

Q.   -- and the other testing that you have testified about here today, yes or no there is a thirty to ten percent variance?

A.   Thirty to ten? By my arithmetic, Dr. Tosie was personally ninety percent sure it was Presley. The other testing that he did with the other voice identification experts and other people in speech therapy and all was seventy. So there is a twenty percent difference.

Q.   Well, if you used the seventy percent, seventy from a hundred is thirty, so I can take that at thirty percent; and if you use the ninety percent, ninety from a hundred is ten, so would you agree with me then?

A.   I'm sorry.

Q.   Depending on which one you use, you got a thirty to ten percent variance, yes or no?

A.   Thirty to ten percent variance between the two tests? There's a twenty percent variance between the two tests. There is a thirty percent in one case that it's not Presley and ten percent in the other --

Q.   All right, sir.

A.   -- so --

Q.   Thank you.

A.   -- I don't understand your question.

Q.   Okay. Well, perhaps I just didn't phrase it properly. I believe you also testified that this case, out of all the cases that you've tried, had the greatest chance of appeal -- of success on appeal. Is that a rough paraphrase and roughly correct?

A.   I think at that time, okay, I had probably -- well, yes.

Q.   Okay, sir.

A.   Yes, that's correct.

Q.   And with already a twelve thousand dollar or more out-of-pocket loss to your firm and what you estimated to be a five hundred thousand dollar gain to your firm should Mr. Jackson and his colleagues prevail on this claim, you did not see it to be economically advantageous to your firm to pursue the appeal?

A.   Well, at the -- you know, once you got the case reversed on appeal, then, you know, you couldn't get a quote reverse and render. You would have to come back down and retry the case again. Okay?

Q.   Yes, sir.

A.   Now, initially, whenever I took the case, I wholeheartedly believed at that time, due to past experiences with Judge Leftwich, that I could get a continuance in the case because my opinion was there was some additional things that had to be done and needed to be done.

Q.   Can you elaborate on that, sir?

A.   Well, yes, sir. In point of fact, we had one particular individual who was allegedly a cousin of Mr. Elvis Presley called us and indicated that he in fact was with Elvis Presley when Elvis Presley recorded that song in Phoenix, Arizona. That particular individual, arrangements could not be made to get that individual into Dallas, Texas during the trial of this particular lawsuit. His particular deposition was going to have to be taken or arrangements made to try to bring the man in or do whatever was necessary to get his testimony in that trial. The whereabouts of that particular individual was only noticed to us within a period of, say, couple of weeks or so prior to trial. All right?

Now, there were some additional testing that could have been done in connection with the recording itself and other expert witnesses obtained, comparative spectrographic analysis where we impose on -- on mylars, clear plastic sheeting, to prove that RCA had in fact monkeyed with the master tape to try to build a case.

You know, I think that conservatively speaking, another twenty, thirty, or forty thousand dollars could have been spent in connection With preparing that particular lawsuit for trial and getting it in the best shape, it could have been to present to the new jury.

Now, I was looking at eight thousand dollars. It was like pulling hen's-teeth out of a hen to get Dennis Brewer's firm to come up with any particular expenses in connection with the lawsuit because they were a little bit reluctant to spend their money. They didn't have it or whatever. So I was looking at a situation where, for the most part, I was carrying the lion's share of the lawsuit.

I felt like I was doing a competent job. I was having difficulty with the particular lawyers because I wanted to try the lawsuit myself. I don't like to set second chair to someone else.

At that time, I prided myself in being a very good lawyer. I still pride myself in being a very good lawyer, and I felt like if I could get the case in shape where I could take it myself without the interference from another law firm and lawyer, yes, I would have gladly paid the eight thousand dollars, but there were other considerations involved in the lawsuit such as these other lawyers in there for a much higher percentage than me with either an unwillingness or an inability to contribute their fair share of the expenses involved in the lawsuit.

Q.   All right, sir. Now, as I understood your testimony earlier, all the other parties wanted you to pursue the appeal; is that correct?

A.   That's correct.

Q.   And, they didn't discuss with you terminating the, employment of their other attorneys to handle the appeal ?

A.   They could have easily terminated them, but the problem was in getting them to give up their percentage interest in the record, and I was unwilling to do so and fight another legal battle over whether or not they were entitled to their percentage. They were entitled to their percentage. What they would have to do is Come off their percentage, but they were not willing to do so.

Q.   So you -- you could have tried it yourself, just you, gotten your percentage, which if everything goes right in the long run nets you four hundred thousand dollars or more, and appealed this case; is that correct?

A.   Well, there was still the element of risk involved on whether or not the public would, quote, accept the record. Okay? That was involved in the deal.   Plus there was a certain amount of uncertainty involved in connection with whether or not if you did retry the case and you spent thirty or forty thousand dollars more in discovery expenses-- you know, keep in mind the expense that we spent over a period of approximately forty-five days. What I spent, the law firm of Dennis Brewer matched that, so we spent somewhere in terms of -- for that short period of time, we spent somewhere in the neighborhood of twenty-four -- to say between twenty and thirty thousand -- well, more than that, twenty to thirty-six thousand. Okay?

Q.   Yes, sir.

A.   And that was only a semblance of what needed to be done. Now, for the percentage gamble involved in it, I was not willing to carry the entire bag for an interest that amounted to probably less than ten percent in the recording rights. Could have been fifteen. I don't know, but I think in all that I would be willing to state under oath that it was probably somewhere in the neighborhood of eight to ten percent.

Q.   But that eight to ten percent, I believe earlier you testified, would net you four hundred to eight hundred thousand dollars; is that correct?

A.   Correct.

Q.   Okay, sir.

A.   Correct.

Q.   The testimony --

A.   Pardon, me. Repeat that. Did you say net me how much?

Q.   Four hundred to eight hundred thousand dollars to your firm.

A.   Well, I'm talking about in terms of gross dollars that might be derived in connection with the deal, so it depends on what you did with the expenses whenever you say net.

Q.   We'll change that to gross your firm four hundred to eight hundred thousand dollars, 1979 dollars, which I would think --

A.   But at the same time be grossing other individuals something, you know, two or three million dollars, and me carrying the total expense of it? I had objection to that, yes, sir, I sure did.

Q.   You mentioned Elvis' cousin who indicated that he was with Elvis when he recorded this recording of Tell Me Pretty Baby.

A.   Let me say this to you.

Q.   Can I finish my question?

A.   Clarify that. I did not speak with that cousin. Okay?

Q.   All right, sir.

A.   I did not speak with the cousin.

Q.   Were those facts detailed to The Court and set out for The Court in a motion for continuance? Yes or no, if you can answer the question.

A.   I don't know. I don't know.

Q.   Were the need to prepare the additional technical testing, the comparative -- I believe you said comparative spectrograph testing and so forth and any other additional testing that you feel was necessary to get this case ready in its best light to present to a jury, were those matters presented to The Court and Judge Leftwich in a motion for continuance?

A.   I'm sure, sir, that, you know, there were numerous grounds contained within the motion, for continuance seeking a continuance, and I'm sure it may have been in general terms and then the argument made in connection with, you know, what was in those general categories. Now, the specifics of what was contained within the motion itself I can't tell you because it's ten plus years ago.

Q.   All right, sir. Outline for me, if you will, what actions, if any, you took to assist Mr. Jackson in perfecting his appeal in the Presley Versus Jackson case.

A.   Well, plainly, what I did first was try to see if I could -- because Mr. Jackson's interest were such that it was not sufficient for me to take percentage points from him or anything. He did not have a large enough

233

percentage. Neither he nor I combined together probably had a large enough percentage to go out here to peddle to get -- because, like I say, I was not trying to just merely raise sufficient funds for eight thousand dollars, period. That wasn't the objective because I foresaw that a fairly sizable amount of money would need to be spent in connection with a retrial.

In any event, those efforts were exerted to try to drum up some money in some fashion because Mr. Jackson was in the penitentiary for life and had no resources, funds or property at all other than the percentage interest in a recording that a judge in Dallas County had said you can't sell.

Q. Can I correct you on that? That a jury.

A. That a judge, sir.

Q. And a jury.

A. We had a jury verdict. We had a judge that entered the judgment, and the judge is the one that entered the order telling us not to sell.

Q. But a jury verdict --

A. The jury didn't tell us whether to sell or not sell. The jury said they believed it not to be Elvis Presley is what they said.

Q. All right, sir.

A. Okay. So I am correct. Then after it was apparent that those efforts failed, then discussions were had with -- had with whoever. Like I say, I know that Mr. Jackson had a girlfriend that was seeing him.

Q. Do you recall the girlfriend's name, sir?

A. Gosh. I've raked my mind, but I cannot remember her name, no.

Q. All right, sir.

A. In point of fact, the first -- the first occasion that I met Mr. Jackson, that girlfriend accompanied me in my car to the penitentiary as I talked to him.

Q. I'm sorry. Are you stating that you visited Mr. Jackson at the penitentiary?

A. Pretrial.

Q. Pretrial. All right, sir.

A. And then, of course, I prepared whatever I sent to him that I can remember advising him about the necessity that he do the pauper's oath and pauper's affidavit and, I'm sure, advised him at the same time there were other instruments that had to be filed because I was not real sure myself if he got that thing docketed and his pauper's affidavit filed that I would accept the appeal at that point because it was my feeling that that appeal might perfect just a small percentage of what might be recorded in the record, so the particular problem was there was also other things, designation of matters that have to go in the appeal, numerous other documents that have to be filed subsequent to the time the pauper's affidavit was filed.

Q. So that to say that you're not sure -- even leaving to one side the affidavit, am I understanding you to say that leaving aside the affidavit, you're not sure that he would have perfected the appeal anyway?

A. Well, you know, that depends on whether or not he complies with the rules in connection with it. There are other -- there are other requirements. You've got to file briefs within a certain period of time. You've got to, you know, get your transcript filed and your statement of facts filed as well as --

Q. Yes, sir.

A. -- numerous other matters.

Q. You're not certain in your mind all of those things would have been completed; is that correct?

A. No, I'm not saying that at all.

Q. All right, sir.

A. Assuming the man could -- I'm sure if he could have either gotten legal representation or sat down with the rule books themselves and interpreted them, you know, I would have surely advised him what all the deadline requirements were as far as filings were concerned.

Q. All right, sir.

A. So I'm sure he got the lawsuit filed, so I'm pretty sure he could have done that deal.

Q. If he succeeds in filing his pauper's affidavit, then that reduces any costs that you would have to assume in taking the appeal; is that correct?

A. Sir, the particular problem in connection with that is whatever percentage Mr. Andrew Jackson had at that time, okay, whatever it was, you know, you still have a judgment that is probably binding on the other parties defendant. Okay? And had the restraining order been lifted, all right, as to Andrew Jackson's capacity to sell the record, you know, then Andrew Jackson may have in fact received a hundred percent of whatever royalties or revenues generated in connection with the thing.

Q. Well, let me ask you this then. Do I understand you to say that Jackson, prevailing on his appeal alone, may not have freed up the record to be sold?

A. May not --

Q. To be distributed?

A. No, no. If he would have prevailed on appeal and got a new trial and a jury would have said yes or if they would have failed to have found that it was, quote, not Elvis Presley, all right, then it could have very well been sold at that and Mr. Jackson received a hundred percent of the revenues attributable to that record.

Q. All right, sir. So is that not all the more reason to pursue Mr. Jackson's appeal, that a hundred percent of that pie of your percentage goes to you?

A. That was Mr. Jackson's choice in connection with -- well, let me back up. The other parties defendant, whenever the record or appeal got docketed, they were going to maintain their interest or maintain their claim in the recording rights -- or not recording rights, but the revenues generated in connection with the sale of the recording.

Q. All right, sir.

A. There would be a legal question involved concerning whether or not if they did not perfect appeal themselves, that judgment would have been binding on them and, therefore, prevented them from sharing in any further revenues. That's a legal question that I never researched to determine the answer to. Okay?

Q. All right, sir. But at the very least, Mr. Jackson would have either been entitled a hundred percent of the revenues or his share of the revenues if he can perfect his appeal and prevail on appeal arid prevail on retrial, yes or no?

A. Yes.

Q. All right, sir, and, yes or no, if he is appealing as a pauper, it's going to reduce your costs to carry his appeal.

A. He --

Q. It's going to reduce your out-of-pocket costs to carry his appeal should you choose to represent him on appeal. Yes or no, if you can.

A. If all you were concerned about is the appeal, yes.

Q. Thank you. Is there anything else that I have not allowed you to or you haven't gotten to yet that you did in the way of helping or assisting Mr. Jackson perfect his appeal?

A. The particular problem, sir, whenever the affidavit came back in late, his appeal was gone. There was nothing I could do for him.

Q. Did you attempt to file a motion with The Court asking The Court to receive his affidavit out of time?

A. Sir, the -- the rules are fairly specific in terms of posting appeal bonds and posting appeal bonds or affidavits or whatever, and one day late is too late.

Q. I understand that, sir, but my question was: Did you file a motion with The Court asking The Court to accept it --

A. I do not know whether I did or didn't.

Q. -- out of time?

A. Don't know.

Q. Did you, to the best of your recollection, attempt to contact Mr. Jackson prior to the running of that time other than the letter that you sent him on the 10th?

A. I'm sure I did, but to answer the question yes or no, there were possibly phone calls attempted or -- because I had no way to contact Mr. Jackson other than to personally go down to the penitentiary. He couldn't receive any phone calls, and whether or not -- I'm sure, you know, that I spoke with his girlfriend.

Q. As his attorney, you're stating that as his attorney, he could not receive a phone call from you, that if you made a legal call to him, legal phone call to him, that it would be rejected, that it would not be received?

A. Well, I may have to back up a little bit. I don't know that I've ever tried to place a phone call to an individual in the penitentiary ever before, so I must say I don't know whether you can or can't.

Q. All right. Thank you, sir.

A. Okay. You may be able to. I don't represent very many people -- very many criminals.

Q. Okay, sir.

A. Very, very few.

Q. What was the nature of your practice -- well, strike that.

Financially, economically, how was your practice, your firm doing in '78 and '79?

A. Oh, gosh, that's hard to say. '78, '79. Probably at that point making somewhere around I don't -- best I can do is give you a range.

Q. That's fine, sir.

A. Okay. Ballparkish, fifty to seventy-five thousand.

Q. Are we speaking in terms of profit?

A. Taxable.

Q. All right, sir. Could you give me a ballpark estimate of your profit after taking out expenses and so forth?

A. When?

Q. In '78 and '79. I'm sorry.

A. I'm saying -- what I said to you was a ballpark range, taxable, you know. We are a, quote, general partnership. Okay? So what I'm saying is I would have paid taxes on somewhere in the ballpark of fifty to seventy-five thousand dollars annually.

Q. I understand that, sir, and my question, I believe, was what was your profit after taking out your expenses, overhead, and so forth in that year in those years; calendar year '78, '79?

A. Your definition is not taxable income, sir?

Q.   Well --

A.   What is your definition? I answered you.

Q.   If that's your definition of what your profit was, that's fine, your taxable income. Okay.

A.   All I said to you is the best response I can give you --

Q.   All right.

A.   -- is the taxable income on my personal tax return would have been somewhere in the neighborhood of fifty thousand dollars.

Q.   Okay, sir.

A.   Okay. Approximately.

Q.   All right. That's fine.

A.   Could have been forty. Could have been sixty. Could have been seventy. I don't know.

Q.   That's fine. To the best of your recollection, did you ever receive a document from Andrew Lee Jackson postage -- marked postage due?

A.   I don't know. I don't know.

Q.   Do you recall anything about the document that you did receive whenever you finally received the affidavit -- the pauper's affidavit from Andrew Lee Jackson?

A.   You know, our practice was -- it's not uncommon even today for us to get an envelope maybe that is a little bit too heavy, and the post -- it will you know, the girl takes it out of the cash drawer and pays the postman.

Q.   All right, sir.

A.   -- or out of her purse or whatever, so I don't know. I don't recall anything about the document. I don't -- you know, to be honest with you, okay, I don't know whether it was sent to me. Could have been sent directly to The Court. I don't know.

Q.   So you have no recollection of whether you filed it or not. Is that what you're stating?

A.   That's correct. The only thing I do know -- well, let me back up. You know, keep in mind this is ten -- in excess of ten years ago.

Q.   I understand that, sir.

A.   Okay. My recollection seems to tell me that, yes, it was sent back to me, and the day that it was received by me, it was carried down because I knew it was late.

Q.   Were your offices at that time here in Grapevine?

A.   No, sir.

Q.   Where were your offices, if I may ask?

A.   At that time at 1035 One Main Place.

Q.   Which is downtown Dallas --

A.   Yes.

Q.   -- a couple blocks from the courthouse; is that correct?

A.   Yes.

Q.   All right. Can you state your full name and your bar number for the record?

A.   Joe Dow Gregory, 08436500.

MR. NELSON: All right, sir. Thank you, sir. And I pass the witness at this time.

MR. BEVANS: I have just a couple.

REEXAMINATION

BY MR. BEVANS:

Q.   In normal correspondence with a client such as Mr. Jackson, who would be imprisoned at the time, was all your correspondence certified return receipt? Was that your normal business practice?

A.   Gosh, I don't know.

Q.   Okay.

A.   It would strictly depend on what I was sending to him or whatever. Whether or not the particular letter that was sent to him explaining about the pauper's affidavit, the necessity of its being filed would have been one that was sent certified mail, I don't know.

Q.   Have you represented other inmates?

A.   No.

Q.   Okay.

A.   That's the only one I ever represented, to my knowledge, that I remember.

Q.   You testified that the jurors said that the voice on the recording was not that of Elvis Presley.

A.   What they found was, by a preponderance of the evidence, that the recording was not -- the artist recording the song was not Elvis Presley.

Q.   Were any of these jurors known to you to be voice experts?

A.   None of them to my knowledge were.

Q.   You made a comment about possible jury misconduct in this case. What did that -- question involve there?

A.   For the life of me, I cannot remember. I just can't remember. I've been thinking about it ever since yesterday.

Q.   Earlier on when we were discussing Judge Leftwich off the record, you indicated that he saw your clients as promoters and early on made up his mind how he was going to --

A.   You know, that's just -- I had tried lawsuits before Judge -- or I say I tried. I had not tried. I sat second chair with one of the attorneys from

Burford, Ryburn & Ford when we were representing Tom Thumb Food Stores and Cullum & Companies in connection with the defense of a lawsuit, and I got along tremendously with Judge Leftwich but noticed in that particular case that Judge Leftwich was prone to be opinionated, and, depending on his opinions, whenever it came to a judgment call, would go a long ways towards trying to help in connection with the trial of a lawsuit; so, you know, I can't -- you know, that's the best way I can respond to that question.

Q.   Earlier when Mr. Nelson asked you a question, somehow I didn't understand the question or else I got lost in the question and then the answer. You said something about the judge making a determination and the jury making a determination in this case. Would you explain that?

A.   Well, his question was that the jury -- I think he tried to correct me and indicated that the jury said I couldn't sell the record. That's not true. The jury responded to a fact question, and then on the basis of that jury verdict, the judge entered a judgment, and that's what we were addressing.

Q.   That judgment was that they could not promote the record?

A.   Well, the judgment itself was -- what they had done, the relief that they were seeking, they were seeking relief in terms of attempting to prevent the sale, distribution, advertisement, or whatever of this particular recording, and they were also seeking attorneys fees. Okay? The judgment itself came down and restrained them from advertising directly or indirectly or intimating directly or indirectly that this was a recording by Elvis Presley and also awarded attorneys fees against them, against Mr. Jackson himself. My memory tells me fifty thousand dollars, but that may not be correct at all.

MR. BEVANS: I have nothing further.

MR. NELSON: Just a couple more brief questions.

REEXAMINATION BY MR. NELSON:

Q.   You're not saying, Mr. Gregory, that had the jury found in fact that the recording was of Elvis Aaron Presley that the judge would have ruled that your client was -- client and his codefendants were not entitled to distribute that record as an authentic recording of Elvis Presley, are you?

A.   Sir, the judge can find as a matter of law whatever he wants to find and enter a judgment on the basis of whatever he finds as a matter of law, so your guess is as good as mine as what Snowden Leftwich would have done had the jury in fact had failed to find in favor of RCA.

Q.   Can you elaborate, sir, on what indication you had that if the jury would have found that that was indeed a recording of Elvis Presley, that Judge Snowden would have entered a judgment against your clients and restrained them from distributing said record?

A.   Sir, if the judge feels like that the weight of the evidence is such that reasonable minds could not conclude other than a given fact, the judge, regardless of what a jury finds, can enter a judgment on that basis.

Q.   Yes, sir, and that would be a judgment not withstanding a verdict, would it not?

A.   That's right.

Q.   And do I understand you to say that you believe that there was a significant possibility that the judge would have entered such a judgment no withstanding a verdict --

A.   No, sir.

Q.   -- had the jury come back --

A.   No, sir. That's not my -- your statement to me initially was -- your question to me initially was that the judge couldn't do it, and I said, yes, sir, he can, and the only thing I was responding to is your question that the judge couldn't do it.

Q.   All right, sir. Without entering a judgment notwithstanding of the verdict, is it your opinion that the judge could have entered an order and judgment restraining your clients from selling -- your client from selling and distributing the recording that the jury had found to be an original, authentic recording of Elvis Presley?

A.   You're going to have to repeat your question. I lost it somehow.

Q.   All right, sir. Let's assume that the jury found in favor of your client that the recording was indeed an authentic recording of Elvis Presley. Can we assume that fact?

A.   Well, actually, that question was never submitted to the jury.

Q.   All right, sir. Tell me, if you will, what question was submitted to the jury.

A.   There's a difference between saying whether a failure to find constitutes an affirmative finding of the negative, and I think the appellate courts will tell you it does not.

Q.   Well, that's not what I asked you.

A.   Yes, you did.

Q.   No, excuse me. I asked if you would tell me what question was submitted to the jury.

A.   The question was, if my memory serves me correctly, do you find from a preponderance of the evidence -- RCA had the burden of proof.

Q.   Yes, sir.

A.   That the artist was not Elvis Presley or was someone other than Elvis Presley, phrased in those terms to put the burden of proof on RCA where it belonged.

Q.   All right, sir. And if the jury would have come back and --

A.   And said no.

Q.   found -- pardon?

A.   If the jury would have responded no, that does not constitute an affirmative finding by the jury that it was Elvis Presley.

Q.   All right, sir.

A.   It just constitutes a failure to find that it was not Elvis Presley.

Q.   Do you believe -- I'm not going to waste the court reporter's time and my time on this.

MR. NELSON: I don't believe I have any further questions.

MR. BEVANS: Nothing further for me.

MR. NELSON: Defendant's Exhibit 3, which was the petition that I asked them to copy for me, I want to attach that to the record of the deposition.

(End of deposition.)